"I need someone like you, Sam,"

Kate said. "You're as straight and true as an arrow. I need that kind of man to help me save our ranch… our home."

Sam stared at Kate's upturned face. Her cheeks were flushed, and he saw the pain and pleading in her huge, wide eyes. Was the longing he saw in her eyes for him?

He grazed her flushed cheek with his hand. Kate pulled away from him, her hand on her cheek where he'd just touched her. The startled reaction caught him off guard. In that moment, Sam realized that she didn't like his touch—or him. Could the love they'd had between them long ago really be dead and gone?

He studied the wariness in her eyes. "I'll help you, Kate," he said finally.

She had always been like a wild mustang, he reminded himself. But a mustang could be tamed. It just took patience and time.

And he had both.

Dear Reader,

In the spirit of blossoming love, Special Edition delivers a glorious April lineup that will leave you breathless!

This month's THAT'S MY BABY! title launches Diana Whitney's adorable new series duet, STORK EXPRESS. Surprise deliveries bring bachelors instant fatherhood...and sudden romance! The first installment, *Baby on His Doorstep,* is a heartwarming story about a take-charge CEO who suddenly finds himself at a loss when fatherhood—and love—come knocking on his door. Watch for the second exciting story in this series next month.

Two of our veteran authors deliver enthralling stories this month. First, *Wild Mustang Woman* by Lindsay McKenna—book one of her rollicking COWBOYS OF THE SOUTHWEST series—is an emotional romance about a hard-luck heroine desperately trying to save her family ranch and reclaim her lost love. And *Lucky in Love* by Tracy Sinclair is a whimsical tale about a sparring duo who find their perfect match—in each other!

Who can resist a wedding...even if it's in-name-only? *The Marriage Bargain* by Jennifer Mikels is a marriage-of-convenience saga about a journalist who unexpectedly falls for his "temporary" bride. And *With This Wedding Ring* by Trisha Alexander will captivate your heart with a tale about a noble hero who marries the girl of his dreams to protect her unborn child.

Finally, *Stay...* by talented debut author Allison Leigh is a poignant, stirring reunion romance about an endearingly innocent heroine who passionately vows to break down the walls around her brooding mystery man's heart.

I hope you enjoy this book, and each and every story to come!

Sincerely,

Tara Gavin
Senior Editor and Editorial Coordinator

Please address questions and book requests to:
Silhouette Reader Service
U.S.: 3010 Walden Ave., P.O. Box 1325, Buffalo, NY 14269
Canadian: P.O. Box 609, Fort Erie, Ont. L2A 5X3

LINDSAY McKENNA
WILD MUSTANG WOMAN

Silhouette®

SPECIAL EDITION®

Published by Silhouette Books
America's Publisher of Contemporary Romance

To all my faithful readers. A big hug back to you!

SILHOUETTE BOOKS

ISBN 0-373-24166-6

WILD MUSTANG WOMAN

Books by Lindsay McKenna

LINDSAY McKENNA

is a practicing homeopath and Emergency Medical Technician on the Navajo Reservation in Arizona. She comes from an Eastern Cherokee medicine family and is a member of the Wolf Clan. Dividing her energies between alternative medicine and writing, she feels books on and about love are the greatest positive healing force in the world. She lives with her husband, David, at La Casa de Madre Tierra, near Sedona.

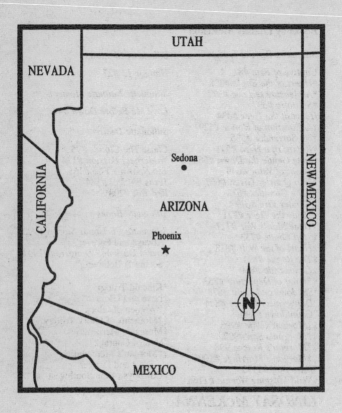

Chapter One

Kate Donovan wanted to run and hide—again. In a few moments, the only man she'd ever loved would be picking her up at the halfway house in Phoenix, Arizona, to take her home. Home to the Donovan Ranch just north of Sedona. Her stomach roiled and the butterflies fought with one another as she stood on the porch of the rambling ranch house. Shame ate at her, as it always did.

She had just been released from an eighteen-month prison term when Sam's shattering phone call came, ripping open every other festering wound within her. When she'd been put into prison, only her two younger sisters, Rachel and Jessica, had been there to support her through the embarrassing trial. Kelly Donovan, her drunkard father, hadn't come near her or the courtroom. He had been too ashamed of her.

And now that she was coming home, he wouldn't be there for her, either.

Tears burned in Kate's eyes and she forced them back, as she'd learned to force everything else in the last eighteen months. Sam had called her last night to tell her that her father was dead. He'd died in a head-on collision with a drunk driver the morning of her release. Suddenly the irony of the situation struck her: Kelly had hit the bottle when his only son, Peter, had died in the closing days of the Vietnam War. Kate's brother had been Kelly's whole world. All his love, what there was of it, had been pinned on Peter—not Kate or her sisters. Why should she expect him to be there for her now?

Lips parting, Kate stared down at her plain oxford shoes, long past due for the trash bin. She felt just like that leather—beat-up, stretched beyond the point of usefulness. She felt *old*. Oh, how old she felt! And Kelly's death lay like a numb, heavy blanket over her already deadened senses. Going to a federal pen on trumped-up charges of ecoterrorism had stolen her life from her.

She still knew she was innocent. The FBI, frightened by the extreme views of the environmental group she belonged to, had planted an agent in their midst. And the agent had used her and developed a plan to blow up the nuclear plant outside of Phoenix. The worst part was it had been the FBI agent's idea! Kate had argued against it, but the more militant members thought it was a plan worth considering.

Now she was going home again. And now Kelly was dead. Her father was dead. Hell, he'd never been a father! He'd been a ghost in their lives after Peter died.

Rubbing her wrinkled brow, Kate drew in a deep, ragged breath. When Sam had called last night—out of the blue—she had been stunned into silence by the sound of his deep, healing voice. She'd never forgotten that first, trembling kiss he'd given her when she was barely a women. And now, at thirty-seven years of age, she still filled with warmth at the memory.

She moved woodenly along the porch, feeling the remnants of the late November heat. The halfway house was designed to give women coming out of prison a few days to adjust to being on the outside once again. Kate was grateful for the space—a room of her own, no clanking and clanging of bars, or the endless noise of women talking.... She shook her head, feeling a little crazy.

Placing a hand on a wooden post that needed to be sanded and given a new coat of paint, Kate stared sightlessly past the brown lawn and the bare cottonwood trees that stood at the end of the property. The house was not in a good neighborhood, and though it was almost noon, the sidewalks and street were empty. Suddenly she felt frightened. Was it her father's unexpected passing that scared her? Or was it that she would be seeing Sam today when she thought she'd never see him again? Both? Probably. She dug her fingers briefly into the wood of the post and felt its dried, splintered texture. Arizona heat sapped the life out of everything. Kelly Donovan had sapped the life out of her.

Kate wanted to feel something at her father's death, but she felt nothing. The numbness that inhabited her

had begun with her capture by the FBI agents; it had
protected her as she faced the accusations made during the trial, and as she was locked away behind bars.
For almost two years, she'd felt nothing. Kate
laughed—a short, explosive sound. Well, she was
feeling plenty now, but it had to do with Sam Mc-
Guire.

Gripping the post, she hung her head and felt tears
crowd into her tightly closed eyes. Sam... The memory of their youth, their beautiful innocence as they'd
fallen in love was one of the few unsullied things in
Kate's life. Another was her mother, Odula, who had
died ten years ago of a sudden heart attack. Kate was
lucky her mother had loved her and her two sisters
with a fierceness that defied description, that Odula
had tried to make up for Kelly's behavior as a father,
a negative role model in their lives.

Sam is coming....

Opening her eyes, Kate groaned, her gaze pinned
on the end of the street, where she knew he would
turn to come down to the halfway house. What must
he think of her? He'd probably swallowed the FBI's
lies, blasted out in the newspaper headlines. He hadn't
come to the trial, as Rachel and Laurel had—but why
would she expect him to? She'd had no direct contact
with him since she'd left the ranch at eighteen years
old. Absolutely none. Back then Kelly had been drunk
most of the time and Kate was just glad to grab her
high school diploma and get the hell off the ranch.
After graduation, Sam had married his high school
sweetheart, instead. And Kate had eventually left the
state entirely to start her own life.

Some life... Once more humiliation flowed through

her. She was the oldest of three daughters and she was the one who had managed to screw up her life the most. Rachel had become a world-class homeopathic doctor who taught in London, England, and Jessica ran her own healing-arts business in Vancouver, Canada. Kate had nothing to show for herself— just endless low-paying jobs that she usually got fired from because she was smarter than the guy who owned the business—and she made the mistake of telling him so. Kate the hothead. She'd been that way ever since Peter died. How much she had loved her older brother! They had all grieved deeply for his loss. Only Kelly had never gotten over his son's death like they had.

None of her sisters had stayed at the Donovan Ranch after age eighteen. They had fled just as she had. And why not? Kelly had made it clear he didn't love them or need them or want them around to run *his* ranch. Peter had been the heir apparent, chosen to take over the Donovan Ranch and give it another glorious generation, replete with grandchildren for Kelly. Yep, Kelly had had all his dreams in place—and none of them had ever included his three daughters. Well, his dreams had died with Peter. And now he, too, was gone.

Kate heard a low growl, the unmistakable sound of a heavy truck. Her heart raced as she lifted her head and turned to look down the street. There was a dusty Dodge Ram pickup turning the corner. The truck had obviously seen a lot of hard use and more than likely earned its keep in the ranching world—just like the man in the black Stetson behind the wheel. *Sam McGuire.*

Suddenly Kate felt anxious, more frightened than the day they had pronounced her sentence to the maximum-security prison. Her eyes widened as the truck pulled to a halt along the curb and she saw Sam McGuire for the first time in eighteen years. Her hand slipped from the post and she moved to the front steps. *Sam.* Oh, how she still ached for him! How many dreams during how many nights had she had of Sam kissing her, loving her, holding her? *Too many,* her wounded heart screamed. *Too many.*

Somehow she was going to have to hold herself together. Somehow she'd have to keep from revealing to Sam how she really felt. Too many of life's events stood between them. He was married. He had a son named Christopher, the last she'd heard. That's what Jessica, her youngest sister, had told her in one of the few letters they'd exchanged over the years.

As Sam eased out of the truck and shut the door, Kate couldn't stop her gaze from moving hungrily over him. At thirty-seven years old, Sam looked wonderful. He'd always been tall, almost six foot three inches, his shoulders broad and square. Kate remembered his proud bearing in high school. Even then, he'd had natural leadership ability. He had always walked with a kind of boneless grace, very male, very in charge.

But the years hadn't been kind to him, Kate realized. His square face was deeply lined at the corners of his gray eyes, telling her of the endless hours he'd spent out in the hot Arizona sun. The deep grooves bracketing his mouth told her he'd held a lot of what he felt inside. His skin was deeply tanned, his dark brown hair cut military short.

She noticed he was wearing a clean, long-sleeved, blue denim shirt, the sleeves rolled carelessly up, and a fresh pair of jeans. Kate knew how dirty and dusty ranching work was. Obviously Sam had taken some pains to shave, shower and put on clean clothes before seeing her. Even his boots, tobacco brown, were not the normal scuffed and scarred pair he would wear while working, but were polished and free of dust.

Raising her eyes, she saw that his black Stetson was set low so that she could barely see those piercing gray eyes of his as they met hers. For an instant, Kate felt a thrill of joy, deep and shattering, as their eyes made contact. And then, just as quickly, she crushed those wild, euphoric feelings.

Unable to hold his searching gaze, Kate broke eye contact. She stood there, her head hung, waiting. Would he judge her? Call her a criminal? Kate knew that word had spread throughout Sedona about her prison term. She knew her name was dirt. Inwardly, she tried to steel herself against Sam's accusations, spoken or not. How badly she wanted to look into his eyes again. At the first contact she'd felt only joy. Joy! How long had it been since she'd felt anything? *Too long,* her heart whispered. *Far too long.*

Sam tried to hide his surprise at the woman before him. Kate Donovan, the girl he'd known in high school, had been a winsome creature, wild like the wind. She had been the spitting image of Odula, her Eastern Cherokee mother, with that thick, black mane of waist-length hair that reminded him of a horse's flowing mane. She had Odula's startling blue eyes, so large and innocent with awe over life itself. Taller than most of the girls in high school, she stood at five foot eleven inches by the time she was a senior. For Kate, who had always tried to hide like a shadow, her height was one more thing that kept her from feeling like other girls her age. Now he saw that it still set her apart.

As Sam slowed his steps, he held Kate's intense blue gaze and felt a stunning force wrap around his heart and squeeze it hard.

Never had he forgotten kissing those full lips that were now compressed withholding back so much emotion. His body went hot with the memory—the memory of holding her, loving her, making her his. As a sophomore in high school, she'd given him her heart and virginity willingly. Passionately. And how he'd loved her—he still did. Shaken by the avalanche of emotion that had somehow, over the years, managed to survive, despite all his bad mistakes, Sam felt a keen, crying ache in his heart—for Kate.

It was her eyes that showed him the extent of her suffering. They had always been special, with golden flecks of sunlight dancing in their depths. As Sam searched her gaze now, he found only dullness and darkness. Could he blame her? She'd just been released from prison. A place like that was enough to kill anyone's spirit. He didn't believe Kate was an ecoterrorist. Yes, she was outspoken, brash, and didn't always think things through before acting. But she wasn't a killer as the media and FBI painted her. Kate wouldn't hurt a fly. She was a warm, loving girl who'd embraced life. And he'd loved her for years.

Now, as he slowed to take the steps up to the porch where she stood waiting for him, he felt naked with pain. Her pain. And he tasted bitter remorse in his mouth for what he'd done to her.

She looked so different from the young girl he remembered. No longer did she have that thick, black mane that swirled endlessly around her proud shoulders. Instead her hair was cut very short and clung to her well-shaped skull. She'd had a thin, model's body in high school. Now, as she stood before him in a pair of Levi's and a pink, short-sleeved shirt, he saw she had filled out in the right places, had some meat on her bones.

Sam could feel the internal strength in Kate; he always had. Her body was firm, and he guessed that she'd exercised a lot in the prison just to keep from going insane. How else could she have stood being locked up for a year and a half? Of the three sisters, Kate was the wild mustang among them. Sam had seen mustangs die, literally, of grief when imprisoned in a corral or box stall. Such was their need for freedom, for the wide-open spaces where they could run at will.

Kate was like that—wild, free and untamable. That was why he'd fallen in love with her so long ago. That's why he'd never gotten her out of his mind or heart. And he'd tried.

Studying her oval features, her high cheekbones set off by beautiful, wide-set, sky blue eyes, Sam saw the years of suffering in her face. He saw lines at the corners of her eyes, slight but present. And more than anything, he saw how the corners of her mouth were pulled in, a sign of the emotions she held at bay. He laughed to himself. Didn't he do the same thing?

When he saw the sudden panic in Kate's eyes, her

uncertainty, he automatically took off his hat and halted at the base of the steps. He recognized that look of fear. He'd seen it in mustangs when he approached them too quickly. They were wary and distrustful, just as Kate was now. Could he blame her? He'd had so many dreams for them—hell, he'd managed to kill all his dreams and destroy Kate in the process. His heart ached as he saw that deep, ingrained fear in her eyes. What had prison done to her to make her react like that to him? When she was a wild, young filly, she'd been fearless. Bitterly, he remembered how life could make one scared and cautious. He had been stung a couple of times over the years. He no longer felt reckless or fearless himself.

He wanted to say so much, and yet it all jammed up in his throat. Suddenly the red bandanna he wore around his neck felt tight, and trickles of sweat slid down his temples as he played nervously with the edge of his Stetson.

"It's good to see you again, Kate," he said, meaning it. He saw a glimmer of tears in her eyes and felt her desire to move closer. At that instant, all he really wanted to do was open his arms, whisper for her to come forward so he could hold her. Just hold her. He knew that was what she needed, then as well as now. Of all the Donovan girls, Kate had taken the most abuse from Kelly because she'd fought back like the rebellious teenager she was. And she was the most injured by her father's ways. Sam saw that now as never before. So instead of reaching for her, he slowly lifted his hand in welcome. He had to move slowly in order not to scare her into running—again.

Without warning, the past came tunneling back at

him, sharp and serrating as a knife blade stuck in his chest, hot and passionate as her breath had been when he'd found her crying outside her locker in the hallway of the deserted high school one evening. Oh, Sam had known Kate was an outsider at school. He'd been the star running back of the football team, while she was a quiet, mouselike sophomore who hid out in the library between classes.

He'd just come in from a very late football practice. Weary, his helmet dangling from his long, bruised fingers, he'd seen a darkened figure crouched beside a locker at the end of the highly waxed hallway. It was almost nine p.m., and there were only a few lights on. Sam frowned, shoved his damp hair off his furrowed brow as he walked softly toward the hunched, sobbing girl.

As he drew closer, he saw that it was Katie Donovan. His heart lurched and his steps slowed. She was wearing jeans and a white tank top, her thick, black hair like a cascade around her shaking shoulders. The sobs coming from her twisted his heart. For so long, Sam had wanted to meet her, but she evaded him every time he tried. Yes, he'd heard the stories about Old Man Donovan. No one in Sedona had missed hearing about his infamous drunks. Sam could understand why the three Donovan girls were like shadows around school. If he had a father like Kelly Donovan, he'd be ashamed, too, and probably hide out like they did.

Sam halted beside Kate, who sat on the floor next to her open locker, her knees drawn up tightly against her, her face buried in her arms. As he leaned down, the light casting long, gray shadows around them, his eyes narrowed. *What the hell?* He saw blood drying on her arm. His gaze traveled to her tank top, where a rusty stain appeared. Shocked, he realized that Kate was hurt.

Without thinking, he took the white towel from around his neck, crouched down and reached out.

"Kate?"

Her head snapped up. Sam heard her gasp. She jerked her head to the right, toward his low, concerned voice. Her red-rimmed, tear-filled eyes widened.

Sam heard himself gasp. His hand froze midair, the towel in his fingertips. Kate's left eye was blackened and swollen. Blood was leaking out of her nose. Her lip was split. Gulping hard, Sam realized someone had beat her up. Who?

"You're hurt...." he rasped, before getting down on one knee and pressing the towel gently into her hand. "Hold on, let me get you some water...."

Still in a state of shock, Sam went to the lavatory down the hall. He found a cup and brought it back, filled to the brim with cool water. Kate refused to look at him as he knelt back down beside her.

"What happened?" he demanded, dipping the edge of the towel in the water. He saw her fighting valiantly not to begin crying again as he slid his hand beneath her trembling jaw. As gently as he could, he wiped the congealing blood away from her soft, full lips, nose and chin. She was so scared. Her eyes were wide with shock and fright. Never had Sam felt more protective—or more angry at whoever had done this to her.

"I—I got thrown off a horse," she rasped.

He grinned a little, one corner of his mouth lifting. "Try me again. No horse is going to give you a black eye and a split lip. You trying to tell me you caught a horseshoe in the face? I don't think so. 'Cause then you'd be dead."

Choking, Kate closed her eyes. "N-no...."

"Here," he said soothingly, dipping the towel again and carefully folding it up. "Put this on your eye."

She did as he instructed.

Sam put his hand on her shoulder. He felt her tremble. She wouldn't look at him. "Heck of way to encounter a girl I've always wanted to meet," he weakly joked.

When Kate hid her face in the towel and leaned heavily against the locker, Sam realized that something was terribly wrong.

"Kate?"

She didn't answer.

Grimly, Sam maneuvered around and placed his hands on her shoulders. She was quivering like a frightened animal. "Kate, what happened?"

She sobbed and refused to look up at him.

Smoothing the curtain of black hair away from her damp, flushed face, he muttered, "Come on, we're getting out of here. Can you walk?"

Sam helped Kate to her feet. He was a lot taller than her, but she was tall for a girl. Slipping his arm around her waist, he allowed her to lean against him, her legs none too steady.

Later, out at the quiet football field, sitting in the bleachers—his arm around her shoulders, her face pressed against his neck—Sam had finally pried the truth out of her. Kelly had beaten her up. Her own father had struck her repeatedly.

Sam sat there till late that night, chilled by the wind off the Mogollon Rim. Kate's words and sobs tore huge chunks out of his heart, and he felt her pain.

In the next two years, Sam would come to know Kate intimately. Would see for himself the trouble between her and Kelly. And he would love her. Wildly. With abandon. Together they would weave dreams. Dreams that he would later smash by his own foolish actions.

Sam's face wavered in front of her. Kate swallowed abruptly and blinked rapidly to make her tears disappear. She stared at his proffered hand, a hand scarred and callused from years of laboring on a ranch. His voice, low and deep, moved through her like a healing salve. The shame that consumed her lessened momentarily, too. He was holding out his hand to her. Was it a gesture of peace? Of welcome? Or was he just performing a necessary social grace? She wasn't sure.

Kate wanted to believe that Sam was welcoming her. But she knew better. He'd never showed up for her trial, never wrote her a letter or tried to call her. Why should he? There was nothing between them now. He was married and had a son. He had a life of his own. He owed her nothing. Absolutely nothing. A two-year high school crush did not make him responsible for her after they'd broke up. As her gaze moved from his strong, square hand up to his barrel chest and the dark hair that peeked out at the top of his shirt collar, she swallowed convulsively. If Sam knew how many torrid dreams she'd had of him over the years, even he would blush. And not much made him blush, as she recalled.

Her gaze ranged upward to his mouth, and she began to feel heat pool in her lower body. It was a warm, wonderful sensation. She remembered that well-shaped mouth as no other; it was wide and quite capable of a wicked, boyish grin. Kate had always loved Sam's rolling laugh and she hotly recalled his mouth closing commandingly over her lips, to fuse them to his own. Now that strong mouth was compressed and Kate grew frightened. She'd seen that kind of response to her before: she was bad news, tainted, an awful person. Yet as she met his gaze, that curious warmth still flowed through her. The sensation caught her off guard.

Kate knew Sam could be a hard-nosed son of a bitch when he chose to be, and usually with reason. But that side of him wasn't present now. His eyes, usually gray and glacial looking, were a warm slate color at the moment, and she could feel her response to him building. She hadn't expected warmth from him. Without thinking, Kate lifted her slender hand and slid it into his waiting one. Sam was just being civil to her because Kelly had died the night before, that was all.

The strength of Sam's hand enclosed hers. Her flesh was damp with fear as she felt the monitored strength of his callused fingers. Heat jolted up her arm at the contact, and almost as quickly, Kate pulled her hand away. If she allowed Sam to touch her for one more second, she'd burst into tears and take that dangerous step forward, falling into his arms.

"Sam..." She choked and broke off for a second. "Thanks for coming to pick me up. You didn't have to."

Shaken, Sam settled the well-worn Stetson back on his head. Kate's handshake had been weak, clammy and unsure. How unlike the Kate he used to know. Anger stirred in him as he wondered how much prison had beaten the life and spirit out of her. There was so much to ask, so little time. Other things had to take priority right now.

"I wanted to, Kate. It was the least I could do. I'm sorry about Kelly's passing. At least he went fast and didn't feel a thing."

Sam's deep murmur fell over her like a warm, nurturing blanket. Kate absorbed his care like a love-starved child. Standing uncertainly before him, she felt his gaze ranging over her from her head to her toes, and it made her feel painfully vulnerable. Her fingers tingled where he had held hers briefly. Did Sam realize that even now his gentle strength fed her spirit? When he'd touched her, she felt the first spark of hope in many years.

As she risked a quick glance up at him, she wondered if he knew the power and sway he held over her. Probably not. It was her neediness, her love for him that was making her feel this way. If nothing else, Sam always did what was proper. He could be counted on to do the right thing—just as she could be counted on to do the wrong thing.

Grimacing, Kate took a step back. "You've got a life of your own to run," she said. "You didn't have to come and get me, too. I appreciated your phone call last night about Kelly."

Sam moved up the stairs and worriedly assessed Kate. She was pale. Although she had Odula's dark, golden coloring, her skin seemed bleached out. He guessed it was from too many hours spent in the prison and not enough in sunlight. Kate had always been a sun lover. She hated being indoors, and had spent most of her time outside working on the ranch, laying wire for fencing, helping with the cattle or the horses—any excuse not to have a roof over her head. The three sisters had built a huge tree house in the white-barked arms of the Arizona sycamore out in their front yard. Kate had spent many nights sleeping out there under the sky, rather than in her bedroom where such starry beauty couldn't be seen.

"Listen," Sam told her heavily, "I called Rachel in London and Jessica in Vancouver. I told them Kelly was dead. Rachel will be here tomorrow evening. Jessica will come in the next morning. I…" He shrugged. "I took it upon myself to set the funeral for the third morning."

Kate's mouth thinned. "That's fine, Sam. Thank you. I don't imagine there was anyone else there that cared about Kelly's passing."

"No, not too many at this point."

She pinned him with a dark look. "You didn't have to do this, either."

"I worked for Kelly for five years, Kate. I owe the man something."

She shrugged. Sam was that way. He had loyalty to others regardless. Kelly had destroyed any loyalty Kate had to the Donovan Ranch—or to him. Her father had killed his daughters' love, their dreams of being a part of the ranch's growing history. He'd driven them all off. According to Kelly, only Peter had been capable of carrying on the legacy. He was a man. They were women. Women couldn't possibly do a man's job, Kelly had told them repeatedly.

"Who's the ranch manager now?"

Sam shook his head. "No one, Kate."

She glanced at him quickly. How strong and stalwart Sam seemed. She ached to take those few steps and move into his arms. Every cell in her body cried out for his touch. He was so big and tall and solid, as if he could weather any of life's storms and live to tell about it. Well, she'd suffered through one too many storm and had been beaten down once and for all. She felt weak. At this point she was incapable of finding any strength left in her battered soul to dredge up and call her own.

"But...I thought Kelly had a ranch crew—"

"He fired them over time. The last foreman, Tom Weathers, quit two years ago. Kelly was running the entire ranch by himself when he wasn't hitting the bottle."

Grimly, Kate took in a ragged breath. "Yeah, Kelly had a way of firing people, scaring everyone off with his drunken rages. Nothing changed, did it?" She looked at Sam and saw tenderness burning in his eyes. And though Kate hadn't expected that from him after all that had happened, she reveled in it.

Rubbing his mouth, Sam said, "After your mom died, Kelly hit the bottle pretty continuously. Over the years, he did chase off everyone."

"He fired you?"

Sam smiled slightly. "Yeah."

"That was stupid. But then, Kelly was known for

doing stupid things.'' She laughed sharply. ''Of course, I'm his daughter and I'm well-known for doing stupid things, making lousy choices, too....''

Sam hurt for her and had to stop himself from reaching out to touch her sagging shoulder. Kate had once walked so proudly. Now he could see she how broken she was. Broken, hurting and badly scarred. ''Look,'' he rumbled, ''you're nothing like Kelly, believe me....'' Sam caught himself before he said too much. He saw the suffering on Kate's angular features. How badly he wanted to reach out and stroke her short hair, a touch to tell her everything would be all right. But it wasn't the right thing to do at the moment.

''Kate, I know you just got out of prison, and I know you have plans for your life, but right now, one of you Donovan women has to come home. You've got a thirty-thousand-acre ranch to run and no one is there to do it. There's beef to care for, roughly fifty Arabian horses that need tending. You need to come home and decide what you're going to do with the ranch now that Kelly's gone.''

She stared at him. ''There are no cowhands or wranglers at all?''

He shook his head. ''None.''

Stunned, Kate stared at him. ''But the cattle and horses—''

''I know. I was over there early this morning doing the watering and feeding. I did a little vetting on a couple of Herefords. Probably the last place you want to be right now is on that ranch, but without one of you there, the place is going to turn into a disaster. The animals will suffer and die...I know you don't

want that. I can come and help you out a bit, but I've
got a job at the Cunningham ranch next door.''

"I didn't know...." she whispered. "Oh, Lord,
Sam, Kelly never wanted any of us running the
ranch...especially me...."

His fingers ached to reach out and touch her. Comfort her.

Kate rested her brow against the post, her eyes
closed. She felt the bite of the warm wood pressing
into her flesh.

"It's a hell of a time, Kate. You deserve better than
this. You have what it takes to run that ranch. I know
you do. But if you don't come home, the ranch is
going to die. It's in rough shape, anyway. Maybe,
when you and your sisters get together after Kelly's
funeral, you'll make a plan and decide what to do
with it.''

Lifting her head, Kate nodded. "Kelly has probably destroyed the ranch like he has everything and
everyone else," she said woodenly.

Sam stood there, feeling every nuance of the rejec-
tion and pain her father had caused her. There were
times when he hated Kelly for chasing off his children. The sisters had loved the ranch with a loyalty
unlike any other he'd seen.

"The ranch is gutted, Kate. You might as well
know it now, so there're no surprises when I pull in
the driveway. Are you ready? I've got to take you
over to the funeral home in Cottonwood first, where
Kelly's being laid out, and you have to fill out some
papers.''

Pain crawled into her heart. For a moment, Kate
felt grief over Kelly's passing, despite the fact that

she hadn't spoken to him since she'd walked out at age eighteen. All he'd ever told her anyway was that she was no good. A loser. That she'd never amount to anything.

Kate looked over at Sam and found his face deeply shadowed, his mouth a hard, set line, his gray eyes burning with that same tenderness that fed her. "Okay, take me home, Sam. But I'm not staying long. Kelly killed my desire to stay on that ranch one more day than I have to. It was all his and Peter's, and he never wanted us around."

Chapter Two

Sam wondered what was going on inside Kate's head as she sat, seat belt on, looking straight ahead as they drove toward Sedona. For the past hour she'd been silent. How mature and beautiful she looked, yet so different from the teenage girl he'd once loved. Life had a way of changing everyone, he decided.

"You need to know something about the ranch, unless you've been in close contact with someone about it."

Kate slanted him a glance. "I usually got in touch with my sisters once a year and that was it. Since Mom died, none of us had a clue as to what was going on at the ranch." And then, more softly, she added, "And we didn't care, either."

"Kelly made sure of that," Sam agreed sadly. He frowned.

"Do you really hate the ranch?"

She shrugged. "How can you hate the place where you were born and grew up?" Kate waved her hand helplessly as she drank in the sight of the desert surrounding them. They were on I-17, heading toward Black Canyon. From there, they would climb from near sea level to five thousand feet, to the high desert plateau. The tall saguaro cactus that dotted the landscape here would disappear, replaced by shorter prickly pear cactus, which could stand the colder temperatures of winter better than the sensitive saguaro.

"I recall you seemed to love the ranch back then."

"Yes," Kate whispered, "I loved the ranch. I guess in my heart of hearts I still do. In a way..."

"The past has a funny way of looking better than it did at the time?" he teased gently, glancing at her and then focusing on his driving.

"Doesn't it always?"

"Sometimes. Sometimes it gives you hope for making the future turn out the way you want it." Sam shrugged. "I used to have dreams a long time ago. I don't anymore. Maybe you still have dreams...."

His enigmatic answer was too deep for her to delve into. Instead, Kate absorbed Sam's proximity. In the cab of the Dodge Ram, Sam McGuire seemed even larger—and as solid as the truck he drove. He had about as many scars as this vehicle did, too. She noticed them not only on his hands, but on his arms and face as well. Ranching life was hard. Brutal sometimes. It demanded your blood upon occasion. Such as now. They had already talked about the funeral arrangements, having stopped at the funeral home and gotten them mercifully out of the way. Kate still didn't feel anything about Kelly's passing. Maybe it would hit her later.

Her heart was expanding, though, with euphoria. She knew it was because of Sam—his guiding, steadying presence. She stole a peek at his rugged profile. He was not a drop-dead-handsome man. His face was wind worn, sun beaten, his flesh tough and dark. His dark brown eyebrows were thick and straight above those gray, frosty eyes that had always reminded Kate of an eagle's. Those eyes never missed anything and she doubted Sam missed anything now. Inwardly, Kate waited for him to bring up her prison term or in some way use it against her.

Sam hadn't been that kind of man in the past, but things changed, she reminded herself. She wasn't the wild, rebellious fighter of her youth, either, anymore. Questions about him begged to roll off her lips, and finally, she broke the pleasant silence between them.

"You said you work for Old Man Cunningham?"

His mouth twisted. "I'm their ranch foreman. Have been for the past five years."

Raising her brow, Kate laughed a little. "Old Man Cunningham. Who could forget that bristly old peccary?" she said, comparing her ornery old neighbor to the wild pig that ranged across the Southwestern deserts. The analogy was a good one. The boars, which weighed well over a hundred pounds, had savage, curved tusks on either side of their mouth. They had poor eyesight and, if frightened, were known to charge the unlucky person and shred him to pieces. Cunningham was like that. Not only did he wear thick glasses that made his watery blue eyes look huge, he had an explosive temper. He abused everyone verbally, beat up his three sons with his fists and generally made everyone who had to deal with him miserable. Cunningham had the largest spread in central Arizona, over seventy thousand acres, which unfortunately ran alongside the Donovan ranch. Kate couldn't count the times Cunningham and Kelly had gotten into range fights over infractions. It had been ridiculous.

"I'm surprised you traded the Hatfields for the McCoys," Kate murmured wryly.

Sam turned and caught her slight smile. It wasn't much of a grin, but it was a start. He could feel Kate beginning to relax by degrees. How badly he wanted to tell her how much he missed her presence in his life, but now was not the time for such a revelation. "Yeah, well, Old Man Cunningham's last foreman quit on him just as Kelly fired me. I got wind of it and went over and asked for a job."

"Talk about going from the frying pan into the fire."

He chuckled and saw her smile deepen. Kate had a soft inner core to her she rarely let show. But now he was seeing her softness. "At the time, I was saving a lot of my paycheck for my son's college tuition," he admitted. "Cunningham made me an offer I couldn't refuse."

"Oh, I see...." Pain stabbed at Kate. How could she have forgotten that he was married and had a son? Her blind heart still wanted to see Sam as that fifteen-year-old football star she'd fallen so madly in love with—and was still in love with, she reminded herself. How did one erase love from one's heart? Kate had tried in many ways. She'd run from the ranch and from Kelly. And soon afterward Sam had married, at age seventeen, when he'd gotten Carol O'Gentry pregnant. Kate, right or wrong, couldn't stand knowing that her two-year relationship with Sam had been built upon sand. He'd loved Carol all along, she figured. He'd taken the love she herself had willingly shared with him, but his heart had never been hers. Well, that was the past. They were older now and life moved on.

Sam saw the flash of pain in Kate's darkening blue eyes. He felt it. But then, he'd always been in close psychic touch with her. It was as if he sensed more than heard her words, or maybe he read her thoughts from her expression. But Kate wasn't one to give much away in her voice or face or body language. Kelly had probably driven all those normal reactions out of her early on. So Sam had always relied on his feelings and sensitivity where Kate was concerned. He could always pick up nuances in her low voice. Or he would see the gold flecks in her eyes blotted out by some thunderstorm within her, and he knew that she was upset. She was a hard woman to read by most standards, and he was glad he'd gotten to know the soft, gentle, womanly Kate in his youth. That was the woman he'd fallen helplessly in love with until…

Sam frowned, shutting the door on his own bitter, stupid errors. He'd made a lot of mistakes, but the worst was what he'd done to Kate. Maybe now, in some way, he could make up for his transgressions.

"Cunningham is still meaner than a frightened peccary," he told her. "He's in his seventies now, partially blind because of his diabetes, and he still drives his sons into the ground."

"Nothing's changed." Kate shook her head. "He and Kelly deserved one another."

"They were a lot alike," Sam agreed.

"So, how do you tough it out with the old bastard at the Bar C?"

"A day at a time."

Kate laughed for the first time. It felt so good to laugh again. Sam joined her, and she marveled at how that tough, hardened mask on his face dropped away temporarily. It was a precious moment she grabbed and held in her heart. His eyes grew warm, his strong mouth curved, and she reveled in that thunderous, rolling laughter that she'd always loved to hear.

"He's meaner than a green rattler," Kate muttered. "He always beat his boys. I remember going to school and seeing Chet and Bo with strap-mark bruises on their arms. I don't see how they took it."

Sobering, Sam said, "Unfortunately, abuse begets abuse. Chet and Bo are still at the ranch. The youngest son, Jim, is an EMT and firefighter in Sedona. He got out at age eighteen, like you did."

"He was smart."

"Yes," Sam agreed slowly, weaving around some slower traffic on the freeway. "Jim was. He's stationed at Sedona Fire Station #1. He lives in town now. I know he's tried to heal the rifts in his family, with very little luck so far."

"Bet he doesn't go home to visit much, does he?" Kate knew Jim was smart enough to stay out of such a dysfunctional, abusive household, as she had.

"When he was a hotshot with the forestry service up at the Grand Canyon, Jim used to come home once a year, for Christmas, and that was it. Usually things erupted in a fight and he always left sooner rather than later. But he'd always come home again the next year to try and heal the family. He had a girlfriend, Linda Sorenson, who lived in Sedona. He was going to marry her, but that soured, too. Now that he's an emergency medical technician in town, I see him pretty regularly.''

"Cunningham is angry at the world and takes it out on everyone. Nothing changes, does it?''

With a shrug, Sam said, "Some things do and some things don't.'' He glanced at her. "I hope you're prepared to see the ranch. It's pretty much a class A disaster area.''

"I'm more worried about getting the livestock water and food.''

"I know. When we reach home, I'll give you a hand.''

She warmed to his care. "You ought to get a medal, Sam. You don't have to help us.''

"A long time ago a certain pretty girl taught me a lot of things. Good things.'' He slanted a glance at her and saw color rising to her wan cheeks. "I don't think you ever knew how much influence you had on me back then, Kate.'' Sam wanted to say, *You taught me about loyalty, for one thing. And being responsible.* But he didn't, because he'd been disloyal and irresponsible toward her. His brows dipped as he focused his attention on his driving once more. "Maybe I can return the favor a little now.''

Kate drew up one knee and clasped her hands around it. She felt the heat of a blush working its way up from her neck into her face. How long had it been since she'd blushed? She couldn't remember. Sam had that effect on her. He always had. Muttering, she continued, "I'm surprised. All we did was fight during those two years we were going together back in high school."

Chuckling, Sam said, "I'd call them constructive discussions, not arguments. Kelly and you got into hot fights with a lot of yelling. We never did that. And a lot of your anger was because of him, not between us. You had to let off steam somewhere." He shrugged. "I understood you, Kate, and I didn't mind if you got cranky and temperamental every once in a while. I knew what it was like living with Kelly and I saw what he did to you and your sisters...." Sam stopped. The past hurt too much for him to go on. He replayed again that first poignant meeting with Kate at her locker. Although Kelly had fought with Kate a lot, he'd beaten her up only once—that night. Sam had found out later that Odula had given her husband an ultimatum: that if he ever laid a hand on one of her daughters again, she'd divorce him. Kelly had backed down. To Sam's knowledge the rancher never *had* laid a hand on Kate or her sisters again, but he'd mercilessly badgered Kate mentally and emotionally, instead. Sam figured those beatings were no less injurious.

"I guess you and I really didn't fight," Kate replied, studying his harsh profile, his hawklike nose and that chin that jutted out proudly, daring anyone to take a swing. She remembered touching that face, running eager fingers across it, feeling his lips kissing her palm, her arm, her... With a broken sigh, she said tiredly, "That was a long time ago, Sam. Water under the bridge. We've both changed. A lot."

"In some ways, yes, but in others—" one corner of his mouth crooked a little as he met and held her fearful glance for a second "—you haven't. You're just as pretty as I recall. Your hair is shorter, but your eyes still remind me of the wide, blue sky we live under." Sam stopped himself. He hadn't meant to get intimate with her. Cursing himself for lapsing into how he felt, he added, "But you're right. We all change."

The abruptness of his last comment hurt her. How often during the last eighteen months had Kate remembered all those affectionate words Sam had used with her during their relationship? If he knew, he'd be embarrassed. "I've changed all right."

"The question is," he murmured, "once you see the ranch, will you stay or go?"

"Knowing Kelly, the ranch is probably pretty much destroyed. That's what he did after Peter's death. Then he killed Mom with his drinking. She didn't die of a heart attack. Her heart was broken. There's a difference. Mom had such dreams for the Donovan Ranch."

"And not one of them came true," Sam agreed. Broken dreams. Yeah, he knew a lot about those, too. And he had no one to blame but himself.

"She envisioned a place where all things lived and grew. She hated to see the cattle raised and then slaughtered." Kate shrugged. "So do I."

"You're a lot like Odula," Sam said. "You not only look like her, you have her big heart, as well."

Kate held out her hands, studying her long fingers, the bluntly cut nails. "As a kid growing up, I always had dirty hands. But it was the dirt of Mother Earth under my nails. I loved it. I loved being with Mom out in our huge garden. I even liked weeding.'' Kate smiled fondly at those memories and clasped her hands around her knee again. ''And all Kelly wanted to do was cut down more of the forest on our property, use it for more fencing for more cattle.'' She shook her head. ''I remember times, Sam, that my mom would go for a walk away from the ranch house. I'd find her sitting on her favorite rock behind a juniper tree, crying.''

Sam heard the pain in Kate's voice. ''Why was she crying?''

''Because, as I found out when I was older and could understand it all, Mom had agreed with Kelly to start a farm, not a ranch. She came from the Quallah Reservation in North Carolina. Her people, the Eastern Cherokee, were farmers, not ranchers. It grieved her to see the cattle slaughtered. One day she told me about her dreams for all of us. When she got done, I cried with her, because our lives had taken another direction instead.''

''Kelly's direction?''

''How'd you guess?''

''He was known to be a hardhead.''

''You're being kind, Sam. But then, you always were. I was the one who called him what he was.''

''Kelly came from this spread. He was a dyed-in-the-wool Arizona rancher, Kate. He didn't know anything else.''

''But that didn't mean he couldn't have given in and let Mom realize some of her dreams, too.'' Angry now, Kate muttered, ''He could have given her that apple orchard she wanted. What would it have hurt that selfish bastard to buy five hundred apple saplings and plant them for her? What he did instead was give her for a garden an acre of land that she had to till with the tractor. Trained in traditional healing arts, she wanted an herb garden to make medicines for her family, but he said no. She wanted to take the fruit of the earth and make this place an Eden. Kelly turned it into a perpetual slaughterhouse with the cattle. Everything hinged on those cattle." Grimacing, Kate glared at Sam. "It still does."

"He could have given Odula some of her dreams," Sam agreed quietly. "One person doesn't have the right to destroy the dreams of another." Like he did. He was no better than Kelly.

Kate winced and stared out her window at the dry desert, the prickly cholla, the saguaros that stood like sentinels, their huge arms raised toward the endless, bright blue sky. "Kelly destroyed four women's dreams," she said finally. "It was his dream or no dream at all."

"Maybe if Peter had lived things would have been different."

Shrugging tiredly, Kate said, "Maybe you're right, Sam. But it's too late for all of us. Peter died in a war without reason. Rachel, Jessica and I grew up in a war zone afterward. The war in our house killed my mother. It drove us all away—until now."

Without thinking, Sam reached out briefly and settled his hand on her shoulder. He felt her internal tension through his fingers.

"You're coming home, Kate. The ranch is in bad shape, and I don't know what your dreams are anymore. Maybe you'll sell it off before it goes into bankruptcy. Maybe you'll decide to stay and fight for your mother's dreams and make them come true after all.''

Kate shut her eyes, her heart pounding, at Sam's brief touch. His fingers had a strong and steadying effect on her reeling emotions. Somehow, in his presence, her numbed senses were coming alive. She was shocked but grateful. Kate thought prison had destroyed a vital part of her. Apparently it hadn't. Sam was able to bring that part of her out from hiding deep within herself. For the first time, she felt a glimmer of hope.

Lifting her head, she looked into his warm gray eyes.

''Sam, in some ways, you haven't changed at all. Hope for the hopeless—that's you. I'm going to let the ranch go bankrupt. I don't have any money—not a cent. Let Kelly's dream die. It doesn't deserve to live any longer, as far as I'm concerned.''

Nothing could have prepared Kate for what she saw as Sam drove through the huge entrance gate of the Donovan Ranch. It was a ranch with a hundred-year history behind it. A colorful history. A tragic one. The gate itself had been made by Kelly's grandfather out of large, flat chunks of red sandstone, white limestone boulders and black lava that had been mortared together. The twin towers rose ten feet in the air, joined by a huge black piece curving across the top on which was written Donovan Ranch.

Kate looked hungrily down the rutted dirt road. She knew it led back off the highway for five miles, to the main ranch headquarters. On both sides, she saw cattle ambling about, looking for sparse bits of grass to eat. The cattle looked thin. Almost starved. It angered her.

"The cattle seem in bad shape."

Sam drove gingerly down the road, avoiding the worst of the ruts. "We've had drought for two years, Kate. There isn't the normal forage available."

"I suppose Kelly didn't supplement with hay?"

"He couldn't. He was out of money. The local feed store refused to loan him any more money. He never paid his bills."

"Do you know how much in debt he was?"

Sam pointed to the glove box. "Kelly kept all his important papers in the rolltop desk in his office. I got them and put them in there. His will is in there, too."

"Kelly never believed in banks or safety deposit boxes, did he?" Kate asked as she opened the glove box. She glanced at Sam.

"Have you looked through his stuff?"

He shook his head. "No. That's not my business, Kate. Maybe when I was ranch foreman it was. But not now."

"So," she murmured, unfolding the will, "how much in debt was he?" Kate knew that all the local ranchers knew a lot about each other's business. There were only one or two feed stores to get grain and hay from, so information was concentrated and gossip was normal.

"I heard a hundred thousand dollars in debt," Sam said almost apologetically. He saw Kate wince. Her lovely, full mouth thinned as she read over the two-page will that Kelly had written some time ago. "The local bank is foreclosing on the mortgage,'' he warned her. ''And unless you or your sisters can come up with a hefty chunk to salve the bank's continuing loss with Kelly, they will foreclose.''

Kate skimmed the handwritten document, made out in her father's scrawly, almost unreadable writing. Her heart squeezed in pain. He had made her executor, leaving everything to Kate to dispense with as she wanted. The discovery was shattering. Unexpected.

''I don't believe this,'' she whispered, gripping the papers with both hands.

Sam slowed as the road began to snake back and forth.

''What's wrong?''

''This is crazy!'' Kate held up the will to him. ''Kelly's leaving everything to me! Me, of all people. I thought he hated me. We fought so much. He disowned me....''

''I don't think he hated you, Kate. You were a lot like him in some ways. You two had a lot of fights, but I find it hard to believe that a father could hate his own daughter.''

''How could he love a daughter who is hardheaded? Stubborn? A daughter with a hair-trigger temper?''

''You are all of those things.'' Sam glanced at her. ''You have your mother's heart, though. And that's where you two parted company. A lot of your arguments with Kelly were over rights for your mother and two sisters.''

Kate tried to think despite the shock and pain. ''Kelly wrote this a year ago. I was in prison. And he left me everything. How...why?" Tears burned unexpectedly in her eyes, and for once, Kate let them come. Distractedly she wiped at them with trembling fingers, barely able to breathe. "He never came to my trial, Sam. I thought he hated me. That he was ashamed of me. I thought that was why he didn't come. So if he was ashamed, why did he write his will this way? I don't understand it. I just don't..."

As gently as he could, Sam said, "Listen to me, Kate. You're in shock over Kelly's passing. You're probably pretty numbed out from being in prison, which had to be a hell in itself. You haven't had time to come up for air and adjust. Your father just died. You've inherited a ranch that's got a broken back. You're a hundred thousand dollars in debt in a blink of an eye. That's a lot to handle, Gal."

Gal. He'd often called her that as a term of affection when they had gone together so long ago. Kate felt the tenderly spoken word sink into her shaken senses and take the edge off her pain for a moment. Her fingers tightened around the will and the print blurred before her eyes. The jostling of the truck on the endless ruts brought her back to reality.

"Prepare yourself," Sam warned, as they climbed a small hill.

Almost eagerly, Kate looked up. She knew this knoll; just past it the land dropped a thousand feet into Echo Canyon, where there were black walls of lava created millions of years ago when volcanic activity was high. Oak Creek meandered along the bottom. A moment later she saw the layers of red sandstone beneath the white limestone cap of the canyon.

The last mile of the road wound like an angry snake downward.

There was only enough room for a single vehicle. To her right was Deer Mountain, a huge rounded hill covered with prickly pear cactus, junipers and large, smooth black boulders. The mountain got its name because the small deer of the area laid under the junipers and slept during the noontime heat, only to come down the mountains at dusk to drink from the creek near the ranch house before they began foraging.

Down below, Kate caught glimpses of the Donovan homestead. Over the years, many cottonwoods had been planted—her mother's wish, because cottonwoods were sacred to Native Americans. Now the darkly polished leaves of those tall, spreading trees were in fall color and hid the ranch from prying eyes. Odula had loved privacy. Kate recalled the bitter fights her mother had gotten into with Kelly. She'd fought for every tree she'd planted around the main buildings of the ranch. Kelly had refused to help, saying it was a waste, but Odula had wanted the shade and coolness, not to mention the privacy.

Kate recalled helping her mother plant those magnificent cottonwoods that now graced a good ten acres of the ranch's central core. The red, yellow and orange leaves, combined with the red, black and white of the canyon walls, made a kaleidoscope of colors.

"It looks so beautiful," Kate murmured, her voice wobbly as she strained to drink in the familiarity of the place where she had grown up. "I've been gone so long...." And how could she have stayed away? This was such a magnificent place. Her mother had called this canyon Rainbow Canyon, not Echo Canyon as Kelly's forebears had named it. Yes, it was a rainbow of living, vibrant colors. Kate's gaze darted here and there. She saw the many caves up on the wall of the canyon, some of which she and her sisters had played in as youngsters. They'd found many Indian relics, some quite old, but had left them undisturbed.

The memories came flooding back...hundreds of them, good and bad. Kate found herself drowning in her feelings from the past. As the truck took the last curve onto the flat canyon floor, Kate gripped her hands in her lap, afraid to breathe. Sam had said the ranch's back was broken. What did he mean?

She didn't have long to find out. The cooling screen of cottonwoods gave way, revealing the main ranch house for the first time. Built of a creamy adobe brick, it was a sprawling place, the roof angled just enough so that the little rain they got would run off. Kate remembered the flowers that her mother had once planted around the fence surrounding the main house. Now that fence pitched forward, in dire need of paint and repair, with yellowed weeds growing around it.

Kate's heart beat hard as Sam braked the truck in front of the house. She saw that the windows were grimy and dirty and cobwebs were everywhere. The front door was hanging open, the wood split from a kick or two. Several windows were cracked and some had panes knocked out of them. Kelly's drunken rages, Kate thought, as she climbed out of the truck. She felt as if she were in a nightmare.

To the left of the house was a huge barn. Sam hadn't been wrong about a "broken back"—the ridge line of the roof was sagging badly and several shingles were missing. The barn doors hung askew. The wood was gray and weathered, in dire need of a protective coat of paint. Beside the barn were many corrals filled with Arabian horses—too many for the size of the enclosures. Several of the posts were leaning at an angle and barbed wire, which shouldn't have been used to restrain horses anyway, was rusted and poorly strung.

She felt Sam come and stand at her side. He placed his hands on his hips as she surveyed the horse area.

"Kelly did his own trimming and shoeing on the Arabs," he told her in a low voice. "Most of those animals are down on their heels. That's how long it's been since they've been trimmed."

Kate grimaced. "They have water?"

"Yes, plenty." Sam motioned toward them. "What you're running low on is hay. I'm bringing a truckload over for you tonight. There's no sense in letting these animals starve from neglect."

Kate hung her head. "Sam, you're a real guardian angel. Somehow I'll pay you back. I promise...."

He gazed down at her. "You owe me nothing, Kate. Consider this a gift."

"If Old Man Cunningham found out you were shipping a load of hay over here, he'd hit the ceiling."

Grinning a little, Sam said, "He doesn't know where it's going. And he won't, either. I'll pay him for it. The check will go into his bank account and he'll never know the difference."

Kate turned, unable to deal with his generosity. To the right of the ranch house were five other houses,

as well as the outbuildings that housed an aging
grader, a bulldozer, a backhoe, two tractors and other
farm equipment. She could see all the work that
needed to be done. Kelly was a master mechanic, but
he'd often left parts lying around, dirty bowls of oil
here and there, not to mention greasy rags. Some
things never changed.

"You got wheels," Sam said, pointing to a
green-and-white Ford pickup that had seen better
days. "I checked it before I left to come and get you.
It runs, but if I were you, I'd keep an eye on the oil
gauge. This thing had blue smoke rolling out of it."

"That truck looks like it's twenty years old," Kate
said.

"Kelly never threw anything away. He always repaired it himself. And if he couldn't, it sat."

"The place looks like a dump," Kate said grimly.
Gone was the pristine house, the sparkling windows,
the white picket fence with bright wildflowers adorn-
ing it like a colorful necklace. When her mother was
alive, things had been kept clean. The place looked
like a garbage pit in comparison.

"I know," Sam said sadly. He cupped her elbow
and led her through the gateless picket fence. "The
inside of the house is filthy. Kelly lived pretty
sparsely."

Kate tried to steel herself but it didn't help. Her
mother had kept this old, rambling ranch house neat
as a pin, with no dust, no sand on the floor. As Kate
entered the broken front door, which hung to one side,
she gave a little cry of distress.

The interior was dark. Cobwebs laden with layers
of dust hung everywhere, like grayish white chande-

liers. The grit of sand crunched under their feet. The oak floor had once been a pale golden yellow; now she couldn't see it for the dust. Odula's frilly white curtains had been traded for dark maroon ones that were drawn shut across each window. The odor of whiskey assailed her nostrils. The smell of garbage sickened her.

When she got to the large kitchen, Kate gagged. Kelly had left food out on all the counters. Sacks of garbage were everywhere. She saw cockroaches scurry away as they entered the room.

"This is horrible," she whispered, gripping the doorjamb and staring into the dark depths. "Horrible...."

Chapter Three

The screeching crow of a rooster very close to the bedroom window awakened Kate from a deep, healing sleep. Wrinkling her nose, she pushed the covers away from her upper body. Burying her head in the pillow, she lay there for a moment without moving. Every bone in her body ached as she felt the fingers of reality tugging at her. The bed was soft. There were no clanking bars, no chatter of women and guards. Just the blessed sound of a damn rooster crowing its fool head off. Her mouth twitched and she slowly rolled over, luxuriating in the bed and the sense of serenity she'd felt ever since opening her eyes.

The ceiling of her old bedroom met her gaze. The paint was chipped and peeling. The brass bed she slept in had been hers since she was a child. It felt good to be back in it—it reminded Kate briefly of being in her mother's arms. The goose-down quilt was warm and comforting across her tall, lanky form. The window was open to the cool November morning and she could hear the soft snort of horses, the whinny of a foal, the lowing of cattle in the distance.

All those animals were her responsibility now. That made Kate sit up. She rubbed her puffy eyes with the backs of her hands. Wearing only a clean T-shirt given to her by the rehab house, Kate pushed herself out of bed and headed down the hall to the bathroom. She'd managed to make the house more livable yesterday. The last thing she'd done before hitting the bed at one a.m. was to clean the kitchen. She couldn't stand filth. And that was what Kelly had lived in. The place was a pigsty. Although the house still seemed gloomy, she felt strangely buoyant.

As she took a quick, hot shower and scrubbed her hair, Kate's thoughts returned to Sam. He'd remained with her all day yesterday, helping her, working his tail off to feed, water and vet as much as he could. He'd also brought enough hay for the next three days to feed the Arabian horse herd.

After her shower, Kate dressed in a pink tank top and a pair of Levi's, then hunted up her old cowboy boots. Someone—probably her mother—had put them in a box. They were ancient, the leather hard and cracked, but they would have to do until she could buy a new pair. One didn't live on a ranch and not wear protective boots. Running her fingers through her damp hair to put it into place, Kate hurried to the kitchen. To her surprise, she inhaled the odor of fresh coffee perking. Who...?

Warily, she slowed down as she approached the

kitchen. A radio was playing softly, nice instrumental FM music, the kind she'd missed in prison. All she'd heard there was hard rock, until she'd thought she'd go insane from the raucous sounds. The odor of bacon frying tempted her. Someone was in the kitchen. Mystified, Kate halted at the door.

"Sam!"

He was at the electric stove, a skillet full of potatoes and eggs in hand. "You look a lot better than I feel," he muttered, and turned back to his duties at the stove.

"But—how? I mean, I didn't hear you come in." Kate moved to the coffeemaker and poured herself a cup of coffee. Her heart was beating strongly in her breast, and she tried not to stare at Sam like the love-struck teenager she'd once been. He wore a white cotton shirt, the sleeves rolled up his arms, a faded pair of Levi's, a belt and cowboy boots. The red bandanna around his throat emphasized the thick, corded muscles of his neck. The way his shirt stretched revealed the power of his chest and the breadth of his shoulders. There was nothing weak about Sam. There never had been.

He was clean shaven. She saw where he'd nicked himself on the side of his hard, uncompromising jaw. A piece of paper was still stuck on the wound.

"Dress you up, but can't take you anywhere," she murmured, moving over to where he stood. Gently, she eased the tiny piece of paper from the cut on his jaw.

Sam stood very still. He felt Kate's warm presence so very, very close to him. As her fingers brushed his jaw, his heart thudded hard in his chest to underscore how badly he ached for her touch, no matter how brief. When she lifted the paper away, he cut her a sidelong glance. Kate's cheeks were a bright pink color. It reminded him of the few struggling pink flowers outside the picket fence. Her eyes... Lord, her eyes were clear, and for the first time, he saw glints of gold in them. Groaning inwardly, he fought the urge to turn and place his arms around her, crush her against him, find that soft, parted mouth and take her. Take her all the way to heaven. He knew he could. He knew that in his heart and soul.

"Thanks," he rumbled.

Kate dropped the paper into the cleaned trash can at the corner of the kitchen sink. "You must have gotten up awful early to get over here."

"A little," he hedged, pouring the concoction onto two awaiting plates. "Come on, let's eat. We've got a lot to do this morning before I show up at the Bar C at eight a.m."

Grateful beyond words, Kate sat down. "This is almost like breakfast in bed."

Sam lifted a forkful of potatoes and eggs and looked at her over them. "That was kind of the plan. I was going to have a 'Welcome home, Kate' breakfast waiting for you down here when you got up. You beat me to it."

Touched, Kate ate hungrily. She was starved, in fact. Ranch food had a taste all its own. Prison food was like cardboard. "The rooster woke me up."

"You might take the woman off the ranch, but you won't take the ranch out of the woman."

Kate watched him eating his meal. Sam's plate was heaped with food, but then, he would be working a good twelve hours today and he needed that kind of fuel. There wasn't a scrap of fat on his hard, well-muscled body, either. Ranching didn't encourage excess weight. She had none herself, but for different reasons.

Looking around the clean kitchen, Kate marveled at the difference. "This place looks almost livable now."

Sam nodded. "It reminds me of the place when Odula was alive."

"Yes," Kate whispered, suddenly choked up with memories of her mother. "Over the years I've come to realize just how lucky I was to have her as a mother."

"She was special," Sam agreed. He stopped eating and studied Kate's features. He saw the pain and loss in her eyes and heard it in her low voice. "You're so much like her." Kate was the spitting image of her, but Sam didn't say that. She had Odula's dark, good looks, those blue eyes that were so thoughtful and filled with intelligence. Although Kate's black hair was still damp and clung to her shapely skull, she was beautiful, in his eyes. He still saw some of that wild, rebellious mustang in her, although it was deeply hidden.

"I got over here at four-thirty this morning," he said, breaking the silence. "The horses are fed and watered. I let the cattle out of the pens and they can graze for what they can find. This first pasture goes for a hundred acres, so they'll find enough for the next couple of days, until you can get some help here."

"It seems so overwhelming, Sam." She put the

fork down and shook her head. "The last thing I remember thinking last night before I fell asleep was that I need money to get this place on its feet. I don't have any. I didn't earn very much while being in...prison."

Being careful not to respond to the word *prison*, Sam kept on eating. His jaw was still warm where Kate had touched him. She had the touch of a hesitant, wary butterfly, he decided. "Then you're going to keep the ranch?"

Shrugging, Kate continued to eat. "I don't know. I'm waiting to see what Rachel and Jessica say. If we don't have two pennies to rub together among us, the ranch will go into bankruptcy."

"Do you have any idea of their finances?"

Rubbing her brow, Kate said, "No." She saw him frown. "I haven't been very good about staying in touch with them the last two years...."

"But at least you're talking?"

She nodded. "Rachel and I have had our fights, and Jessica, bless her spacy little self, stayed in touch, too. I'm on good terms with them, Sam."

"Good, because right now, if you're going to save your home, it's going to take the three of you, all the money you own and a hell of a lot of elbow grease, time and miracles."

Wouldn't it though? Kate remained silent. She knew so little about her sisters. A letter or phone call once a year had maintained the ties, but she knew hardly anything about how life had treated them. She focused her attention back on Sam.

"Why are you doing this?"

He raised his head and held her soft blue gaze. "Why?"

"Is there an echo in here?"

He grinned a little, wiped his mouth on the paper napkin and put the plate aside. "Why wouldn't I?"

"Don't answer a question with a question, Sam McGuire. So what if you worked for Kelly for five years? What did he ever do to make you this loyal and helpful to us?"

Sam withheld the real answer to her question. Instead, his mouth curved into a lopsided grin. "Cowboy's code. You help your neighbor when things go to hell in a handbasket."

She studied him ruthlessly, combing his innocent features with her eyes. "I know you better than that, Sam. How about the truth?"

"That *is* the truth," he said gently, slowly getting out of the chair. The wooden legs scraped against the linoleum floor.

"Humph," Kate said, rising in turn. "No one from the Bar C came over here in the last ten years except you." She took her plate to the sink, rinsed it and put it in the newly cleaned dishwasher. Leaning against the counter, she took the mug that Sam handed her. There was such a wonderful familiarity with him. Things had always been so easy between them—until the breakup of their relationship. Kate had had a terrible fight with Kelly one day and, in desperation, she had run way from home, but not before leaving Sam a note saying that she couldn't take it anymore. She'd planned on leaving not because she didn't love Sam, but because at home she was trapped in a bad situation that had no end. She'd left the note at Sam's house, saying goodbye—forever—and then had hitched a ride to Phoenix, truly intent on leaving.

For two weeks, Kate had walked the streets of Phoenix aimlessly, alone, hurting and confused. A policewoman, sympathetic and helpful, had finally picked her up, and Kate went back home. Kelly had tried to be apologetic. Her mother, who had been crazed with grief and worry, welcomed her back with open arms, as did Rachel and Jessica.

It was when she went back to school the next day, her nerves in knots about trying to find some way to apologize to Sam, that Kate had heard the news. In her absence, Carol had walked into Sam's life. Carol had stolen him from her. Maybe that wasn't entirely true, Kate acknowledged. Her own decisions played a key role in all of this. Sam had thought she was gone forever. Carol was pretty, a cheerleader, and Sam was the star of the local football team. It was a natural pairing. And Kate? She was a ranch brat who worked several hours before going to high school and afterward until dark, taking care of the cattle and horses, with her family. She didn't have time for clubs or after-school activities—certainly not cheerleading. But then, Kate reminded herself, she'd never have made it as a cheerleader. She just wasn't the outgoing, bubbly type. She had too much Indian in her; she was too deeply introverted.

"Does Old Man Cunningham know you're over here?" Kate wondered, sipping the fragrant coffee.

Sam leaned back against the counter, leaving about a foot of space between them. "No."

"Do you live at the foreman's house at the Bar C?"

"Yes."

"I don't imagine your wife appreciates you being over here."

He raised his brows and studied her briefly. "She doesn't care."

"Why?"

"Because Carol and I got a divorce last year."

Kate felt the blood drain from her face as she stared up into his dark gray eyes. "Divorce?"

He shrugged and looked away. "You don't need my tales of woe on top of your own right now. After our son, Chris, went off to college in California— Stanford—Carol and I decided that it just wasn't working."

Kate swallowed hard, wanting to know more. But it wasn't the time or place to ask questions. Stunned by his admission, she felt her head reel and her heart pound. Sam was as loyal as they came. What had caused him to consent to a divorce? Looking away, Kate muttered, "At least you stayed together until your son was raised. That's something a lot of couples don't even consider nowadays."

"Yes," Sam said, pushing away from the counter, "and they should. At least, Carol and I did. We agreed that Chris needed that kind of stability."

"So you made the best of it."

Sam's mouth quirked. "We did what we had to do." He paused thoughtfully, then said, "Listen, we need to move about thirty of the Arabs into a new pasture area. Let's saddle up and get it done. That way, it will give you about a week's grace on feed for them."

* * *

The familiar, soothing sound of creaking saddle leather, the jangle of a horse's bit, was like music to Kate. She and Sam rode on two of the ranch's Arabian horses as they moved the herd to an upper pasture, much closer to the Mogollon Rim area. The Rim, as they called it, was a huge jutting masterpiece of black lava, red sandstone and white limestone. It rose two thousand feet straight up from the desert floor of the ranch. The north pasture hugged the foot of the Rim and Oak Creek flowed through it, a natural source of water for the horses.

As Kate and Sam rode, their legs briefly touched every once in a while. Kate thrilled to the unexpected contact with Sam. He sat so straight and proud in the saddle, born to the rocking motion of the bay gelding beneath him. The November chill made her feel alive, though she was glad for the denim jacket she wore over her tank top. The air was sweet with the odor of the pine trees that topped the Rim ahead of them.

The huge, carved canyon was over twenty miles long, ending at Flagstaff, and the Donovan spread included four miles of it, so that the canyon mouth actually occurred on the ranch.

Kate loved the canyon area of the ranch. It was a startling contrast to the prickly pear and juniper of the hot desert. The tall Ponderosa pines stood like proud sentinels on the Rim, reminding her of Sam's proud stance when he walked.

The horse she road was a bay mare named Cinnamon, a long, rangy Arabian looking more like a Thoroughbred at fifteen hands high. She sighed as Cinnamon danced. How good it felt to have the move-

ment of a horse beneath her! How much she had
missed this!

"You're looking awful pensive," Sam observed.
He saw the joy in Kate's eyes as she turned her attention to him. For the first time, he saw the soft corners of her mouth turned upward, not in. The flush
on her cheeks only made her more desirable in his
eyes.

"I was just thinking how much I missed all of
this," she said, gesturing toward the mouth of the
canyon directly in front of them. "How could I have
left this place? It's heaven. It really is."

"Sometimes when a caged animal is freed, the taste
of freedom is pretty heady."

Kate understood the analogy. Her gaze dug into his,
though the rim of his black Stetson was tipped so that
she could barely see his eyes. "You're right," she
admitted. "I hated prison. I hated everything about
it." She inhaled the pine-scented air, the dampness
that flowed out of the canyon to the dryer reaches of
the desert. And then she regretted her words because
she saw Sam's face close. No longer was there that
wonderful openness they'd just shared. Internally, she
tried to prepare herself for his judgment.

"You're no killer," Sam told her in a low voice,
holding her startled glance. "I never believed what I
read in the papers about you...about that group you
got tangled up with."

Relief sheeted through her and Kate could no
longer hold his dark, burning stare. Then she forced
herself to look at him again. He deserved her courage,
not her cowardice. "You're right," she whispered,
her voice raw with emotion. "I did get tangled up

with the wrong bunch. They were hotheads, Sam. At least some of them were. Stupid. Just plain stupid. I was stupid, too. But I never was involved in the plans to blow up that nuclear power plant, I swear to you. It was the undercover FBI agent who suggested it and then whipped the men into planning it. I was against it from the beginning, but they just laughed at me.''

"So the men who planned it skipped across the Mexican border and you took the fall for them?''

Grimacing, Kate nodded. "Yes, the three men who planned it are somewhere in South America.'' Free. Not imprisoned as she had been.

"Sounds like the FBI wanted a scapegoat, Kate. You were at the wrong place at the wrong time and they wanted to make an example out of an extremist environmental group. You got left holding the bag.''

Nodding, Kate compressed her lips. "I didn't think you'd understand, Sam. I guess I was figuring you would swallow the FBI and newspaper stories.''

Chuckling, he reached over and gently touched her shoulder. How badly he wanted to slide his leather-gloved hand around her tense body and hold her. Kiss her senseless. Forcing himself to break contact, he said, "You and I have a long history, Kate. You're like a wild mustang. You want your freedom and you want to have your say. Nothing wrong with that. Maybe you made some poor choices about who to hang out with, but that's all. I remember when a calf or foal would die, you'd cry. I recall a time when the horse you were riding hit a gopher hole and broke its leg. I was with you when that happened. You couldn't shoot the horse, even to put it out of its misery. So why would I think you were capable of blowing up

a damn nuclear power plant that might kills thousands
of human beings?''

Tears swam in her eyes and she looked away, trying to get hold of her unraveling emotions. A lump
formed in her throat. She was so close to sobbing.
Her fingers tightened around the reins as she continued to avoid Sam's probing gaze.

"I—I just made some very stupid choices with
people," she agreed. "I can't kill. I never could. But
they wouldn't believe me, Sam." She turned to him,
tears burning her eyes. "Do you know how angry and
frustrated I was? I was so ashamed. I could barely
look Rachel and Jessica in the eye when they came
to my trial. I didn't blame Kelly for not coming. I
knew I was the worst disappointment in his life...."

Pulling his horse to a halt, Sam turned the animal
around so he was facing Kate. Their legs touched, his
dark leather chaps against her slim jeans-clad leg.
"Listen to me," he growled, reaching out and cupping her jaw. He felt her tremble. "Not everyone is
ashamed of you. I'm not—I never was. Yes, there are
going to be people in Sedona who have judged you,
Kate. But folks who know you will know you are
innocent." He brushed his thumb against her cheek
where the tears had fallen. The suffering on her face
nearly cracked his massive control. As her lips parted
and trembled, all he wanted to do was kiss her and
take that pain she was suffering into himself. Right
now he was stronger emotionally than she was. He
knew he could do that for her, but would she let him?
Sam was very unsure. The old Kate he'd known well.
This was a new Kate—a woman damaged badly by
prison, by being unfairly branded as a terrorist. He

had no idea what those wounds had done to her—yet. And until he did, he could do little but be supportive and try to nurture her in small ways.

A breath escaped Kate as she closed her eyes and laid her cheek into his gloved palm. How strong Sam felt. She wanted desperately to be in his arms, to once more feel those iron bands closing around her and holding her safe. "I feel like raw meat inside," she continued, unable to look at him. The hot tears beaded on her thick lashes and then fell down her cheeks. "I'm so afraid to go into town, into the feed store, and sense their eyes on me, to feel them judging me, Sam."

"I know," he rasped. "I know."

Pulling away from his touch, Kate blinked her eyes rapidly and then wiped the tears away. "But I've got to do it. I can't keep running and hiding. I started that habit at seventeen. And when I was eighteen, I ran away from this ranch—and Kelly—for good. I've been running ever since. I've made a mess of my life, Sam. I feel bad inside. I'm ashamed. My sisters are successful. They made something worthwhile of their lives. I haven't. I'm the oldest and I've screwed up everything I ever touched."

Sam forced his hand down on his leather chaps. Kate's voice tore at him. She had no idea how much he still loved her—had always loved her. And she wouldn't know, either. He was a failure, too—at his relationship with her in high school, and later with his loveless marriage. Kate would never love him after all the lousy mistakes he'd made. He was the real loser here, but she didn't realize it. All the dreams they'd shared during those two years together were shattered. Gone.

But Sam had to put aside the past for the time being. There was enough going on right now. He knew Kate was suffering over Kelly's death. As much as she hated Kelly, he was still her father, and she had much grieving to do. After eighteen months in prison, she was suddenly free and that had to be causing her a hell of a lot of readjusting, as well. And then to have the ranch going into bankruptcy, to have her roots, her heritage taken away from her—something he knew was so intrinsic to her—made him wonder how she could handle it all.

One thing Sam had discovered early about Kate was that her hellish years growing up with an alcoholic father had made her strong. She had a backbone of steel. Sam knew some steel was flexible and could be tempered by heat and fire, while other steel was brittle and couldn't stand stress at all. What kind was Kate made of? What had life done to her? Had it tempered her strength and courage so that she could bend and weather all of this? Or would she crack under the strain, broken like this ranch was? Sam had no answers. And as much as he wanted to help Kate, he knew the outcome depended solely on her own grit, her spirit to fight back, to reclaim her rightful heritage—no matter what odds were staring her in the face.

"Well," he told her heavily, "I'm no prize either, if you want to look at it that way."

Sniffing, Kate wiped the last of the tears from her face.

"What are you talking about?"

"I made the worst decision of my life by marrying Carol. It was eighteen years of hell. A prison. So, if you made a mistake and spent only eighteen months in a prison, who's the stupid one here?" He grinned a little, trying to lift her spirits.

Kate stared at him, openmouthed. "But—I thought you *loved* Carol."

Grimacing, he took off his hat and rubbed his furrowed brow with the back of his arm. "You talk about mistakes. Kate, when I got your note that you were running away for good, I believed you. I knew how bad it was for you at home, and you'd often told me you thought that running away, leaving Sedona, was the only thing that would help." He stared down at his leather-clad fist. Forcing himself, he looked up into Kate's eyes.

"I got roaring drunk three days later. I'd been in touch with your mother. The police were looking for you. I knew you'd really left this time. Not that I blamed you...." He shook his head sadly, his voice dropping with regret. "A couple of my friends saw how down I was by your leaving. They talked me into going to a party. Carol was there and she was drunk, too. I remember passing out. The next thing I knew, I was on her parents' bed, buck naked, and so was she. I should have had a condom. I should have said no, but things got pretty hot and I had sex with her. Talk about stupid mistakes." He rubbed his jaw. "It was my fault as much as hers. Grieving for you being gone, I was drunker than hell, with hormones raging and no condom. Well—" he glanced at her grimly "—Carol ended up pregnant from that one time. My parents were heartbroken. They had college in mind for me. Instead, I married Carol out of responsibility to our baby.''

Kate's heart ripped with pain. Sam's pain. ''I'm so sorry, Sam! I never knew.... When I left that time, I thought I was running away for good.'' She tried to take a deep breath, but her heart hurt so much, it was impossible. Her voice was barely above a whisper. ''What a mess I made by doing that. I felt horrible leaving you, but I had nowhere to turn. As much as you tried to protect me, Sam, you couldn't. I knew that. Kelly had threatened to come after you, too. He knew we loved each other. I was afraid if I ran to your house, he'd follow me and hurt you, so after leaving that note, I hitched a ride to Phoenix.'' Shrugging painfully, Kate held his saddened gaze. ''I spent two weeks just wandering around. I was so hungry.... I didn't have any money, so I begged for food at the back of restaurants.'' She sighed. ''I'd always thought you'd fallen in love with her and out of love with me because I left you. Not that I blamed you....''

''No, Kate.'' Sam cleared his throat and looked up at the sky, now alive with high clouds turned a dark pink and lavender as the sun approached the horizon. ''I was so damned ashamed of what I'd done—how I'd fouled up my life, college plans, and hurt my parents—that I let you think that. I was just too damned cowardly to really tell you the truth. Until now.''

Joy and shock suffused her. Kate stared at his grim features. ''And the past eighteen years was to—''

''To give Chris, our son, some stability. I owed him that much. It wasn't his fault we screwed up. As it stands, he's going to college and he'll get a good start in life. I made my bed and I laid in it, Kate. I never was angry at you for leaving me that note. If anybody understood, I did. At least you didn't make the kinds of mistakes I made. You made others, that's all. But nothing worse, in my eyes, than the one I made with you.''

He'd been in a loveless marriage for eighteen years. Kate sat in the saddle, her feelings in turmoil, her head spinning with realizations and guilt over her own adolescent rebellion, over running away. By doing that, she'd set both herself and Sam on a course with disaster. ''I guess,'' she murmured, ''there's all kinds of prisons, aren't there?''

''Yes,'' he answered. ''The key is to survive them, Kate. That's what you've got to do now. Somehow you have to find the internal strength, the guts, to get through this—Kelly's passing, your responsibilities for the ranch. There's a great burden sitting on your shoulders, a hell of a lot of decisions in front of you. But you're Odula's daughter. You've not only got her blood, and her love of the land, you have her spirit.'' He swept his arm toward the canyon walls. ''I couldn't have survived my time in prison without being on this land. There's something special here, Kate. I don't know what it is, but it has me by the throat and I don't ever want it to let go.

''This land fed me, nurtured me through those years with Carol. I love my son deeply, and I was able to impart my love of this land to him. It's a part of him now, like it's a part of you and me.'' He sighed, looking down at his hand on the saddle horn. ''I hope that you stay here. Stay and try to root yourself here—for a lot of reasons. Some of them are purely selfish on my part. Others are not.'' He glanced at her through slitted eyes. "You're like a tree torn up, roots and all. Now you're getting a chance to come back, dig a hole and replant yourself. It won't be easy. It'll take back-breaking work. A commitment like I gave to my marriage, really. I don't know where the money will come from. I hope one of your sisters has it."

Shrugging, Sam reined his horse away from hers. "Come on," he said gruffly, "we've got to get the herd moving. I have to be at the Bar C soon or Old Man Cunningham will fire me for sure."

Chapter Four

Late in the afternoon, after vetting several young Arabians, Kate sat near a long wooden water trough. She dipped her hands into it and splashed her face, finding the water cool and refreshing. Murmuring over the luxury of it all, she straightened and wiped her eyes. This was a far cry from being in prison!

In the corral where she stood, there were twenty young foals, all black for the most part. It was amazing that the broodmares were bay, chestnut, white and gray, but the foals turned out black. Her gaze moved to a barbed wire enclosure away from the mothers and babies.

A black stallion, his coat gleaming in the November sun, paced back and forth endlessly. Gan, which was Apache for devil, didn't deserve such a name, Kate thought. Sam had told her that Kelly had won the black Arabian stud in a poker game in Sedona with some of his old cowboy buddies ten years earlier—shortly after Odula's death.

Her father had gotten drunk one night and gone to the Red Rock Inn, a famous landmark where cowboys frequently gathered to drink whiskey, smoke and play cutthroat poker. It was on that night that Kelly had bet his entire herd of prized, registered Arabian mares against Ben Turner's black stud. Luckily, Kelly won. But he hadn't won much, according to Sam. The horse, a hellion, was unmanageable. No one could ride Gan. No one could get near him except with a crop or some other protection in hand. The only reason the stud had been kept alive was the fact he could throw black foals a high percentage of the time. And in the world of Arabian horses, the color black was rare, so people paid more money to have one.

Kate's heart went out to the black animal. She decided that the stallion had probably met with heavy abuse in his younger days and had turned on humans as a result. Sam had told her that Kelly, in his drunken rages, would go out and throw rocks and jeer, tease the animal unmercifully. When Sam found him doing it, he'd haul Kelly away from the nervous stallion, which would be shaken and enraged. More than once Kelly had been bitten by the stud. Kate shook her head as she stood there watching the beautiful horse. Kelly had had it coming, there was no doubt.

Sam had left hours ago and she felt the emptiness inside her. Kate already missed his larger-than-life presence. She missed *him*, but was afraid to admit it to herself. Picking up the plastic toolbox containing vetting supplies, she leaned down and slipped between the slats of the fence. The work was endless, but she loved it. Being outdoors again, breathing fresh, pine-scented air and experiencing the dryness of the desert, was far preferable to being incarcerated in a prison.

Her muscles ached here and there; the long horseback ride with Sam had been heaven, but she hadn't put a leg over a horse since she'd left the ranch years ago. Now the muscles in her legs were tightening up. Her arms and shoulders were sore from helping Sam move fifty bales of alfalfa hay from his truck into the barn. But it felt good to be physical again. More and more Kate realized how much she'd missed this ranch, her roots.

When she thought of Rachel arriving tonight, her heart squeezed in fear. Her sister was two years younger than she. In high school, Rachel had been the popular one, voted school president her final year. And despite all her ranch chores, she'd managed to be a member of the debate club, too. Everyone knew and liked Rachel. She was beautiful, Kate acknowledged, with thick, long, brunette hair, dancing green eyes, a willowy figure. And she was smart as a whip.

Making sun tea later, Kate placed a gallon jar of cold water with four tea bags out in the sunlight, then sat down on the porch. It, too, needed a coat of paint. Everything did around the ranch. As she sat there, her arms resting on her knees, Kate wondered how she could revive the place. Hourly, she found herself wanting to save it more and more. Sam was right— her roots, her history, were here. Everything she was and was not came from this old ranch. Now it looked like her—battered and nearly destroyed from years of neglect. She'd nearly destroyed herself with a lot of bad choices, Kate acknowledged. But the circumstances of her life weren't anyone's fault but her own.

The fact that Kelly had left her as executor of the will and owner of the ranch bothered Kate more than she was willing to admit. How many times had he said she'd never be able to run a ranch of this size? That she and her sisters didn't have what it took to do so? So why had he left it to her? Why?

Near sundown, around six p.m., Kate heard a truck pull into the driveway. She wiped her hands on a towel and hung it on a peg. The odor of a pot of chili cooking on the stove permeated the kitchen as she moved through the room. Was it Rachel? Her heart sped up in anticipation.

The knock at the door, which she'd repaired earlier, echoed through the living room.

"Come on in," Kate called from the kitchen entrance.

Sam poked his head in the doorway.

Blinking, Kate halted midway through the living room. "Sam?" He'd said this morning that he wouldn't see her until the weekend.

"Howdy. Sorry to drop by unexpected," he said, standing uncertainly.

Frowning, Kate gestured for him to come in. "That's okay. What's wrong? You look worried."

With a grimace, he took off his hat and entered the room after wiping his dusty boots on the mat. "No more than usual. I just thought I'd drop by and see how you were getting on." If he'd been brazenly honest, Sam would have added, *I had to see you.* And he did. Almost every minute of his day, he'd rerun one of their conversations or visualized the precious smile that shadowed her so very serious mouth. He craved to see more of that dancing light in her eyes. Sam knew he didn't have the right to be here. At all. But he couldn't help himself as he stood there, hungrily absorbing the sight of Kate into his being.

"I was just going to eat some chili. Come on in," she invited. He looked tired, but then Sam had been up since four this morning, put in half a day's work here at the ranch and then gone over and put in eight solid hours at the Bar C. She noticed his jeans were soiled and his once-white shirt was dusty and had splotches of sweat across it. How handsome he looked even now, she decided, as she walked back to the kitchen with him. Automatically, her fingers grazed that spot where he'd cupped her face earlier that morning. The love she felt for him welled up in her, and she was unable to stop it. The feeling was good, strong and grounding. Another part of her, the scared, frightened mustang, wanted to run—again.

Automatically, Kate filled two bowls with chili and took some freshly made cornbread out of the oven. She cut several thick slices and gestured for Sam to sit down at the kitchen table.

"Dinner?" Sam grinned, looking at the hefty bowl of chili filled with onions and green Mexican chilies. The smell was mouthwatering.

"Why not? You've earned it. Wash your hands at the sink and then we can sit and eat. You can tell me over the dinner table what my next problem is."

Once they both sat down to eat, Kate marveled at how delicious the spicy chili tasted. Her mother's recipe. Mexican food was a main part of their fare, but so was fry bread, cornmeal and a lot of vegetables from her mother's background. By contrast, Kelly liked Irish stew, corned beef and cabbage and plenty of potatoes. All these things drifted back to Kate as she ate hungrily. Sam sat opposite her, eating just as much as she did. He went through half the cornbread, and she wasn't surprised. The sun tea made the meal complete. This was the first meal she'd made at home and it tasted marvelous.

"So," Kate murmured, placing her empty bowl in the sink after eating, "how did your day go? Like mine? Busier than a one-armed paper hanger?"

Sam took one more piece of cornbread, slathered it with butter and squeezed some honey from a plastic container over the top of it. "That sounds about right," he growled, giving her a slight grin. Kate was a damn fine cook, he'd discovered. But then, she was good at anything she set her mind to. As she stood at the kitchen counter, her back against it, sipping sun tea from a glass and studying him, he saw exhaustion around her eyes. Knowing her, she'd worked nonstop. Kate was a worker of the first order. She always had been.

"Listen," Sam said gently, as he wiped his hands on the napkin, stood up and walked over to her. "Why don't you rest a little, Kate? You're looking pretty worn out." Fighting himself, Sam cupped her shoulders. He ached to lean down and kiss her parting lips. He saw the surprise and then the molten longing in her blue eyes. And just as quickly, it was replaced with hurt. How badly he'd hurt both of them. Sam wished there was a way he could apologize enough to Kate on that account.

Kate held herself very stiffly, afraid to move, afraid to breathe. His hands felt stabilizing. Wonderful. How she wanted simply to surrender, lean against his powerful, strong form. Uncurling her fingers, she whispered unsteadily, "Please..."

Sam could smell her clean hair, and he longed to press his face against her head and inhale the sweet fragrance. He felt her tremble violently as he held her shoulders. Allowing his hands to drop back to his sides, he realized she didn't want him to touch her. He'd overstepped his bounds—damn his own selfish need and hunger for her! Moving away from her, he said gruffly, "Look, you have Kelly's funeral in a couple of days. Your sisters will be here. Right now you need them more than me."

Bitterly, Kate turned. She saw the dark, hooded look in Sam's eyes. Her body ached for his continued touch. "They may not want to save the ranch. They may not care anymore, Sam. Not that I could blame them. Kelly ran us off. He made it clear we weren't capable of running a ranch. As far as he was concerned, women were good for only one thing—having kids."

Sam raised his eyes toward the ceiling. "Kelly was old-fashioned."

"He was of caveman mentality," Kate retorted. "He *never* respected the three of us. Hell, he never respected our mother, and she was ten times smarter than he was. But he was too proud, too stiff-necked to listen to her counsel." Kate looked around the kitchen, her voice wobbling with sudden grief. "He didn't think women were worth a plugged nickel. Only a man could run this ranch.'' Her eyes hardened and she put her hands on her hips. ''I swear, Sam, if I can, I'll save this ranch even if I have to kill myself doing it.''

Sam knew there was no love lost between Kate and her father. Kelly had made sure of that. ''Look,'' he soothed, ''wait until Rachel gets here. You ladies have your mother's intelligence. My bet is that among the three of you, you'll come up with a plan to save the ranch.''

When Kate saw Rachel climb out of her rented vehicle, all her fear left her. Whatever their past, it didn't matter at that moment. Her sister was home. Rachel's long, reddish-brown hair was still thick and curly, falling below her shoulders. At thirty-five, she was tall, proud looking and still just as thin and ballerinalike as she'd been as a girl. Slightly shorter than Kate, Rachel wore a long-sleeved, dark green sweater, a black skirt that fell to her ankles and sensible dark brown shoes.

Kate flew off the wooden porch, her arms wide. ''Rachel!'' she cried.

Rachel smiled tiredly and opened her own arms. ''Hi, sis....''

Kate squeezed her hard, tears coming to her eyes as she stepped back to look at her sister. Behind her, the night was coming on, a dark cape over the twilight sky. ''I'm so glad you're here.''

''Me, too.'' Rachel smiled unsteadily, tears in her eyes. ''How *are* you?''

Kate shrugged. "I'm free of prison, if that's what you mean," she said a little defensively.

Rachel picked up her leather traveling bag from the rear seat, then a black physician's bag. "Let's go inside, shall we? I'm beat from a nine-hour flight across the Atlantic and then a five-hour flight out of New York."

Warily, Kate took the rest of her luggage and led her into the house. "You'd better prepare yourself," she warned.

Somehow, Kate felt responsible for the bad condition of the house as Rachel walked through it to her old bedroom, down the hall and across from Kate's.

"Kelly really let the place go, didn't he?" Rachel said, dropping her luggage on the recently made bed.

"Yes. Everything around here is either broken or ready to fall apart. Are you hungry?"

Rachel pushed her dark hair away from her face. "No...thirsty though."

"Come to the kitchen. I've got fresh coffee made."

Rachel smiled. "No coffee for me. I'm on a homeopathic remedy for grief and coffee will antidote it."

Kate smiled a little, falling in step with her sister. Despite her fears she was glad to see Rachel and already felt the effects of her solid, soothing nature. "That's right, you're a homeopath. I tried to figure out what you did from those once-a-year letters we sent to one another. It's a type of alternative medicine?"

"Yes," Rachel said, "it's a natural medicine discovered over two hundred years ago in Germany, and it's practiced around the world."

"You said you're teaching at Sheffield College near London?" Kate poured her some iced tea and they sat down at the table.

"Thanks, Katie. Yes, I'm one of the instructors there." Rachel reached out and gripped her hand. "How are *you,* though?"

"I'm home," Kate said simply. "It feels good, Rachel. Really good. Better than I thought it would."

Sipping the tea, Rachel studied her as a comfortable silence fell between them. "I'm talking more about how you're handling Kelly's death. Where are you at with that?"

Rachel's hand was warm and dry as she folded it over Kate's. Kate had always marveled at her sister's beautiful hands. They were so long and artistic looking. Hers, in comparison, were large knuckled with blunt-cut nails and lots of old ranching scars covering them. Moving her gaze back up to her sister's face, Kate saw that Rachel's green eyes were filled with concern, and she tightened her grip.

"I heard it from Sam McGuire," Kate continued. "He called to tell me about Kelly at the halfway house I was staying in when I got out of prison a couple of days ago."

Gently, Rachel said, "How are you *feeling,* Kate?"

Frowning, Kate pulled her hand away. "I'm not feeling anything," she said flatly. "Not a damn thing, and I don't care if it's right or wrong."

"There's nothing wrong with that response," Rachel said. "Grief has many faces."

"I'm not grieving," Kate said, her eyes flashing.

"I am." Her sister sighed. "I took *ignatia amara,*

a homeopathic remedy for grief. When Sam called me, I started to cry."

"Why? All Kelly ever did was make *us* cry. I'm not shedding one tear for that bastard after what he did to all of us."

"He was a very injured human being," Rachel said slowly.

"He injured all of *us!*" Kate lowered her voice. "I'm sorry. I'm just upset. So much has happened since I got home."

"Tell me about it?"

How like Rachel, Kate thought, to be the listener. She always had been. Having her here was good. Kate felt less threatened now. Almost relieved. Rachel was the cool-headed one in the family, more like their mother, who had always listened in silence and then chewed over everything internally before speaking her thoughts. Kate, on the other hand, had inherited Kelly's hair-trigger temper, his brusqueness and lack of diplomacy.

"It's almost eight. You have to be dead on your feet," Kate protested.

Shrugging, Rachel smiled warmly. "Hey, I haven't seen you in so long. So what if I'm tired? I'll sleep in tomorrow morning. We have a lot to catch up on, Katie." Looking around, Rachel's voice lowered with emotion. "And I want to know about our home, and what is going on with it."

Kate snorted. "Our 'home' is a hundred thousand dollars in debt and a week away from being foreclosed on by the bank unless we declare bankruptcy. Either way, we're going to lose it."

Chapter Five

The next morning Kate, with Rachel's help, fed the cattle and horses. It was nearly eight a.m. when a small red compact car came zooming down the dirt road of the canyon. The two sisters stood on the porch and watched the vehicle's progress and the huge cloud of dust it kicked up in its wake.

"That's Jessica," Kate said with a laugh.

Rachel laughed in turn and dusted off her hands. "Yep. Jessica's never slowed down." She looked over at Kate. "She's how old, now?"

"Thirty, I think." Kate shook her head, then studied her sister, who had traded her professional clothes for a long-sleeved white blouse, jeans and boots, and braided her hair into two long, thick plaits. They reminded Kate of their mother, who'd always worn her hair in braids prettily decorated with pieces of colorful yarn and feathers. Absently, Kate touched her own short hair. She wanted to grow it long once more to try and reclaim her Native American heritage. "Last night when we stayed up late talking, I got to thinking that we three haven't stayed in touch like we should have. We just sorta scattered like a flock of startled quail and went three different directions."

Rachel nodded. "And to three different countries. I live in England. Jessica lives in Canada."

"Kelly did it." Kate knew she sounded bitter and didn't care.

Rachel reached out and squeezed her hand. "Katie, some day you'll be able to let go of your anger over what Kelly did to us. He did the best he could. He was just a very wounded human being."

"Aren't we all wounded?" Kate demanded, her anger rising. "Just because we are doesn't mean we go around beating the hell out of our kids or pushing them away and telling them they're no good because they happen to be female and not male." Her voice shook and Kate forced herself to take a deep breath. "You're right. I've got a lot of anger."

"I can give you a homeopathic remedy to help you start processing it," Rachel said.

"Maybe," Kate muttered as she watched the red car pull into the driveway. "I'll let you know." She didn't know that much about homeopathy, and thankfully, Rachel didn't push it on her. Right now, they had a ranch to try and salvage. Kate would use her anger constructively this time around. Maybe she would do something right, for once.

She couldn't help but grin as Jessica, who at five foot six inches was the shortest of the three, came leaping out of the car like a colorful whirlwind in a bright red cotton skirt, a purple-and-pink blouse with long puffy sleeves, and a violet scarf around her neck. The youngest of the sisters had Odula's long, black hair, sparkling gray eyes and Kelly's thin, wiry build.

"Katie! Rachel!" Jessica shrieked, running toward them with her arms outstretched.

Kate laughed and stepped off the porch. Jessica looked so fresh and unscarred by life. Her small, fine features, like delicate porcelain, showed no sign of stress or aging. She was the same little elfin sprite Kate had grown up with. As Jessica threw her arms around her, Kate could smell the perfumed fragrance of some flower.

Rachel joined them, and more laughter, tears and embraces followed. How good it felt to have the arms of her younger sisters around her! Kate felt Jessica squirming like a wildly happy puppy—she was never able to be still for more than a heartbeat. As Rachel's husky laughter fell over them like a warm, welcoming blanket, Kate felt her anger dissolve, replaced by an unparalleled joy surging upward. How much she loved her sisters! And how much she had missed them—their counsel and shining personalities—in her life. As they stood in a small circle, hugging one another, she realized for the first time just how much she'd lost by running away from the ranch. She should have stayed to watch them grow and mature. Would she ever learn not to run?

Finally, when they all separated, Kate looked at them. Rachel had tears in their eyes and Jessica was crying unabashedly. Pulling out some tissues she had in her pocket, Kate said, "Come on, you crybabies, we've got a lot to talk about.'' She gestured for them to come into the ranch house. ''Blot your eyes and let's get down to business or we'll have a lot more to cry about.''

Jessica sat with a cup of tea between small, delicate hands, each slender finger of which was ringed in silver or gold. Kate served Rachel a cup of hot tea also, and after pouring herself a cup of strong coffee, she told them the bad news about the ranch, not sparing her sisters the bottom line.

''Kelly left the ranch to me in his will,'' she told them in a low voice.

Jessica brightened. ''Oh, that's wonderful, Katie! You're the firstborn. It should go to you.''

''Kelly wanted it to go to Peter,'' Kate growled.

Rachel reached out and touched Kate's hand. ''No matter how much you dislike Kelly, he loved you, Kate, the best he could. I think he showed that by giving you the ranch.''

She wasn't willing to agree with Rachel's assumption. ''I haven't got two cents to rub together. I'm flat busted.'' She looked at them, her voice earnest and low with passion. ''I love this place. When I first came here, I was ready to let it go, but…I can't now. I can't explain why.''

Jessica sighed. ''Oh, Katie, this is our home. Our *roots*. How could any of us let it be taken from us?''

''Are you saying you want to save the ranch?'' She prayed that they did.

''Why not?'' Rachel said, sipping the tea. ''This ranch has a hundred-year history. It has Donovan blood, sweat and tears in the sand. I feel it's worth trying to save."

Jessica removed a wispy lock from her brow with a graceful motion of her hand. "Katie, you may not have any money, but you have heart. I have some money saved from my business. It's not much, but…"

Kate looked at Rachel, who was by far the most successful moneywise of the three of them. "What about you, Rachel? We need money. Do you have any you want to pour into this broken ranch we call a home?"

"I lay awake half the night thinking about that," Rachel admitted slowly, turning the white, chipped mug around in her hand. Her broad brow wrinkled and she slanted a glance toward Kate. "All my life, since I can remember, I've wanted a healing place, a clinic to take care of the poor, the elderly and the babies. When I discovered homeopathy, I knew it was the vehicle for my dream." She shrugged and tried to smile. "That's why I went to England, to get the very best training in the world. That's why I've worked over there, teaching as well as running my private practice. I didn't want to leave the U.S., but I had to in order to get the education."

"So, this clinic," Kate prompted. "Are you building it over in England?"

"No…" Rachel laughed softly. "The other part of my dream was to have it here, on the ranch. Remember how Mom used to tell us she had a dream of a medicine house? A place where she could use her herbs, flowers and poultices on people who needed healing?"

Jessica nodded and smiled tenderly. "Mama *was* a healer. Look at you and me, Rachel—we're in the healing arts. I've got my own natural essence company and you're a homeopath. Both are alternative medicines. Both of us got our training from Mama's herb garden. She taught us everything she knew and we just carried it forward, that's all."

Kate felt like a failure—again. Odula had shown the three of them her healing skills, taught them her tremendous herbal and floral knowledge, and Kate had stupidly walked away from all of it. All because of Kelly. She saw now the mistake she'd made. In getting rid of Kelly, she'd also cut out and run from the good things she'd been given and taught. Thankfully, Rachel and Jessica had not done what she had. But that made her feel even worse. Fighting her own feelings of inadequacy, she looked at Rachel.

"What is your bottom line on this, Rachel?"

Opening her hands, Rachel said, "I can't leave in the middle of a school year at Sheffield. My contract is up December of next year. I could leave at that time, come back here and work with you to try and save the ranch. I have fifty thousand dollars saved."

Kate gawked at her sister. "You're kidding me! That's a lot of money!"

Rachel grimaced. "Katie, that money was squirreled away over a fifteen-year period for my dream of having a homeopathic clinic."

"I've got it!" Jessica cried, pushing her chair away from the table. "I know what we can do!" She whirled around on her tiptoes and clapped her hands. "It's so simple! Rachel, you come back home a year from December. I can make it home by May at the earliest. My company can't be picked up and moved just like that—I have to do some serious planning." Eagerly, she placed her hands on the table and looked at them. "I've got twenty thousand dollars in assets I can give, Katie. Why can't we all come home as soon as possible? Rachel, you can still have your clinic. Build it here, on the property! And I can build my greenhouses and the other buildings I need for the natural essences I make. We could do our work here, at home. Oh, wouldn't that be a wonderful dream come true? Mama always wanted us to stay on the ranch!"

Kate sat there, feeling Jessica's boundless hope. It all sounded so good and so easy. "I guess the only thing I can bring to this deal is my elbow grease," she joked weakly.

Rachel grinned. "You're the one who's going to be working herself to the bone, with us unable to be here to help at first. Besides, Katie, it's your *heart* that's really invested in saving our home. We have money, but so what? You'll be here, working dawn to dusk." Worriedly, she added, "And you can't do this alone, Katie. We're going to need a foreman. Someone who can help you out daily."

"We don't have *that* kind of money," Kate protested. "I've been running some figures in my head. We could sell off half the cattle herd. That would cut down on the needed hay for the coming winter and stop some of the financial hemorrhaging. We could also sell off about fifteen head of the black Arabians for the same reason. They'll fetch a decent price because black is rare and in great demand."

"If we did that," Rachel said, "would it pay off the hundred thousand owed on the ranch?"

Kate grimaced. "No. We can probably get twenty thousand out of the cattle and horses we sell off. If you put in your fifty thousand, and Jessica her twenty, that's getting us up there." She clenched her fist. "But the bank may want the whole hundred thousand dollars no matter what we try and do."

Rachel nodded. "The funeral is tomorrow morning. How about if I call up the banker for an appointment with him tomorrow afternoon? I can only stay three days and then I've got to get back to England. Let me handle this part of it, okay?"

Kate was relieved. "No kidding. Your diplomacy is a hell of a lot better than mine! Hoof-in-mouth disease, you know?"

Jessica giggled. "Katie, you have other strengths that we don't. Let's all of us use our skills to the best we can. The three of us can do this! I'm so excited!" Her eyes shone with hope.

"Still," Rachel warned, "as soon as I can get the banker to give us some breathing room and refinance the ranch, we need a foreman."

"We don't have the kind of money it would take to get someone, Rachel." Kate sighed. "Foremen are special. They know everything from accounting to calving and then some. I can't just hire some wrangler looking for work."

"You mentioned Sam McGuire last night," Rachel said primly.

"What about him? Can you lure him back from the Bar C to take over here? You know, he worked here for five years. Maybe he wants to come back."

Instantly, Kate was on her feet. The chair she was sitting on tipped, but she caught it before it fell over. "Sam's got a job already."

Jessica frowned and tugged at a lock of her hair. "So what? Can we lure him away from it? I'll go see him, Kate—"

"You will not!"

Rachel frowned. "Kate, don't get stubborn about this. You need help. Sam McGuire is a known quantity. You're right—we can't just hire some tumbleweed wrangler that drifts from ranch to ranch looking for work. Sam's a hard worker. He's loyal and he's smart."

Panic set in and Kate began pacing the floor of the kitchen. Rachel's argument was on target, she acknowledged as her heart pounded hard in her breast. "But he's already got a good-paying job."

Rachel laughed. "Oh, yes, at the Bar C. Come on, Katie! Old Man Cunningham is a mean old peccary. His wranglers work for a season and then quit on him. He can't keep anyone for long. He's got high turnover because he's grumpy." She grinned mischievously. "I'd like to give him *Bryonia* to sweeten his disposition up a little."

They all chortled.

Rachel shrugged eloquently. "I'm sure Sam would consider coming back now that Kelly's gone. He *loved* this ranch. I talked to Kelly one time on the phone about Sam and he told me that Sam was like a son to him."

Kate halted and stared at Rachel. "He said *that?*"

"Yes, and a lot more, but I'm not going into that

now.'' She eyed Kate. ''Do you want me to ask Sam or do you want to do it?''

Swallowing hard, her throat dry, Kate rasped, ''No...I'll approach him.''

''He's been helping you out ever since you came back,'' Rachel said gently. ''I've got to think he cares about our ranch or he wouldn't have done it.''

Standing very still, Kate realized Rachel's wisdom. ''You're right,'' she whispered, ''I've got to get out of the way and let the ranch be helped, not hurt by me. Okay, I'll ask Sam sometime after the funeral. He'll be coming to it.''

Rising to her feet, Rachel smiled. ''Good. Don't look so glum, Katie. It's not the end of the world, it's the beginning. Come on, I'm going to give you some *natrum muriaticum.* I think you need it.''

At that moment, Kate felt too enmeshed in the violence of her own feelings about Sam to care about a homeopathic remedy. A huge part of her hoped he would say no to their request. Another part had never stopped loving him, or wanting his daily presence in her life. How could she keep her feelings toward him separated from the hard, demanding ranch activities? He didn't love her. Too much time and hurt and life responsibilities stood in the way, Kate knew. But that didn't stop her from loving him. Even now.

Sam would live in the foreman's house, not in the main ranch house, but that was still too close for comfort. Kate was scared—more than she ever had been before. She'd known fear when the sentence for an eighteen-month prison term was announced by the judge, but this was different—and far more personal.

She was afraid that she couldn't keep her feelings private from Sam.

Tasting the fear, she watched Rachel walk over to her homeopathic kit, which sat on the kitchen counter. Her sisters were so solid and normal compared to her. They were successful, had saved money, had dreams and goals, and worked hard toward them, while she'd made a mess of her life.

"Here," Rachel murmured, patting several small white pellets in Kate's hand. "Take these. It's potentized table salt. It's for people who bury all their feelings, Katie."

Wryly, she looked at Rachel. "Me?"

Laughing, Rachel slid her arm around her shoulders. "Yes, you, Miss Toughie. Go on, put them in your mouth and let them melt away. And then take a shower and go to bed. You'll feel better tomorrow morning." Rachel lost her smile. "Tomorrow, we bury Kelly."

"Bless him," Jessica whispered, her eyes filling with tears. "He was such a tortured soul. He's in a far better place now, with Mama."

Kate didn't know what had happened to her emotions, but the funeral for Kelly hadn't been as arduous as she thought it might be. Kelly Donovan was buried on the family plot on the ranch, surrounded by heavy wrought-iron posts that needed painting. Ten other graves were in that rectangular enclosure on a hillside covered with Ponderosa pine. Mercifully, the ceremony was short. The minister said all the right things and then shook their hands and left. Jessica paid him the $120 fee for his services.

Sam McGuire had come and stood next to Kate during the funeral. Afterward, he settled his dark brown Stetson on his head. Today he wore a dark brown blazer and a white shirt with a big bolo tie sporting a turquoise stone in the center. His Levi's were clean, and he wore his go-to-town cowboy boots, the same ones he'd worn when he'd picked her up at the halfway house down in Phoenix. Kate had watched the warmth of Rachel's and Jessica's welcome for Sam. Her's had been a curt and short greeting in comparison. She chided herself relentlessly. Why couldn't she be just as warm and outgoing as her two sisters? She was a crab compared to them. She always had been. It was her anger against Kelly, Kate decided. Damn him, he'd always ruined her life. Always. And now, as she stood alone under the pines near his fresh grave, she was the one on whose shoulders the responsibility fell to try and save the ranch. Could she do it? They had enough money to probably give them breathing room, but to make a ranch profitable was another thing all together.

Hands damp, she saw Sam excuse himself from her sisters and purposefully walk toward her. She felt heat leap to her face as his dark gray gaze settled on her. He looked grim—she could see sadness in the set of his mouth and in the darkness of his eyes. Sam wasn't the kind to pretend something he didn't feel, Kate thought.

"Want to go for a walk?" he asked, tipping his hat to her.

Kate wished the heat in her face would subside. She'd blushed like this in high school every time Sam looked at her that way. "I guess...." she murmured.

Kate knew her sisters didn't need her right now. Rachel was meeting with the banker at two p.m. today and she'd fill them in on whether or not the bank was going to foreclose on them. And Jessica had some of her own business to attend to back at the ranch.

Sam gently placed his hand on her elbow and led her down a well-worn deer path, moving more deeply into the woods. "You look mighty pretty in that dress."

Kate tried to steady her reeling senses. Sam's hand was firm yet careful. He was so strong and tall—like the mountains. But she felt like a raging river without banks right now. "It's not my dress. It belongs to Rachel. She loaned it to me because I didn't have any...."

Sam smiled down at her. The dark blue, long-sleeved dress was conservative and fit Kate well. Small pearl buttons down the front stopped at a white belt around her waist, setting off the white collar. The material was soft and flowing and fell around her slender ankles. Sam noted that she was wearing different shoes, too. Knowing Kate had little money, he suspected Rachel had loaned her them, as well, but he wasn't going to inquire and embarrass her further. He saw the wariness in her eyes. Always the wild, untamable mustang, he reminded himself.

He smiled inwardly. A mustang could be tamed, but doing so took patience and time. He had both. But what gave him the right to try and tame Kate? To try and win her heart again? He was a miserable failure at so much in his life.

"Well," he murmured huskily, "the dress brings out the sky blue color of your eyes."

His compliment went straight to her heart and Kate absorbed it greedily. She tried to think through the haze of feelings and desires that Sam automatically stirred up in her. "Thank you...."

"You ladies talk about the fate of your ranch?" Sam asked, halting beneath a huge pine. He didn't want to drop his hand, but he did anyway. He stood before her, taking her in more fully. Kate's hair had been coiffed, he was sure, by Jessica, who had those feminine skills. A pair of gold earrings with small pearls adorned her delicate earlobes. Even a touch of lipstick graced her lips. But her real beauty was completely natural, Sam thought. Kate was a living, breathing part of this harsh, extreme land that either tore a person apart or built character. Kate had character.

"Yes," she said in a strained voice. She twisted her hands and looked down at them. "Sam, they had an idea. It was this...I mean, no, it's a good idea, I think." Kate took a huge breath and forced herself to look up at his craggy, sun-darkened features. She was so scared. "Rachel thought it would be a good idea to hire a ranch foreman—I mean, to help me—us— because they can't come home for six months to a year from now due to their other commitments. It would be just me. And I don't want to hire just any old person to help me. They felt I should ask you to come to work for us...." She looked away, her voice strained. "We can't pay you what you're worth, but as soon as we got the ranch back on its feet, we could pay you more and more over time."

In that moment, Kate had never wanted anything more than to have Sam say yes to her proposal. The fear that he'd reject her lingered. She still loved him, even if he didn't love her.

Sam took off his hat and ran his fingers slowly across the rim of it. "I see...."

Opening her hands in frustration, Kate blurted, "You worked here before but it'll be different this time, Sam, I promise. I'm not Kelly. I need someone who's got business savvy about ranching. I've forgotten so much over the years. I need help. It's true that Rachel and Jessica are giving the money, but I can't run this place single-handedly." She earnestly searched his face for some kind of a sign. Right now, Sam's face looked like the craggy cliffs of Oak Creek Canyon—completely unreadable. More panic set in, and she began to talk very fast, stumbling over her words.

"Look, I know I'm an ex-con. I know I have a bad history with people around here. I'm sure you're concerned about your reputation, but I'll try and be good. I'll try to make good decisions and I'll listen. I really will. I know I'm stiff-necked and pop off at the wrong time. But I'm older and I've learned. Please, could you consider it? I'll stay out from underfoot. I'll handle the accounting, the money part of it, and you just tell me what to do and I'll do it—"

Sam gripped her arms. "Kate," he rasped, "stop it. Stop it and listen to me. You don't need to cut yourself down like this."

Helplessly, she stared up at him. "I'm no prize," she said in a choked voice. "I know that. And I'm a hothead. I know that, too. But Sam, this ranch is my *heart*. My *soul*. I'll do *anything* to save it, I'm discovering. But I need someone like you. You're as straight and true as an arrow. You don't lie. You don't play games. I need that kind of man to help me save our ranch...our home...."

His nostrils flared as he stared at Kate's upturned face.

Her cheeks were flushed and he saw the pain and pleading in her huge, wide eyes—the eyes of a hurt child in some ways, he thought. His fingers tightened slightly on her arms. He had a tough time believing she was asking him to come back to the ranch to help her. For an instant he saw longing in her gaze. For him? How was that possible, after all he'd done to her?

"Rachel said Kelly thought of you as a son. Is that true?"

Sam nodded, still looking into her wide, beautiful eyes.

"Did he mean that? He was so hung up on his grief for our brother...."

Gently, Sam allowed his hands to slide downward. Kate felt good beneath his fingers, though he felt her tense a little. "I think," he admitted, "at some point Kelly realized his grief for Peter had torn the family apart. But by the time he realized that everyone was gone. He told everyone in Sedona I was like a second son to him, and for a couple of years, he was a fairly decent man who didn't hit the bottle too often."

Kate stared up at him. "But the three of us weren't good enough, were we?"

His fingers stilled on her hands. They felt damp and cool in his. "If that was so, why did he make you the owner of the ranch, Kate?"

She avoided his burning look.

"Kelly might not have been one for a lot of truth or honesty, but when it came down to it, I think he was apologizing to you. Maybe letting you know he loved you in his own way by making you executor."

Though pain crawled through her gut, Sam's hands felt comforting on hers. She compressed her lips, her voice low and trembling. "But you said he treated you like a son."

"For a while," Sam reminded her wryly. "He got over that, too."

"How? By hitting the bottle again?"

"'Fraid so, Kate."

"I feel so confused," she whispered unsteadily, and then looked up at him. Kate felt the tenderness of his gray gaze enveloping her like a warm, embracing blanket. She felt his fingers tighten momentarily around hers. "I'm sorry, Sam, I didn't mean to lay all this on you. I know how badly Kelly wanted a son. It's not your fault."

"No insult taken, Kate." He tried to smile, but failed. "I'll give my two-weeks notice today. All right? Stop talking about yourself this way. So you made some mistakes. So what? What's more important is that you've learned from them. I can see that better than anyone else can." He lifted one hand and grazed her flushed cheek with his index finger. The startled look in her eyes caught him off guard. Kate pulled away from him, her hand on her cheek where he'd just touched her. In that moment, Sam realized that she didn't like it—or him. Whatever had been brought to life between them so long ago was really dead and gone.

The pang in his heart felt like a stake had just been

driven through it. Settling his hat on his head, he looked up beyond her to the mountain cloaked in pine. Kate and her sisters needed his help. Kate didn't want him back on a personal level—that was obvious. All right; somehow, he'd rein in his feelings for her. He'd work damned hard to keep how he felt about her to himself. She wanted a foreman, not a lover or possible partner in her life. His mouth compressed. Lowering his gaze, he met her wide, pleading eyes.

"I'll do it, Kate. Did you hear me?"

Still disbelieving, she nodded. "You really will?"

"Yes," he said heavily, turning to go back down the slope, "for you and your sisters."

Kate reached out, wrapping her fingers around his lower arm. "Sam...wait...."

He stood perfectly still. Kate's fingers were warm and soft against his hard flesh. "What is it?"

"If Kelly saw you as a son," she began, searching his somber features, "I don't understand why he didn't leave you the ranch, instead."

Sam pulled out of her grip, because if he didn't, he was going to haul Kate into his arms, crush her against him and take that ripe, soft mouth with his. His lower body ached with need—need of her and only her. More harshly than he intended, he rasped, "Kelly saw me as Peter's replacement, that's all. Don't make anything out of it. I think he loved you, Kate, and leaving you the ranch was the only way he could show you he did."

Kate stood there, still dizzy with realization as Sam walked in long, steady strides down the slope to where the vehicles were parked near the grave site. In her wildest imagination, she couldn't envision

Kelly calling any man his son except Peter. Rubbing her brow, she slowly started back down the hill. Her mind spun with more questions than answers. If Kelly had adopted Sam like a son, he'd obviously wanted him to marry one of them, hadn't he? That was silly. They had all left the ranch. What kind of harebrained scheme had Kelly thought up? Sam had worked for Kelly after Odula had died, and Kelly had been hitting the bottle pretty regularly around that time, grieving, she suspected. That was it. Kelly was probably roaring drunk when he'd said those words, that was all.

Still, as Kate stepped carefully around the black rocks sticking up through the carpet of brown pine needles, she was shocked by the implications of her father's words. Who had Kelly seen as Sam's wife? It couldn't have been her, that's for sure. Jessica? Rachel? With a shake of her head, she jammed her thoughts on the matter deep inside her. Right now she had to focus entirely, along with her sisters, on saving the ranch—if the bank would allow it to be saved.

Chapter Six

Kate felt loneliness eating at her. It was exactly one week after Kelly's funeral and her sisters were gone. Already she missed them terribly. Their support as far as the ranch was concerned was enormous. But more than anything, they had helped ease the shame she felt over her recent past. They had listened to her story of what had happened. Jessica had cried. Rachel had told her that something good always comes of bad experience. Kate wasn't so sure. Standing on the porch of her home, watching the sky turn lavender before the sunrise, she wondered how she had remained sane in prison.

This morning, now that the feeding and vetting were done, she wanted to ride out to a particular pasture that needed repairs on the fence. Chet Cunningham had nastily called over and demanded they fix

their rotting fence posts and string some new barbed
wire to keep their cattle off the Cunningham property.
In her leather saddlebags were pliers, wire cutters and
heavy leather gloves. Plus a new homeopathic first-
aid kit that Rachel had absolutely insisted she take
with her. Rachel had even made one for Kate to carry
in her truck! Kate had laughed, but she was grateful
for Rachel's care.

There were five houses on the ranch property and
new guests had arrived two days before Rachel and
Jessica had left. Morgan Trayhern, the man who had
commanded her brother's company, had been written
about glowingly by Peter in a number of his letters
to Kelly and Odula before that tragic day he'd died
on a hill in Vietnam. Many years later, Morgan had
flown in to talk to Kelly about his son's death, and
apologize. Now Morgan and his wife, Laura, had
asked to come and stay at the guest cabin for a couple
of weeks.

Apparently, Morgan and Laura had been involved
in a very traumatic kidnapping. Kate was uneasy
about the South American drug connection, but had
some of her fears eased when she was told a crack
Army officer, Major Mike Houston, would be guard-
ing the ranch during their stay. Morgan was recov-
ering from his recent imprisonment and coma. Dr.
Ann Parsons from Perseus, Morgan's mercenary outfit, was also on call at the ranch during their stay.

Kate had approved their visit because Rachel had
urged her to fulfill the old family obligation. Kate had
no reason not to. There were houses available down
in the canyon for Morgan and his wife, as well as the
major and the doctor. Kate had met Dr. Parsons ear-

lier in the week, and a part of her wanted to mingle more directly because she liked the tall, thin doctor. Maybe it was Ann's large, compassionate blue eyes that drew Kate. Or maybe it was simply because Ann was around Kate's age. Kate had found out via Rachel, who was inquisitive when she met new people, that Ann had been an Air Force flight surgeon and a psychiatrist until Morgan had snatched her from the military and asked her to head up their medical trauma section. Ann was, according to Rachel's whispers, more like a sister to Morgan, which explained in part why she was here at the ranch to take care of him.

Kate walked a long circle around Morgan's other friend, Army Special Forces Major Mike Houston. Part Quechua Indian, with his mother from Mexico, Mike was a big, barrel-chested, square-faced man in his thirties with frosty, dark blue eyes that reminded Kate of a cougar she'd once met up on the Rim. Though Mike's intelligent eyes were not yellow like the cougar's, his huge black pupils seemed to drill right through her, just as the cougar's had on that fateful day. And there was an air of danger as well as mystery around Mike.

Jessica, sensitive as she was, was mesmerized by Mike Houston from the moment she met him. More than once she had drawn Kate aside and whispered that he reminded her a lot of her friend Moyra, who worked at Jessica's company up in Vancouver. Moyra, who was from South America, was a member of the highly secret and mysterious Jaguar Clan, and according to Jessica, Mike had the very same lethal energy around him that Moyra did. The fact that he'd been down in Peru for nearly ten years, working as an American advisor to halt shipments of drugs into the U.S., told Kate a lot about the man.

Kate pooh-poohed a lot of Jessica's psychic information, while Jessica was dying to ask him if he was a member of the Jaguar Clan, but was afraid to. Kate just laughed and shook her head over her little sister's curiosity about the soldier. Though Houston was laid-back, Kate could feel an air of tension around him. It was nothing he broadcast directly, because his mouth would often curve into a casual Texan smile of welcome that would make most folks feel at ease.

As Kate walked to the barn, she saw her two ranch guests out at one of the Arabian broodmare corrals looking at some of the growing foals. Ann and Mike each stood with one foot propped up on the lowest rung of the corral, their arms draped lazily over the uppermost one. Even though they wore jeans and short-sleeved cotton shirts, there was no hiding their military background. As Kate drew nearer, she could see that Mike often stole a swift glance at Ann when she wasn't paying attention. Kate saw the familiar look of longing on his face. She'd seen that expression on Sam's face when he looked at her.

A slight smile tugged at her lips. The major seemed very interested in Ann—man to woman—if she was reading the situation correctly. And why not? Ann was an attractive woman, with shoulder-length hair that fell in a soft pageboy about her oval features. Though the color seemed almost black, Kate saw the reddish gold cast as a slight breeze lifted a few strands in the early morning sunlight. If Ann was aware of Houston's keen appraisal, she didn't show it. Maybe it was a one-way street, Kate thought as she drew close enough to speak to them. Just as her love for Sam had turned out to be. Suddenly, she felt very sorry for Mike Houston. It was hell to fall in love when the other person didn't return the feeling.

"Good morning," Ann exclaimed, turning and smiling at Kate.

"Hi, Ann." Kate nodded in Mike's direction as he turned. That easy Texan smile came to his square face, while those frosty blue eyes warned Kate that this man was a warrior in every sense of the word. "Watching the babies?" she asked, slowing her pace and pointing to the corral, where several foals three to six months old frolicked at their mothers' side.

With a soft laugh, Ann nodded. "I love babies."

"That's good to hear," Mike said enigmatically, turning and watching the foals kicking up their heels.

Ann raised one eyebrow, but said nothing. Her blue eyes sparkled as she met and held Kate's gaze. "How are you doing today?"

Knowing Ann was a psychotherapist as well as a medical doctor, Kate really didn't want to reveal too much. "Okay," she murmured, standing near them, her gaze on the horses in the corral.

"Mmm," Ann said, "one day at a time. I understand."

Opening her mouth, then closing it, Kate realized that Ann *did* understand. If Mike hadn't been nearby, Kate would have been tempted to confide in Ann. But of course, Ann was a guest here. The doctor was here for Morgan and Laura, not her. Changing the subject, Kate said, "Will you go for a ride later?"

Mike twisted his head and grinned. "Us Texas

boys just can't stand not throwing a leg over a good horse.'' His gaze settled warmly on Ann, who had her back to him. "What about you, Ann? I know you're from Oregon, and you've probably never been around horses much. Would you go riding with me?''

Kate saw the merriment in Ann's eyes as she turned and held the major's teasing stare. She sensed a warmth between them. Maybe Mike's ardor wasn't one-sided after all.

"Just because I'm from Oregon doesn't mean I never saw a horse before.''

Mike held up his hands in surrender. "Now, Ann,'' he drawled good-naturedly, "I didn't say there weren't any horses in Oregon.''

Kate grinned. She liked the parry-riposte between them. They made a handsome-looking couple. Mike was like Sam in the looks department, with a rugged, weathered face that had been shaped and molded—sometimes brutally—by life's circumstances. Ann was beautiful in Kate's opinion—even if she was skinny as a rail. That woman could stand some meat on her bones, Kate thought, studying her thin hands—a surgeon's hands. Often Kate had seen her embroidering or knitting out on the front porch of the house where she was staying.

"I think,'' Ann said seriously, "us folks from Oregon ought to teach you Texas men a lesson in horseback riding.'' She glanced over at Kate. "Don't you think?''

Laughing, Kate nodded and pointed a finger in Mike's direction. "I think you just stepped into a bear trap, Major Houston.''

"Ouch,'' he jested with a widening smile. "Okay,

the gauntlet has been thrown. I'm just dumb enough
to pick it up.''

Ann smiled. "You'd pick up any gauntlet that was
thrown, Mike, and you know it. And dumb? No, I
don't think so. I might accuse you of many things,
but that's not one of them.''

"Oops, guilty twice over.'' With a sigh, Houston
said, "I guess I'll just have to go saddle up two horses
and find out.''

"How about if I saddle my own?'' Ann said point-
edly.

"That's three,'' Mike said, deflated. "I think I'm
getting the message. Not only do women from
Oregon know about horses, they know how to saddle
them.''

Ann winked at Kate. "Not only that, we can ride
like the wind, Major.''

Kate lifted her hand. "Okay, you two go riding.
I'm sure you'll enjoy it. There're two geldings, a
chestnut and a bay, on the left side of the barn aisle.
They're good, gentle trail horses. I've got some work
to do, so I'll see you later.''

As Kate walked on past them into the barn, where
Cinnamon greeted her from the box stall at the end
of the aisle, she heard Mike's deep, husky laughter as
he continued to tease Ann. Somehow, Kate knew that
Ann would handle that Texas know-it-all cowboy just
fine. Mike was intelligent, but Ann had a street smarts
that would get him every time.

Kate chuckled, eager to saddle her mare and get to
work. Earlier, she'd heard that as soon as Mike was
done with his assignment to guard Morgan and Laura
for the next two weeks, he was going back down to

Peru to continue interdiction activities. She wondered if Ann figured into his future plans.

As Kate reached Cinnamon's stall, the bay mare nickered again and thrust her muzzle over the top, looking look for the carrot Kate always carried with her. Feeding the mare, Kate found her thoughts moving back to Ann. Ann had turned her resignation into Perseus before coming to the ranch. Now Kate wondered what a woman like her was going to do after quitting such a high-powered, well-paying job? She'd heard Rachel confide that Ann wanted to work with the poor and underprivileged in Washington, D.C., but Kate wasn't certain that was what the doctor would do.

Patting Cinnamon affectionately, Kate led her out of the box stall, tied her in the aisle and began to brush her down before saddling her. Yes, the day was turning out to be pretty good so far, even if Kate had fence mending staring her in the face for most of it—one of the most dreaded jobs a rancher had to undertake. Still, the day held hope, and this was the first time Kate had actually felt that particular feeling for a long, long time. What would make her day complete would be to see Sam—but that was impossible.

Absorbing the bright blue sky, the dry desert air, the soft scent of scrub juniper that dotted the rocky, red clay and sand, Kate felt peace settling around her. The rhythmic movement of her surefooted horse, the chirping of birds hiding in the dark green arms of the junipers, conspired to make her feel a momentary trickle of happiness. Of late, she'd been slightly less numb inside, which was amazing to Kate. She'd thought her feelings, pulverized by the trial and prison, were dead and gone. Rachel had told her the remedy *natrum muriaticum* would help bring them back. But whether it was the natural remedy or her time on the ranch that had brought her senses alive again, Kate hung on to each fleeting feeling as it arose in her.

The fence line curved up a slope covered with yellowed chaparral, prickly pear and slender stalks of dead grass. The black lava rocks scattered throughout the region poked up through the red clay ground, which was almost as hard as they were. Kate frowned as she noticed some broken strands of wire. Fence mending was hard, dirty work and she was glad the morning was cool. Doing this kind of work in hundred-degree summer heat was blistering and sapping. It wasn't her favorite duty, anyway.

Today Kate wore a red flannel, long-sleeved shirt over a white tank top and a pair of Levi's that were finally getting broken in. Jessica had gone into Sedona one day last week and bought Kate seven new pairs of Levi's, seven flannel shirts in a rainbow of colors, heavy socks to wear with the new pair of cowboy boots Rachel had bought her, and a brand-new black Stetson cowboy hat with a wide brim to protect her face and neck from the powerful sunlight. They'd also purchased several skirts and two dresses, though Kate didn't know when she'd wear them. Her sisters had always been good to her, but now she felt as if she was truly being taken care of by them. Maybe that's why she missed them so much—they were nurturing like their mother had been. How come she wasn't that way? Or maybe she had been at one time, but life had beaten it out of her? Kate was unsure.

Cresting the hill, Kate pulled her horse to a stop and dismounted. The Arabian had been taught to ground tie, which meant that when Kate dropped the reins to the ground, the horse wouldn't move. Pulling on thick, protective gloves, she set to work on the twisted, broken barbed wire. Off in the distance, perhaps half a mile away, she saw another fence crew working—from the Cunningham side of the property.

Kate slowed her step and narrowed her eyes. Her heart sped up. It was Sam and three other wranglers out fixing their fence line. For an instant, she stood very still, transfixed by Sam's seemingly larger-than-life form. He was sitting astride a big, rangy chestnut gelding with four white socks and a white blaze on its face. The blue-and-black checked shirt Sam wore emphasized the breadth of his shoulders and powerful chest. A red bandanna was around his neck, and he wore a denim jacket that matched the color of his Levi's.

Swallowing convulsively, Kate forced herself to get to work. Picking up one end of the barbed wire, she took a twelve-inch strand and twisted it around the broken part. Leaning down, she retrieved the other rusty end and connected them. Though the whole fence line needed to be replaced, as Chet had nastily informed her on the phone, this would have to do for now. At least, until she had more help. Since Sam had given his notice to Old Man Cunningham, he hadn't been over to the Donovan ranch. She couldn't blame him for being cautious. That old bear Cunningham would probably fire him on the spot for disloyalty.

How she missed Sam! How many times had she awakened in the morning, thought of him working with her at the ranch again, and gone into an absolute panic? Often during her twelve-hour workdays the thought of spending more time with him sent her into a spasm of euphoria mixed with fear.

As she connected a second strand of barbed wire, her sensitive ears picked up the sound of a galloping horse. Kneeling on the ground, she finished the connection and then looked up.

It was Sam. Her hands froze on the wire as she watched him riding up the slope toward her like a man born to the saddle. He rode with such ease and grace, his upper body absolutely still, his hips moving with the rhythmic motion of the horse, his long, powerful legs wrapped strongly around the animal. Slowly, Kate forced herself to stand up. She saw the hardness on Sam's face and in those cool gray eyes barely visible below the brim of his black Stetson.

Just getting to see him was wonderfully healing for Kate. She moved to her mare and took off her gloves, stuffing them back in the saddlebag. As Sam drew his horse to a halt, she managed a lopsided smile of greeting.

"Great minds think alike?" she asked, pulling out a thermos of hot coffee.

Sam tipped his hat to Kate. Her cheeks were flushed from work, from the chill of the November air, and her black hair curled around her face, slightly damp at the temples. Did Kate know how beautiful and wild she looked? Sam wondered as he dismounted.

"I think so," he said with a brief smile. Searching her large, blue eyes, Sam saw some of the darkness he'd noticed at the funeral was gone. That was good. He watched as she poured some steaming hot coffee into the thermos cup. Her hand shook a little. "Chet told me he'd called you up a couple of days ago, griping about this fence line." Sam looked back at his hardworking crew down below. "Thought I'd get this done before I left. I've got two other crews laying new wire and post about a mile down the line."

"He wasn't exactly nice about it," she agreed. "I'm glad your men are fixing the rest of it. I wasn't looking forward to doing this all day." Kate offered him the cup of coffee. He shook his head, but thanked her. Nervously, she sipped the hot liquid, almost burning her mouth. It never failed to amaze her how ruggedly handsome Sam was. Sweat stood out on his furrowed brow and his gray eyes were fathomless, as always. Kate wished she could tell how Sam felt by looking into his eyes, but he was like that rock canyon wall—unreadable. As she stared at his mouth, her lower body tingled in memory of his kisses so long ago. Kate had never forgotten his touch, his strength, or his tenderness with her. For a man of his size and power, Sam had always been exceedingly gentle. She had given her virginity to him and he had cherished that moment with her as something not only special, but sacred. Kate had felt like the most loved woman in the world.

Coloring, she looked away and pretended to be watching the crew below. It was a good thing Sam couldn't read her mind! What would he think of her, a foolish young girl in high school who still had a heartbreaking crush on him when she was old enough to know better? The coffee burned her tongue. She frowned.

Cinnamon's soft snort made her glance toward Sam. He was gazing at her. Instantly, her heart slammed against her ribs. His gray eyes were narrowed, thoughtful and burning with that look—the look she'd never forgotten from her youthful days with him. It was a smoldering look, of banked coals ready to explode into life. It was a look that had come into his eyes when he wanted her, wanted to make hot, passionate, unbridled love with her.

She had to be crazy. Kate chided herself and dipped her head, focusing her attention on drinking her coffee. Sam didn't desire her. That was the past. She'd misread the intent in his eyes, that's all.

"How are you getting along without your sisters?" Sam asked, stroking Cinnamon's mane as he stood beside the mare. He'd seen high color come to Kate's cheeks as she'd dodged his look. Damn, he hadn't meant to give away his real feelings for her. Did she notice just a little how much influence she still held over him? Even though she was dressed in work clothes, they could not hide her femininity, the graceful way she moved her hands or quirked her full lips. No, beneath that wide hat brim was a mature woman's face. A face he wanted to touch with his fingers and retrace to see if he remembered it as well as he thought he had.

Kate shrugged and kept a safe distance from Sam. "I miss them terribly."

"I was hoping the three of you would get along." Sam used his thumb to push his own hat higher on his head. "Any word from the bank on what they've decided to do with the foreclosure?"

With a slight smile, Kate turned to him. "Thanks to Rachel's diplomatic skills, she managed to talk the bank president into not foreclosing. My sisters have pitched in seventy thousand dollars against the hundred thousand that's owed. I've got a buyer for half the beef herd and I'm sending twenty Arabian yearlings to an auction that will be held down in Phoenix in a couple of weeks. I'm hoping we'll get another twenty thousand."

"Smart move," Sam said. He watched her toss away the last few drops in the plastic thermos lid. "That's good news."

"The best," Kate agreed, realizing she had to put the cap back on the thermos in the saddlebag that Sam was standing next to. She moved slowly toward him. It was then that she noticed the left side of his jaw looked a little swollen and bruised.

"What happened?" she asked, pointing at his hard jawline. "Did you tell Old Man Cunningham you were giving your two weeks' notice and he nailed you with a right cross?" It would be just like him to do that, Kate thought.

Sam saw the wariness in Kate's eyes as she hesitantly approached him and her horse. He stepped back to give her some breathing room and instantly saw relief in her gaze. That hurt him and he wrestled with the pain. "It was Chet," he admitted. "The kid's a hothead of the first order. Cunningham and I got into an argument after I told him I was giving my notice, and Chet walked in on it. The kid took a swing at me and connected.''

Kate saw merriment in Sam's gray eyes as she quickly twisted the cap back on the thermos and tucked it down into the saddlebag. ''Somehow, knowing you, Chet got the worst of it in the long run.'' She pulled her leather gloves back on.

Chuckling, Sam moved around the head of the mare, his hands resting on his hips as he surveyed his line crew. ''He's nursing a broken nose.''

Laughing, Kate went back to work on the third strand of barbed wire. ''Well deserved, I'm sure. He's the youngest?''

''Yeah,'' Sam rumbled, kneeling down beside her and picking up the broken end of a strand of barbed wire. ''Mean as a green rattler.'' Green rattlesnakes were the most poisonous of all the rattlesnake species in Arizona.

''He was always that way,'' Kate murmured as they worked together. Their fingers met briefly. Kate inhaled sharply and dropped the wire. How silly of her! Scooping it back up, she took the other end Sam proffered. He was so dizzyingly close, she had to force herself to remain calm as she twisted the ends together.

''Chet was the youngest and the most spoiled,'' Sam continued. He watched her work with quick, smooth efficiency. ''For someone who hasn't been doing ranch work for a long time, you haven't forgotten much, have you?''

Laughing a little, Kate shook her head. ''Listen, so much has come back to me since I got home, Sam, it isn't even funny. I thought when I ran away at eigh-

teen that I'd forget all of this.'' She slanted a glance
at him, amazed at how open and readable his face
was right now. The flecks of silver in his gray eyes
warmed her and so did the careless grin shadowing
that strong, wonderful mouth of his.

"You never really left, Gal.'' Damn! He hadn't
meant to call her again by the affectionate name he'd
given her so long ago. Sam saw his words have an
immediate effect on Kate. Her hands froze in midair
for a second. And then she ducked her head and
quickly finished connecting the barbed wire. Scram-
bling to cover his error, he added huskily, ''Your
heart and soul are here, like you said before. I don't
know too many people who can cut those parts out
of themselves and survive very long.'' He eased to
his feet and stepped back a little to give her the
breathing room she obviously needed.

Shaken with longing, Kate stood up and brushed
off her dusty, red-clay-covered knees. ''I guess part
of me didn't leave the ranch. Not really.'' She removed a glove and pushed several curls away from
her temple. Sam had called her his pet name, Gal.
The word had rolled off his tongue like hot honey
across her screaming, sensitized nerves.

Moving over to his gelding and picking up the
reins, he said, ''I'd better get back. Is there anything
you'll need in the next week before I come over?''

Touched by his concern, Kate shook her head. ''I
just need to clone myself and be two people, is all,''
she said, laughing softly. Sam moved with the ease
of a man born to the saddle as he mounted his chestnut gelding. He sat tall and proud in the saddle, his
shoulders back, his posture like that of a military of-

ficer. Yet there was such ease and grace about him even then.

"Look," Sam said more seriously, "if you run into trouble or need help, Kate, call me? You've got my phone number."

"Yes, I do. I'll be fine, Sam." She put the pliers back into the saddlebag.

He liked to watch Kate move. Nothing was wasted in her motions. She was always thinking, and he liked that about her, too. Ranch life was hard and ranchers learned to conserve their energy, finding the shortest routes, watching where they put their feet because rattlers abounded in the area. Even in November, which was hotter than usual this year, some rattlers were still out and about instead of crawling in their holes to hibernate the winter away.

Sam paused before turning his horse toward the Bar C. "I may be out of line," he said, catching her gaze, "but I'd like to take you to dinner, Kate." He saw her eyes grow huge with shock. Girding himself for her answer, he pushed on. "I can't take time out from my normal ranching duties right now or Old Man Cunningham will pitch a fit. I'm free after eight. How about dinner down at the Muse Restaurant in Sedona? They've got the best New Orleans lamb in Coconino County. We could talk business strategy. I've got some ideas, some plans I'd like to discuss with you before I come over as foreman."

Her heart skittered. Her mouth went dry. Resting her hand on the horn of the saddle, Kate gazed up at Sam's tall form silhouetted against the sky, and felt warmth sheet through her. "Well..." she murmured,

"I don't know.... I haven't been to Sedona since I got out of...since I got home."

Sam understood Kate's hesitancy. Her prison experience was so fresh and she was afraid people would look at her, whisper hurtful things. "Kate, I don't dare come over to your ranch right now. I need a neutral place. I don't need another dogfight with Chet, which will happen if he finds out I was over at the Donovan Ranch."

"I see...." She had to say yes, she realized. This was for the good of the ranch. "Okay," she said a little breathlessly. "I'll meet you there for dinner at eight tonight?" The thought of going out with Sam made her giddy. The prospect was scary. And wonderful.

He tipped his hat, the corner of his mouth moving into a slight smile. "It's a date, Gal. I'll see you then."

Pressing her hand against her pounding heart, Kate watched Sam turn the horse around and trot back down the hill toward his crew. What had she just done? It was for the ranch, she chided sternly. It wasn't a date. But Sam had just called it that. And he'd called her by that endearment, Gal. Her hands shook as she picked up the reins and mounted Cinnamon.

There was no sense riding down the slope to repair the rest of the wire, because Sam's crew was coming to fix it. She turned her mare around and went in the opposite direction. There was plenty of wire to be fixed at the other end. As she rode that way, her mind spun. She had refused to leave the ranch last week when Rachel and Jessica wanted to take her shopping in Sedona. Kate just didn't want prying eyes on her. She was too well-known, her past too fresh and herself too raw to handle those accusing stares she knew she'd get.

Now she was glad her sisters had purchased several skirts and two dresses for her during their shopping spree. At the time, she'd told them the new clothes would probably gather dust in her closet, that she really didn't want to go to town or dress up. Well, now she did. Less than a week later! Kate shook her head. Which outfit would she wear tonight?

Sam couldn't stop staring at Kate as she walked into the Muse Restaurant promptly at eight p.m. She looked stunning in a dark brown corduroy skirt that hung to her ankles and a dark blue denim jacket with deerskin fringe hanging from each shoulder. The jacket was tailored so that it emphasized Kate's slim waist, and there was ivory-colored hairbone pipe, four inches long, on each side of the elk buttons. Around her throat was a five-strand hairbone-pipe choker, and on her ears, she wore long elk-bone earrings decorated with red, blue, yellow and black beads, the Eastern Cherokee colors. The dangling earrings only emphasized Kate's long, slender neck. As she walked proudly, the fringe on her gold deerskin shoulder bag swung gently. Sam smiled. She still looked like an Indian, even with her short hair.

If Kate was worried about other people, it didn't show.

Her shoulders were back, her chin lifted with pride, and her sky blue eyes glistened with gold flecks. He took off his hat as she approached the lobby where he'd waited. As she stepped up to him, he caught a faint whiff of a flowery fragrance. Even though Kate wore no makeup, she was the prettiest woman in the very popular restaurant.

He grinned. "Are you the same Kate Donovan I saw this morning stringing barbed wire?" he teased.

Breathlessly, Kate gazed up at him. "I clean up pretty good—is that what you're saying?" She gripped the deerskin handbag hard, her knuckles white, she was sure. Caught between worrying what the Sedona townspeople thought of her and Sam's glittering appraisal of her, she felt nothing but panic. Stepping closer to him, however, she felt protected in some ways. In other ways, she did not.

Hat in his left hand, he placed his right hand on the small of her back as the hostess hurried over to seat them. "Gal, you're decked out like a show filly for a class A horse show and you just took grand prize."

She laughed softly at his drawled comment. "Only another rancher would know that was a compliment, Sam McGuire." How feminine she felt!

The look he gave her, that smoldering gray gaze, made her feel deliciously sensual in her new clothes. As they followed the hostess through the restaurant, part of Kate's worry about prying eyes melted away beneath Sam's steadying hand. His touch was healing. Provocative. Necessary to her. Miraculously, as they were seated in a black leather booth in a dimly lit corner, Kate felt her fears of going out in public abate to a large degree.

Sam ordered hot coffee and so did she as they looked over the extensive menu of food reputed to be the best New Orleans cooking in the Southwest. Glancing at him over the edge of the menu, Kate studied Sam. He wore a tobacco brown suede blazer, a crisp white cotton shirt, a bolo tie with a dark green, crystalline stone Kate recognized to be diopside, a mineral found in copper mines. His dark hair gleamed in the light, and his face was clean shaven. He'd obviously taken pains to be at his best. Even his nails were blunt cut and scrupulously clean though a cowboy's hands were usually rough and callused, with the red clay of the Arizona desert under his nails. When he'd guided her to the table earlier, she'd inhaled the odor of soap and that special scent of him as a man.

The low lighting in the quiet but busy restaurant made Kate feel as if she and Sam were the only two people in the world. As she circumspectly looked around, she realized that she didn't recognize anyone. That made her feel relief. No prying eyes. No accusations. Just Sam and her. Together. Alone.

Setting the menu aside, she laughed a little nervously. "I feel like déjà vu."

Sam looked up from his menu. "Oh?"

Shrugging delicately, Kate whispered, "Like we were teenagers again. Kids. Like so many years hadn't gone by."

He put the menu down and held her warm blue gaze. He saw such life in Kate's eyes. And, just as he had in the past, he reached out, his fingers capturing hers. "Some things time can't destroy," he told her in a low voice laced with feeling. "What we had, Kate, was good. The best. I never forgot it. I never forgot you."

Chapter Seven

As inconspicuously as possible, Kate pressed her palms flat against the linen napkin in her lap to get rid of the nervous dampness. Sam was too close, too virile, and too many memories of what had been— and would never be in the future—were flowing unchecked. Every time she looked at his scarred hands as they played with his coffee cup, she recalled his hands upon her, loving her; she recalled soaring with him in the beauty of their untrammeled passion. Somehow she had to put a stop to this flood of memories and feelings.

"Is Old Man Cunningham making your last two weeks miserable?" she asked.

Sam smiled a little, enjoying the way the shadows lovingly caressed Kate's oval face. "Chet's the one acting out for his daddy. He's got a busted nose, so

I think he'll back off now, but with him, I'm never sure.''

"A hothead is a hothead," Kate said wryly, managing a one-cornered smile.

"You're not a hothead, Kate. You're a passionate woman who lives her beliefs and isn't afraid to put her money where her mouth is. Chet, on the other hand, is a spoiled kid gone sour. His daddy has contributed to his continuing ways."

She sighed. "That was one of the things I was worried about when I came back here—what people would think of me. When I realized you were going to pick me up, I was so frightened." Kate met and held his warm gray gaze. "That was silly of me, looking back on it now. You've always given people a lot of rope to hang themselves with. Even back in high school, you never bad-mouthed anyone. You never said they were useless or bad or—''

"You thought I'd think you were bad, Kate, because you went to prison?"

Avoiding his gaze, she nodded. She placed her hands around the coffee cup, her voice low. "I thought the worst. Kelly always said I had a bad streak in me. He blamed my rebellious nature on my mother's side of the family."

Reaching out, Sam laid his hand over hers. "Kate, life makes people misbehave. They aren't born 'bad.' Take a look at that black stallion of yours. Over the years, when Kelly was drunk, he beat that poor animal. When I was there, I put a stop to it, but the stud is mean now, and he doesn't trust humans. That horse is seen as 'bad' by an outsider, maybe, but knowing that Gan got the tar beat out of him, we know he isn't really." Sam smiled and caught her wary gaze.

"Same can be said of you. Kelly had a lot of failings and he usually blamed them on other people when he could. You were firstborn, and you got it in the neck. Don't let him calling you bad keep rubbing you raw."

She pulled her hand from beneath his, the need for him overpowering and heady. "I went to prison, Sam. That will be with me until the day I die. There's plenty of folks around here that won't let me forget it."

"So? Are you going to live your life for them or live life for yourself?"

He was right. She took a nervous sip of the coffee. "I'm running scared. I'm jumpier than I ought to be. What I need to do is forget about what other people think and put that energy into saving the ranch."

Leaning back in the chair, Sam nodded. "That's the spirit. You have time now, Kate. And I'm sure there will be folks who say things about you, or look at you funny, but just keep your back straight, your shoulders squared and walk proud. If you don't, this will destroy you."

"I know...."

Sam leaned forward and placed his hands on the table. The waitress came and they gave their orders. He was privately pleased Kate ordered the same meal he did—lamb, mashed sweet potatoes and a salad. After the salads arrived, he moved to another topic that interested him.

"You know, I don't know much about your sisters' businesses. You said they're coming back to the ranch six months and a year from now, but what will they do?''

Kate played with her salad, her appetite gone. She nibbled on the romaine lettuce half-heartedly. ''Rachel is a homeopath. That's an alternative medicine that's practiced around the world and gaining popularity here in the U.S.—again. Rachel said that one out of every five doctors here by the turn of the century was a homeopath. And then the AMA came in and things got more political. There was squabbling in the ranks of homeopaths, and they lost out. By 1940, there were very few left. Now,'' Kate said more brightly, ''there's a goodly number of them in the U.S.''

''She's coming back to hang out her shingle in Sedona?'' Sam ventured. He enjoyed Kate's company. She was relaxing now and he saw the eagerness and excitement dancing in her eyes.

''Not exactly,'' Kate hedged, placing the half-eaten salad aside. ''Rachel's had this dream of founding a clinic for the poor and the elderly. She wants to practice from the ranch. We've got one building, a real old one, that needs a lot of work, but it could, over time, be turned into a clinic.''

''And that's how she'll make money?''

''Kind of… She has had a thriving practice over in London and gets paid well for teaching at Sheffield College. The clinic is going to be on a donation basis, so Rachel won't earn a whole lot.''

Sam frowned. ''Is her idealism getting in the way of reality? If you three ladies don't pool your resources and add to a common till, you won't be able to keep that place afloat. There're too many maintenance costs involved. The cattle—''

Holding up her hand, she said, ''I know, I know....'' Kate looked up at the ceiling briefly. ''This is Rachel's dream. She's worked a long time to make it a reality. I can't just tell her no.'' Looking at his scowling features, she added, ''I was hoping that when you got over here, you and I could sit down and create a long-range business plan on how to continue making the monthly mortgage payments on that land Kelly bought when we were kids. That acreage is what is hurting us financially. The ranch is paid for in full, but that land isn't.''

''Running a ranch daily takes a lot of cash flow,'' Sam said. ''Vet bills alone will eat you alive if something goes through a cattle or horse herd.''

''Or drought, like we have right now,'' Kate agreed. ''If we didn't have water rights to Oak Creek, I don't know how the cattle would fare.''

''You'd have to sell them off or have them die of thirst,'' Sam told her.

Kate nodded. ''It's funny how all this knowledge of ranching is coming back to me, Sam. I thought I'd forgotten it.'' She held up her hands. ''Look, blisters. My hands have grown soft over time.''

He captured one hand. Her fingers were long and he saw red blisters here and there on her palms. ''You've been digging post holes?'' Many of the main corrals at the ranch were in dire need of being replaced.

With a laugh, she nodded. ''Sure shows, doesn't it?''

Grinning, he reluctantly released her hand.

"Ranching isn't for wimps," he agreed. Looking up, he saw the waitress coming with their main course. "I don't know about you, Gal, but I'm starved. Let's dig in."

Kate hadn't realized how much fun she would have with Sam tonight. It was as if they were teenagers in love again. He spun story after story over their delicious meal of lamb chops. Sometimes she laughed so hard her stomach hurt.

Sam waved his fork in the air. "Have you seen a black cat hanging around your barn yet?"

Wiping her eyes, Kate said, "Yes, he's like a shadow."

"That's One Ear. I don't know how old he is, but he's been the ranch mascot since the time I was there. I saw him the other day and was surprised he was still alive. One Ear hunts pack rats, exclusively. I don't see many cats living too long doing that, but he's made it an art form."

Kate knew that Arizona had some of the largest rats in the nation—pack rats. They could get to be the size of a cottontail rabbit, and cats often lost the battle to them as a result. Pack rats were a real problem, especially when they found an entrance beneath a house or up into an attic. They would chew through wiring, setting a house on fire while electrocuting themselves, or eat through a wooden frame and drywall. They were highly destructive, not to mention disease carriers of the first order.

"I'm glad One Ear is around."

"You should be. That cat is ornery, but then, hunting pack rats has made him that way. I remember one time Kelly was drunker than a skunk and he weaved his way out to the barn to feed the horses. I guess One Ear was up in the rafters of the barn, going hell-bent-for-leather after a pack rat. Well, the rat lost its balance going across a beam that Kelly was under, and it landed on him. About a split second later, One Ear landed on Kelly's back to get to the pack rat. I heard Kelly shouting and cursing a blue streak and went running out to the barn to find out what was going on.''

Sam chuckled. "Kelly was lying in the aisle of the stable area, twisting, squirming and shouting. One Ear was leaping and hissing. What had happened, as near as I can put together, was the pack rat landed on Kelly's shoulder and made a dive down the collar of his shirt. That black cat was biting, swiping and claw-ing at Kelly's backside, where the pack rat was trying to hide. Kelly was shrieking and hitting at his back with his hand, and rolling around on the floor, trying to get the cat to quit attacking him.''

Kate put her hands to her mouth to stop from laughing too loudly. She loved Sam's face as he told a story; he lost that usual hardness, that implacable look. His gray eyes danced with humor; his mouth hitched into a grin.

"What happened?"

"Well," Sam drawled, wiping his mouth with a napkin and putting his plate aside, "I saw the pack rat zoom out the bottom of Kelly's shirt, which was in shreds at this point from One Ear's clawing attacks. It took off under a box stall and so did the cat. Kelly was lying there in a daze, swearing. His shirt was in shreds. He was a little bloodied, so I took him to the water trough outside and I threw him in it.''

"You threw Kelly in it?" Kate's eyes grew round at the picture that presented. Few people ever stood up to Kelly. Obviously, Sam had.

"Better believe it. I got some soap, took off what was left of that rag of a shirt and scrubbed the hell out of his back while he cursed and swore some more."

"Kelly wasn't known to be grateful to anyone," Kate said. "Did he get any diseases from that pack rat?"

"No, just a tread-marked backside was all. After that, he hated One Ear. He wanted to shoot the cat, but I wouldn't let him. When I got fired, I thought about trying to find One Ear and take him with me, but he's wild and won't go up to a man. It was nice to see him still at the ranch."

"Yes," Kate said with a chuckle, "he survived Kelly, too."

A deep voice interrupted their banter. "Well, well, what's this? The ex-con out on the town?"

Kate's heart squeezed in sudden terror. She looked up toward the source of the male voice. Chet Cunningham stood there leaning against the booth, his nose bandaged, both his eyes blackened. He held a beer in one hand, his dark gaze stripping her.

Sam lifted his head and looked up at Cunningham. "Chet," he said in a low, warning growl, "I'd suggest you amble back to the bar where you came from and leave us alone."

Smirking, Chet raised the bottle to his lips and took a good long gulp from it. Wiping his mouth with the back of his hand, he grinned wickedly. "Now, McGuire, you might be boss on the ranch, but here you're nothing. I don't have to do what you want.'' He straightened up, lightly touching the bandage on his nose. "You broke it.''

"I'll break it again if you don't leave.''

Kate's heart pounded in her chest. She felt shaky. Darting a look around, she realized that most of the people in the restaurant were staring at them. Her worst fear had just come true.

Chet took another swig of the beer. "Big, tough bastard, aren't you, McGuire?'' His lips lifted in a sneer as he leaned over the booth. "Well, I'm not afraid of you, mister. I never was.'' He glared at Kate. "You two rattlers deserve one another. Katie Donovan,'' he crowed in a loud voice. "Man, she's gonna blow up Sedona now that she's home.'' He weaved backward, caught himself and leaned over the booth again. "Blowin' up a nuke plant, huh? Man alive, you're a terrorist of the first order. Who you gonna take care of next? The bank that owns your broken-down ranch? The hay-and-feed company Kelly owes thousands of dollars to? Hell, you're just like your old man—no good....''

At that instant, Kate felt rather than saw Sam get to his feet. He reached out and grabbed Chet by the collar of his shirt.

"That's enough,'' Sam snarled, spinning the younger cowboy around.

Kate saw Chet lift the beer bottle in reaction. She opened her mouth to scream a warning. Too late! She saw the bottle smash against Sam's upraised hand as he protected himself from the coming blow. Glass shattered everywhere. Within moments, Sam had dragged Cunningham to the side door and pushed him out.

Hurrying, Kate left the booth and followed them.

"You son of a bitch!" Chet roared, sprawled out on the concrete sidewalk. "I'll kill you!"

McGuire leaned over him and poked him in the shoulder with his index finger. "You get up and I'll break the rest of your face, Chet. Lie there and get a hold of yourself." Breathing hard, he saw Kate approaching. Damn!

Chet glared up at him. "You're a dead man, McGuire. Deader than hell. You just don't know it yet."

Pain began to drift up Sam's left hand where the beer bottle had struck him full force. Chet had been aiming at the side of his head, and the cowboy could have taken out Sam's left eye if he hadn't reacted when he did. He saw that Chet's round face was red and flushed. Cunningham was so damned drunk he couldn't get up if he tried. More important, Sam worried about Kate, who stood slightly apart, her hand pressed against her mouth, her eyes huge with terror—and pain. A lot of pain. Damn Chet and his big mouth.

Turning, Sam took Kate by the arm and gently steered her toward the parking lot at the rear of the restaurant. He'd get her to the truck, then go back, pick up his Stetson and pay the bill. "Come on," he said, "let's go."

Kate hurried to keep up with his long stride. "I'm sorry, Sam. This was my fault."

"Like hell," he muttered, opening the truck door for her. "Chet's been moody all his life. Me leaving the ranch has made him meaner than usual." He searched her pale features, her broken spirit obvious in her darkened eyes. "I'm sorry this happened, Kate. I really am. Consider the source. Chet's drunk. He's stupid."

"I saw the other people. I saw their faces...."

Angrily, Sam whispered, "Kate, let it go! Stop giving your power away to Chet or anyone else who might think less of who you really are." His adrenaline was making him shaky. He was furious at Chet for hurting Kate. "I'll be back in a minute. Just sit here." He opened the door to his pickup.

Kate nodded and climbed in. She clutched the deerskin purse in her lap. With the door closed, the silence inside the truck was suffocating. Closing her eyes, she tried to deal with the pain that Chet's attack had brought up. In a few minutes, she opened her eyes and saw Sam's large, dark figure emerging from the restaurant. Chet was still lying on the sidewalk, probably passed out. Sam moved around him, heading for the truck, and Kate tried to pull herself together. She didn't want Sam to know just how shaken she really was. He climbed in the driver's seat, and in the gloomy light, she saw his left hand. Dark blood was streaming down his fingers.

"You're hurt," she said in a choked voice, taking several tissues from her purse.

Sam shut the truck door. "Yeah, he got me with that bottle," he grumbled, holding his hand up and looking at it more closely. The blood dripped onto his Levi's. When Kate's hands captured his and she pressed the tissue to the cut, all the anger went out of him. She was leaning against him, close and warm, and her care and attention pulled the plug on his fury toward Chet. Inhaling sharply, he could smell that light, flowery fragrance she wore on her skin. Her soft, thick hair brushed against his jaw as she peered closely at the wound. He felt her breast press against his right arm, her thigh against his. Biting back a groan, he sat very still as she worked to stop the bleeding. His body ached. For her. All of her. In the years since he'd seen her, Kate had matured physically. Now he was wildly aware of her firm flesh against his, the womanly strength, yet incredibly gentle touch of her hands on his.

He hungered for her. As she unbuttoned the cuff of his shirtsleeve and pushed it up his arm, he wanted to lean across those scant inches between them and kiss her exposed neck.

"Sam, this is bad," Kate said, wobbling. "That beer bottle sliced you open. We have to get you to the hospital to get this cleaned up and stitched."

Groaning, but not because of his cut, he muttered, "Let me wrap it in a handkerchief and you can clean it up once we get home."

Kate twisted her head toward him. How close Sam was! She stared, mesmerized for a second, her gaze on his strong, compressed mouth. She saw dots of perspiration on his upper lip. As his gaze lifted and she met his dark gray eyes, a bolt of heat surged through her. Her lips parted. How badly she wanted to kiss him, to feel his mouth once again on hers. And then, just as quickly, she pulled away. How selfish of her at a moment like this—when Sam was hurt—to be thinking of such things.

"Give me your hanky," she said, moving away

from him. "And let me drive. You can make it up to me tomorrow by driving me back to pick up my car."

Sam didn't argue, the cut in his hand hurting like hell itself. He climbed out of the pickup, made a couple of tight wraps around his hand with the handkerchief and allowed Kate to climb into the driver's seat. He saw the worry on her face.

"This isn't anything, Kate," he protested as he climbed into the passenger seat.

"Yes, it is," she whispered fiercely. Backing the truck out of the parking lot and driving into the November darkness, Kate felt some of her trembling abate. With both hands on the wheel, she drove away from Sedona. Away from all the staring, prying eyes that had judged her. And Sam had defended her. Now gossip would spread about him. His reputation was unsullied up to now, she was sure. He didn't deserve to be dragged down in the mud because of her own bad name.

She wanted to get back home just as soon as possible. At least at the ranch, there was safety.

"This is going to hurt," Kate warned Sam as she sat down at the kitchen table. Stitching up animals was one thing. Doing the same for a human being unstrung her a little. Sam sat there, his coat off, the sleeve of his shirt rolled up haphazardly on his dark, hairy arm so that she could get a good look at the damage the beer bottle had done.

Sam watched Kate's face. Her brow puckered and her mouth thinned as she gently laid his hand on a clean white towel. Most of the bleeding had stopped by the time they'd gotten home, but a good two-inch gash was laid open on the outside edge of his left hand. He felt the soft coolness of her fingers against the throbbing heat of his hand.

"You know," he told her huskily as she prepared to stitch the wound closed, "every time you touch me, Kate, the pain in my hand goes away."

Taking a deep breath, Kate put on thin surgical gloves so that she wouldn't infect the just-cleaned wound. "I think this cut is making you loco, Sam McGuire."

He grinned a little. "No, Gal, its you—your healing touch." *It's always been you*, he thought. When Kate lifted her head and looked at him, he saw tears in her eyes. She quickly forced them back and concentrated on the task at hand. Sam decided to remain quiet and watch her work. There was such gentle delicacy to Kate. He wished that she would realize that about herself. Kelly had really hurt her as a child growing up. One day, Sam hoped she'd let those tough, outer walls dissolve so that the old Kate, the real Kate he'd known and loved so fiercely, would emerge.

As she began to stitch up his wound, Sam said in a low voice, "You haven't lost your touch, Kate. Maybe you don't recall this, but I remember times you took care of sick and ailing animals and they always survived. Your two sisters are both in the healing arts. But you're like Odula—you heal with your touch. You don't need a homeopathic remedy or a natural essence." He smiled a little, enjoying her focused care. "A healer. That's you, Kate."

Grimacing, Kate kept her attention on the process. Sam's hand was so large, his flesh work-hardened.

She felt each of the thick calluses that over time had built up on the palm of his hand and his fingers.

"Right now, I'd like to punch Chet Cunningham in the nose. What he did was wrong, Sam. You're going to be laid up with this hand a good three weeks. He really hamstrung you."

"Not too much work for one-handed cowboys, is there?"

She glanced up and caught his boyish grin. Returning to her task, she muttered, "Not really. Old Man Cunningham will probably give you walking papers sooner rather than later."

"So?" he teased. "Just lets me come over here sooner and be a crippled cowboy helping you."

She laughed and felt the tension draining away from her. "No kidding! No post hole digging for you."

"But I can use the time and work out a solid business plan for you."

Kate shook her head. "Sam McGuire, I swear if the good Lord gave you mud to work with, you'd find a way to market and sell mud pies and make a profit doing it!"

Chuckling, he leaned back and closed his eyes. Kate's touch was more than healing, it was opening up his heart and letting him hope for a future with her. Not that he deserved a second chance. Sam knew he didn't, but his heart cried out for her still. "Now, Gal, there's always a silver lining to every cloud. You know that."

Glumly, Kate shook her head as she finished. Taking the white roll of gauze, she carefully wrapped the wound. "Hope? I lost that a long time ago, Sam."

Soon his hand was swathed in a protective dressing. Pleased with her efforts, Kate sat up and took the plastic gloves off and dropped them in the waste basket. In the bright light of the kitchen, Sam looked a little washed out. She suspected he was in a lot more pain than he let on.

"Rachel gave me this homeopathic first-aid kit," she said, opening it up on the kitchen counter. Pulling out a small booklet, she opened it to read. "She said there's information on remedies that I could use around the ranch, both on people and animals. Let me see if there's one here for you."

Sam sat there, his long legs sprawled out. "My hand feels pretty good now."

"Hmm, here's something." Kate brought the kit over to the table and sat down. "It says for cuts to use calendula. Interesting," she said looking up at him. "That's a flower something like a marigold. Anyway, calendula is for open cuts and lacerations. It helps them heal up faster. The only time it can't be used is in a puncture wound."

"Well, give me some," Sam urged. "I don't want to be crippled for three weeks with this thing."

Opening one of the small amber bottles, Kate poured six or seven small white pellets into his hand. "You're supposed to put these in your mouth and let them melt away."

Dutifully, Sam did as he was told. He didn't care if the homeopathic remedy worked or not. For him, just getting to spend time with Kate was all that mattered. She sat watching him expectedly.

"There. I feel better already."

She laughed and it was a sound without strain. "What a fibber you are."

He joined her laughter. In that moment, he felt that familiar closeness he and Kate had shared with one another so long ago. Some of the color had come back to the high slope of her cheeks. Her large blue eyes were no longer shadowed. Sam thought he saw flecks of happiness dancing in their depths. Because of him? Because they were together? He wasn't sure.

The last thing he wanted to do was leave. But he had to. Rising slowly, he smiled down at her. "I *do* feel better." Reaching out, he grazed the soft, warm skin of her cheek. "But it's because of you, Kate. It always has been...."

He saw her eyes widen—beautifully—and he saw desire in her gaze. For him? It was the first time he'd seen that look since they were in high school. When she placed her hand lightly and tentatively against his chest, his flesh tightened instantly. With a groan, he leaned down.

Kate felt his hand still against her cheek, rough, stimulating and making her want him with every cell in her screaming, hungry body. Without thinking, she flexed her fingers against his chest. How badly she wanted to kiss Sam! Looking up through her lashes, she saw his gray eyes burning with raw need of her. Instantly, her breath caught. She read the intent in his narrowed eyes. He was going to kiss her! Why, after all these years, would he want to do that? Her past was so shameful—how could he want her now? The thoughts dissolved the moment his mouth made hot contact with her parting lips.

Suddenly, Kate didn't care any longer. She lost herself in the masterful power of his searching mouth. His breath was warm and moist as it flowed across her cheek. His hand guided her and tilted her head just enough so that he could fully enjoy her. The taste of him was wonderful, his mouth strong without hurting her. Oh, how Kate had needed his touch! With a soft moan, she found herself a willow leaning against the hard planes of his body. His fingers moved through her hair and she felt his other arm encircling her waist and bringing her against him.

All she'd ever wanted, Kate discovered as she returned his searching, tender kiss, was Sam. The years stood between them and yet, miraculously, they melted away. His mouth curved and followed the line of her lips as they yielded to his sweet, molten assault. Her senses reeled and then exploded outward like the heat flowing through her, making her shaky, making her want him in every possible way. His hands felt strong and steadying against her head, against her bottom as he cupped her body to his. She absorbed his strength and felt his harsh control at the same time. There was no mistaking the fact that he was fully aroused. As she eagerly returned his kiss, lost in the light of explosions moving like a golden haze throughout her, all she wanted was to consume him as he wanted to consume her.

And then reality hit Kate. All the old memories, the shame, the fact that she'd led such a bad life, avalanched upon her. As she pulled away, she realized that Sam's kiss had been born out of the excitement of the night's activities—of Chet's attack upon him. That was all. Nothing more. People often did crazy things after a trauma. Hurt flowed through Kate as she stepped away, her fingers touching her wet, throbbing lips. Her heart was thudding hard in her breast. Her flesh prickled everywhere he had touched her.

As she looked up, she saw the molten look in Sam's eyes. At the same time, she saw a question in his gaze and then disappointment. It was obvious to her that he was sorry he'd kissed her. She wasn't. But that didn't matter, she realized as she took another step away from him.

Sam reached over for his cowboy hat, which rested on the table. His body ached like fire itself. He saw the pain in Kate's eyes, the way she was looking at him. How could he blame her? He'd overstepped his bounds completely with her. There was no way she could want him back in her life on a personal basis.

"I'd better go," he said roughly.

As he moved through the darkened living room, heading for the front door, Sam cursed himself. Why had he kissed Kate? Why? All it had done was hurt her. What a selfish bastard he was.

Chapter Eight

Sam knocked several times at the door to the main ranch house but there was no answer. The light was on in the study, where Kate spent a lot of time when she wasn't at his side working hard from dawn to dusk. By this time, she was usually in bed. When he'd left the barn after tending to a number of calves that had recently been born, he saw the lights at the house were still burning. Concerned, he'd decided to drop by.

Looking up to the sky, he saw white flakes start to come down on the gusts of wind. It was late December now, nearly midnight, and the sky was spitting ice crystals that he knew would turn to snow any minute now. After a two-year drought, all of a sudden rain and now snow were being dumped on them.

After a moment's hesitation, he quietly entered the

house and shut the door, taking off his damp hat and hanging it on a peg next to the entry. After he shook the accumulated ice crystals off his sheepskin jacket, he carefully wiped his boots on the rug in front of the door.

"Kate?" His voice rang oddly through the house. Sam waited a moment, sensitive about giving Kate her space, but didn't hear her reply. Ever since that kiss, things had been tentative between them. Sometimes he saw sadness in Kate's eyes. Other times desire—for him. He wasn't sure what was going on, and he was too scared to confront her about it. His gut told him to back off, wait and be patient. Despite his regrets about ruining what might have been for them, Sam found himself hoping for some kind of future that included Kate. He had no business thinking such a thing. His head was clear on why. His heart, however, had a mind of its own. Scowling, he walked toward the office, which was situated on the north side of the house.

The door was open, as always, and the light spilled out into the gloom of the darkened hallway. He placed his hand on the doorjamb and halted at the entrance. His face softened. With the accounting books opened before her Kate was fast asleep. His mouth compressed with concern. Sam knew she was worried about the money. He could see a lot of paper wadded up and littered around the chair where she sat sleeping. Money. Wasn't it always money? The ranch teetered on a thin line between disaster and survival, thanks to mounting feed prices, a drought that had wiped out normal food supplies, a heavy bank debt and constant need for materials for fences and the like.

Kate had her Pendleton jacket hung over the back of the chair. She wore a light pink flannel shirt and a pair of jeans, muddied from helping him calve hours earlier. Her feet were encased in thick, pink socks and her muddy cowboy boots sat on some newspaper next to the antique oak desk. An ache built inside Sam's lower body as he absorbed her soft features. Kate was allowing her hair to grow, and it was slightly curled and ruffled around her face. Beneath the light, he saw the reddish highlights. Her lips... Inwardly, he groaned. Her mouth was one of her finest attributes, in his opinion. So soft and kissable. He ached to kiss her again. If it ever happened—and his heart certainly hoped for that opportunity—it had to be Kate who initiated the kiss, not him. Sam was damned if he was going to be like a thief in the night, stealing from Kate once again. He'd hurt her once and he swore he would never do it again.

Worried about the flush he saw blooming on her cheeks just below her thick lashes, Sam thought about how Kate had been using every bit of her physical strength to keep this ranch going. She was up at four a.m. every day. By ten p.m., she was usually so exhausted she weaved when she walked. On most nights she was in bed shortly thereafter. Yes, he had her pattern of living down pat. The foreman's house sat three hundred feet away from the main house, so he couldn't help but notice such things. His hours were the same as hers, but he was used to the brutal demands of ranching. Kate had just jumped in and was still adjusting.

Sam wanted time with her—quality time. But there had been no opportunities. A series of disasters had occurred as soon as he'd quit the Cunningham Ranch and come over to her ranch. A late thunderstorm had blown up a day after he'd arrived, and lightning had struck nearby, starting a small fire. Fire was always a worry here and the sudden blaze had destroyed three hundred acres before the borate bombers flown in from Phoenix had gotten it under control. All the fence posts had to be removed and replaced with new posts and wire, to keep the cattle from wandering onto Cunningham property.

And then prices on feed shot out of sight, and supplies took a much larger chunk of money. It was as if the bleeding at the ranch changed to a hemorrhage. The effect of the drought in the Midwest, where the wheat, oats and corn were grown, had finally reached Sedona and managing the ranch finances became a juggling act for Kate. She had to rob Peter to pay Paul, as she put it.

The cattle could go without grain, but the young Arabian horses could not if they were to get the nutrition they needed for strong bones in such a desert environment.

How peaceful Kate looked sleeping, Sam thought as he quietly moved closer. He remembered her sleeping in his arms so very long ago. At that time, her hair had been long, halfway to her waist, and he recalled how thick and silky it lay against his chest as she nestled her head in the crook of his shoulder to sleep. An ache spread throughout him at the memory and Sam laughed at himself, stopping inches from where Kate was sleeping. The last six weeks had been a living hell for him. *Hell.* They were so busy trying to keep things going, that they rarely saw one another except while vetting and caring for the animals which wasn't often enough for him.

Sam leaned over and lightly touched the curls near her unmarred brow. His fingers itched to graze the slope of her cheek. *No.* He couldn't. That wouldn't be fair to Kate. He pulled his hand back and allowed it to drop to his side.

When he'd moved into the foreman's house, Kate had helped him unpack some of the boxes. In one, she found the framed photo of Chris, his son. In another, a photo of Carol. He'd seen the look on her face, the pain and sadness as she put the pictures aside. Frustration moved through him. How could he get Kate to understand that he was interested in her? She had shown no overt signs of interest in him, that was for sure. Yet she'd returned his kiss just as eagerly and passionately as he'd explored her delicious mouth.

Releasing a long breath of air, Sam got an idea. He saw the white snowflakes striking the window just beyond the desk. Yes, maybe it would work. Maybe he could devise a way to get Kate to rest, even for part of a day. She desperately needed a small vacation of sorts. Christmas was only two days away and he'd seen two presents sitting on the coffee table in the living room, but no tree was up. Maybe his idea would work.

Gently, he closed his hand over Kate's shoulder and squeezed slightly.

"Kate?" Sam realized just how deeply she was sleeping when she didn't respond to his call. He saw the beginnings of shadows beneath her eyes. She was working herself, literally, to the bone. Matter of fact, she'd lost a good fifteen pounds in the process, from what he could see. The hollow of her cheeks was more pronounced, the flesh tighter against her sloping bones. They were working so hard that they ate on the run or grabbed whatever was easily available. In reality, they needed four wranglers plus themselves to keep this ranch at operating level. Could the two of them continue this murderous pace until next June, when Jessica arrived home?

Sam leaned over, extending his large hand across the soft smoothness of her shoulders. He could feel how firm and physically fit the ranch work had made her. "Gal? It's time to go to bed." He gave her a small shake. Her lashes fluttered and she moaned softly. The beginnings of a tender smile pulled at Sam's mouth as he watched her start to surface from her deep sleep. "Come on, Kate. You can't sleep over the accounting books. You need to get a bath and go to bed...."

Kate felt more than heard Sam's low, vibrating voice. She loved the deep tone of his voice because it always made her feel safe and nurtured. His hand was on her shoulder, gently moving in a slow, provocative circle. Was she dreaming again? Dreaming of his loving her? How wonderful his strong fingers felt against her sore, tired back. Forcing her eyes open, she raised her head. Sam's shadowy features made her blink. Sitting upright suddenly, she felt him remove his hand.

"What's wrong? Does one of the new calves have a problem?" she asked in a muffled tone.

"Whoa, there's no crisis," Sam said, holding up his hand.

He forced himself to take a step back as she sat up and rubbed her eyes. "Everything's fine. I saw the light on in here. It's not like you to be up this late, so I knocked on the door." He smiled a little and rested his long fingers across his hips. "I found you asleep on the books there. It's midnight, Gal. You need to be in bed."

Her skin felt like it was glowing everywhere he'd touched her. Kate was barely functioning. Her heart, all her sleepy senses, were hanging on Sam's husky voice and his nearness. He rarely came into her house. Blinking to drive her exhaustion away, Kate rubbed her face.

"Oh...thanks, Sam.... I was just trying to find some extra money. I was thinking that maybe I didn't add or subtract right...."

Kate looked utterly vulnerable in that moment as she sat there, her hands curved across her thighs. He wanted to sweep her into his arms, carry her to the bedroom, lay down with her and simply hold her against him until she dropped off to sleep. She needed some holding, some attention, and he knew it. This ranch was extruding every emotion she had out of her. He knew Kate was taking the success or failure of the ranch on her shoulders. It wasn't right, but that's what she was doing. She still felt such guilt over her past that she was probably using the ranch as a way to right old wrongs.

Grimly, Sam said, "I want you to sleep in tomorrow, Kate. I'll get up and do the feeding. Then, when

I'm done, you and I are going to saddle up a couple of horses and we're going up into the canyon.''

She stared at him. "What?"

He gestured to the ledger books spread out on the desk. "This ranch is bleeding you dry, Kate. I want you to take a day off. Sleep in tomorrow morning, have a nice, leisurely breakfast. I'll drop by when I get the chores done."

She smiled and rubbed her brow. "Sounds like heaven to me, Sam McGuire." And then she studied his harsh, unreadable features. "Why are you doing this? You're working twice as hard as I am."

He matched her smile. "Because you need a down day, Gal, that's why. Aren't you a little curious about what we'll be doing up in the canyon?"

Sam's teasing warmed her and she laughed a little as she stood up. "Well, yes...."

Nodding, Sam walked to the door. "Good. I'll see you tomorrow around ten a.m., then."

"This is beautiful!" Kate told Sam with a sigh. They rode together through the dark green Ponderosa pines, which were covered with a cape of fresh white snow. The storm that had raged throughout the night was the first big snowfall of the season. Bundled in her sheepskin coat and gloves, her black Stetson keeping her head warm, Kate smiled over at him. "Prison took so much out of me," she confided, absorbing the majesty of the pines as they rode up the snowy slope.

Sam silently congratulated himself on his idea. Behind his black gelding was a packhorse carrying a surprise picnic lunch, hot chocolate in two large thermoses, an ax and enough rope to bring a spruce tree home for Christmas. The weather was cloudy, the sky roiling with dark and light gray shapes. Every now and again a patch of blue could be seen, and even a surprising glint of yellow sunlight briefly shone before the swift-moving clouds swallowed it up.

"Out here," he told her, "you can not only feel your freedom, you can taste it." The rushing and bubbling of Oak Creek was to their right as they followed it higher up the hill. The heavy scent of pine filled their lungs and Sam drew the fragrance deep into his chest.

Kate reached out, resting her gloved hand on the arm of his sheepskin jacket. "This is heaven, Sam. Heaven," she said. How much she wanted to kiss him again! She was afraid to ask. Afraid to explore the possibilities of why it had happened in the first place. More than likely, the kiss had been a knee-jerk reaction after the fight with Chet. If only it had been for other, more important reasons...

Sam's heart expanded powerfully at her touch. Right now, Kate looked like the eager young girl he'd known before life had tripped her up so badly. Her sky blue eyes shone like those of a child. Her soft lips were parted and expectant. The high color in her cheeks simply made her eyes that much more startling and lovely to look at. Despite the fact that he was losing his heart all over again, he grinned at her.

"Start looking for just the right tree to bring home so we can put it in your living room. Christmas shouldn't be celebrated without one."

Sobering, Kate allowed her hand to rest on her thigh. The steady movement of the horse beneath her

was soothing and something she loved. She was
afraid to ask, but she was going to anyway. Kate had
made every attempt to stay on a business footing with
Sam, keeping things from getting personal. She was
afraid if she dropped that decorum she might make a
fool out of herself. She'd seen those photos of Chris,
his son, and Carol, his ex-wife, on top of his television set.

"Sam...do you have plans for Christmas Day?"

Surprised, he looked at her. "Why?"

"W-well..." Kate stumbled over her words. "I just
thought that—that Chris might be coming home. You
said he was on Christmas break from college and I
thought he might be—be visiting you for a while."

He shook his head, noting the wariness in Kate's
eyes. "No. He's going to visit Carol in New York
City."

"Oh, I see...."

"You thought he was coming out for the holiday?"
Sam had wondered why Kate hadn't mentioned
Christmas to him. It was as if she was avoiding the
holiday completely, which wasn't like her. He recalled how much she'd loved Christmas in her
younger years. Odula had always had a party, inviting
many elderly neighbors who could not afford a holiday meal. The Donovan Ranch at one time had been
known for its charity work with the poor and elderly,
thanks to Odula. When she died, the gift of charity
died with her.

"Yes, I thought you might want to spend time with
your family," Kate admitted.

Sam shook his head and watched a huge chunk of
snow slide off a nearby pine. The wind was still

gusty, and the pines ladened with their white covering, began to lose their adornment. "When Carol and I got our divorce, she moved back East. Back to where she was born—New York. I didn't want Chris torn between choosing one or the other of us for holidays. He decided that every other year he could be with me on Christmas. This year, he'll be with Carol and her family."

"I see...." Kate saw a blue jay flit between the pines, its call loud with warning. The horses were beginning to climb steadily, their breath white like steam, shooting from their nostrils.

"How about you?" Sam asked. With the banks of Oak Creek on one side and a heavy brush barrier on the other, they had to ride close together, their legs touching now and then. He didn't mind the closeness and Kate seemed to like it, too.

"Me? Oh...I just arranged for a beef to be sent to the mission in Cottonwood so they would have food to serve to the homeless over Christmas. That steer you took to the packinghouse in Sedona last week is the gift I'm giving them. They're trucking it down this morning to the mission."

He smiled warmly. "Just like your mother."

Blushing, Kate avoided his hooded gray eyes. She heard the emotion in Sam's deep voice and his approval of her charity. "I want to try and bring back some of the traditions we had when Mom was alive. There's no way we can open the ranch up this year to the elderly. But maybe next year... I always loved being able to help the old ones. They don't all have relations nearby to celebrate with them this time of year. We always had a great time. I know the three of us always looked forward to Christmas Day and all.''

Sam remembered very clearly about those times. He'd been part of that special celebration himself when he was going steady with Kate. Odula and her three daughters had worked endlessly in the big kitchen, roasting turkeys, making pot roasts with all the fixin's for the thirty or forty elderly people who would be bussed out to the ranch to enjoy a real family dinner with them. Even Kelly would straighten up his act, get cleaned up and behave.

In that moment, Sam felt the sharpness of his love for Kate. It had never died. It had just hibernated all these years.

Waiting. Just waiting. The joy he heard in her voice as she spoke about helping the elderly, and the golden light dancing in her eyes, made him realize how much he'd missed out on because of his own stupid moment of drunken need. Disgusted with himself, Sam wished he could change the past. He wanted a second chance with Kate.

''Odula's spirit lives on in you, Kate. She'd be proud of you,'' he murmured.

''Thanks, Sam. I'm beginning to realize how much of my mother is in me and how much I never let grow outside of me.'' She gestured to the snow-laden pines that surrounded them. ''We *always* came up here for a Christmas tree as a family every year. I loved it! All of us on horseback, with a couple of packhorses. We made a picnic and day of it.'' Her voice grew heavy with feeling. ''And you remembered this, didn't you? I'd forgotten. I've forgotten so much that's important....''

He pulled his gelding to a halt and dismounted. Without speaking, Sam placed his hands around her waist and lifted her off her horse. Bracketed by the animals as they were, the movement brought them together. Sam took off his heavy gloves and framed Kate's upturned face. The hope of the world lay in her widening eyes. Wordlessly, her lips parted, just begging to be kissed by him. A fire raged, barely in check, within his aching lower body. He felt the smooth warmth of her skin beneath his hands as he looked deeply into her eyes.

"Maybe a lot of things have changed, Kate," he rasped, feeling the movement of the horse pushing her fully against him. "But people's hearts hold memories. Lots of 'em." He managed a wry, one-sided smile. "My reasons for doing this are plenty. You've been working yourself to the bone. You've lost a lot of weight and I'm worried about that. And your family's traditions are important." Looking deeply into her glistening eyes, he continued, "I feel that in some small way I can help you get back in touch with some of those parts of yourself. Let me help you when I can. I've hurt you once. And God help me, I've never been so sorry. This time around, Kate, I'm going to try and be a positive influence in your life, not one that rips you apart like I did before. If you could just trust me a little, Gal—just a little..." He grimaced and scowled. "I know I'm asking for the moon. You have every right to tell me to go to hell and never look back. I can't change the past, but I can make sure the present is different—better—for you...."

His rough, callused hands felt so steadying, so right to Kate. Completely off guard because Sam had only been this intimate with her once since she'd come home, Kate pressed against him, feeling the heat and vibrating strength of his powerful body. She heard his words, understood them too well, and allowed his raw emotions to blanket her in those moments out of time. Without thinking, she lifted her hands and enclosed his as they lay against her face. Hot tears spilled from her eyes, trailed down her cool skin and laced through his fingers.

"Don't you realize how good you've already been to me?" she said in a wobbly voice. "You didn't judge me when I came out of prison. Without you, Sam, this ranch would have fallen flat on its face. Look how much you've done." Sniffing, she gave him a trembling smile, becoming lost in his dark, stormy gaze. "The past is done, Sam." She saw a flare of some unknown emotion in his eyes and his fingers tightened briefly against her flesh. "I don't bear any grudges, believe me. We both made mistakes."

Taking a deep, shaky breath, Sam nodded. "What I did to you, Kate, is unforgivable...."

"You thought I had run away for good," she whispered, allowing her hands to move to his upper arms. "I can understand why you got drunk that night. We loved one another and what I did to you wasn't right. I know that now—hindsight's always twenty-twenty, isn't it?" Her mouth stretched into a sad line. "You made love to Carol out of grief, Sam. That's something else I know and can understand now that I'm older, more mature. I'm sure you weren't expecting her to get pregnant. It probably came as as big a surprise as any you've ever had." She sighed, looking up at him. "At least, you did the right thing. You were responsible to her—and your son. I really admire that, Sam. It says a lot of good things about you. Even though you made a mistake, you rectified it."

Standing here, protected from the chill of the winter air by the warmth of the horses, Kate absorbed the heady scent of the pine and Sam's hands upon her face, and felt as if all her dreams had come true. She reveled in his attention and the care that radiated from him as it began to heal another old wound in her heart, whether he knew it or not.

Using his thumbs, Sam wiped the remnants of tears from Kate's cheeks. Allowing his hands to fall across her proud shoulders, he sighed. "You're right—I didn't fall in love with her," he rasped, holding her gaze. He saw her eyes widened with surprise. "I was shocked by the note you left, but I knew this had been building for a while. Mustangs run when they're threatened, and Kelly had pushed you as far as you could go. Something had to give. And like you said, hindsight is always twenty-twenty." He grimaced. "You ran. You had no choice. I felt so damned helpless. I couldn't protect you from Kelly, or from the hell in that house you had to live in. When I got the note, I knew you meant it. I loved you and I understood, but it made me reel. I got drunk. I did some stupid things. Things I've paid part of my life to try and correct." His hands tightened on her shoulders.

Digesting his admission, Kate studied him in the soft silence of the forest, letting the bubbling sounds of Oak Creek sooth some of her wounded feelings. "You're letting me off too easily, Sam. If I hadn't run away in the first place, none of this would have happened.''

Harshly, he whispered, ''You saw no other choice at the time, Gal. I never blamed you for what you did. I understood why you did it. I might have been stupid, Kate, but I wasn't going to do what some guys did if they got a girl pregnant. I wasn't going to walk away and pretend it didn't happen.'' Anger tinged his words. ''I really screwed up. I had the best thing in the world, and in one night, I threw it away.'' His fingers dug into her jacket. ''I threw what we had away, Kate, and I've been the sorriest bastard ever since. I take responsibility for my choices. Being drunk was no excuse. Having had a lot of time to look back on it, I realize I was an egotistical fool. I was the star running back of the football team. I liked all the attention Carol gave me. She'd been following me around all year and I liked her attention a little too much.''

Standing there against Sam, Kate felt his anguish. ''Teenage hormones and a swelled head to boot?''

He nodded and held her wounded gaze. ''Yes. A bad combination. Hell, Kate, at that age, what did we know? I didn't realize I already had the woman I wanted to spend a lifetime with. I was careless, and I thought I knew everything. I played with fire and it burned me. Worse, it burned you, too. If I could do it all over again—but hell, it's too late.''

''Did you *ever* love Carol?'' Kate asked faintly. Her head swam with the question. How could anyone live for eighteen years with someone they didn't love? That seemed like a horrible prison sentence to her— far worse than the one she'd endured for eighteen months. In one way, Kate was aware of Sam's loyalty and responsibility. Maybe it was his ranch upbringing, where kids were taught from the time they were born that their actions and words carry weight, that their decisions have consequences, and that if they start something, they have to finish it. Maybe it was the code of the Old West, where a man was his word. Where any decision was accepted with the full weight of responsibility to go with it.

Sam allowed his hand to skim the sleeve of her coat. "No. Not real love..." Not like the love for Kate he'd continued to carry in his heart like a torch that refused to go out.

"What a horrible sentence," she whispered.

"Don't feel sorry for me, Gal. I brought it on myself. Carol and I learned to be friends, instead. We had a lot of rough times and we worked on them together. I admire her, too, for what she did for Chris. It says a lot about her commitment and responsibility to the situation." Sam captured Kate's gloved fingers. "What I feel bad about, what I want to repair between us, is what it did to *you*. Somehow I want to make up for all the pain I've caused you, Kate." His mouth became a slash of pain because of all he felt over his stupid actions and decisions. "You were the innocent one in all of this. I saw what life did to you. You ran away from home once and for all soon after graduation. Right after my wedding. You see, I knew your *real* reason for leaving. You left because I'd married Carol."

Feelings surged up through Kate, and she felt a lump growing in her throat. She wrapped her fingers tightly around his, her other hand resting on his massive chest. "No, Sam," she whispered brokenly, "I didn't leave because you married Carol."

He raised head and studied her intently. "You didn't?" They had been two months away from graduation when everyone in school found out that Carol was pregnant and he was going to marry her. It took only a day for the gossip to fly around the school. Then Sam never saw Kate again. She became like a shadow at school and avoided him completely. They had never gotten to talk after that.

"Only my family knows the real reason why I left, Sam. Kelly was drunk all the time. He and I got into the worst argument we ever had when the police brought me home from Phoenix." Kate moved away from Sam, to her horse, and picked up the reins from the snow-covered ground. Her hands shook. "You never knew what happened, Sam. No one did." She couldn't look at him. Instead, she looked at the tall pines behind his massive frame. "Kelly was afraid all along that you and I were going to run off and get married someday. He said I needed to go to college first and get the education that he never got. This happened the day before I found out you were going to marry Carol. Anyway, Kelly and I got into a yelling match. I told him I didn't want to go to college, that I wanted to stay on the ranch and keep learning how to run it. He got angry. Angrier than I'd ever seen him in a long time. He accused me of going to bed with you—which I had. Before, I'd always avoided telling him and Mother the truth. But that time I did."

Sam stood very still. He saw the anguish in Kate's

face as she held the reins tightly in her fingers and stared down at them.

"What did Kelly do to you?" he asked hoarsely.

"It wasn't pretty," Kate admitted hollowly. "He slapped me across the face and sent me flying."

"That son of a bitch."

"My mother came running in, saw what happened, and she flew into Kelly like a hornet." Kate touched her nose. "That's why it's crooked. He broke it when he hit me."

Sam's hands clenched into fists. "That's why I never saw you again at school? You never showed up for the graduation ceremony, either. I was looking for you...but when I called your house, I got Kelly. He told me to never call again or try to come out to the ranch to see you. He said if I did, he'd shoot me on sight. I took him at his word."

With a strained laugh, Kate nodded and turned to him. "Yes, Kelly was good for his word, wasn't he?" The rage banked in Sam's eyes surprised her. His mouth was set and his hands were clenched in fists at his side. "Rachel, bless her, said nothing at school. We were all too ashamed of it, anyway. She got my assignments, my books, and I finished out the last two months of school at home, on the ranch. Kelly never told me you tried to call me." Kate opened her hands. "What a mess, huh? I got my diploma and left the next day. I took a job in Santa Fe, New Mexico, as a waitress. There, no one knew me. By that time, my nose was healed up. I tried to start a life on my own...."

Wearily, Sam walked up to her. She stood alone, suffering, so proud and so distant from him. "I'm sorry, Kate. So damned sorry. I didn't know any of this...."

She twisted to look up at him and saw the agony clearly written on his features. "After I left home I learned a lot of things over the years, Sam. Especially about having an alcoholic parent. All of us, in our own way, supported Kelly's drinking. We enabled him to carry on and hid from the world the best we could what his drinking did to us."

"It wasn't a secret around Sedona," he muttered.

"Yes, and over time, it just got worse and worse."

A shudder worked through him. "Kate, I'm sorry. For everything."

Her mouth curved faintly as she held his saddened gaze. "I know you are, Sam. You are a good man. You married Carol out of responsibility, not love, in order to give Chris a home and two parents. You yourself were raised by your dad when your mother died giving you birth, so I can understand how important it was to you that your son got the things you didn't."

He nodded. "That's how I felt, Kate. I never knew my mother. I didn't want Chris to grow up without two parents. I knew what it was like and I can't forget the hole that's still in me because of it."

"So you walked into a prison where there was no love, to give him that gift." She shook her head. "I don't think I would've had the guts or the heart to do that, Sam. I admire you for it. I really do."

"I don't regret my choice," Sam said. "Chris is a great boy and I love him as much as life. Carol was and is a good mother to him. We made an agreement early on to do the best we could for his sake." Looking up, Sam saw a bald eagle skimming the tops of the pines along Oak Creek, looking for a noon meal of trout. "She was never happy out West. We agreed a long time ago to divorce once Chris left for college. Our duties to him were over at that point, and he's old enough to understand why we got a divorce. Carol's always wanted a career in photography and now she's got one back in New York City. All's well that ends well."

Kate studied him, aching to reach out and touch his clenched jaw. "What about you, Sam? Are you happy? Are you living your life the way you dreamed about doing? Or maybe you don't have dreams like Carol did?"

He raised his head, a sad smile lifting one corner of his mouth. "My dreams died when you left, Kate." He saw her return his smile, hers soft and edged with shyness.

"Surely you must have at least one left?" she asked.

He shrugged painfully. "None, Kate. I had one hell of a great life when I was a kid in high school. You and I dreamed together of getting married, having a ranch and kids.... Well, that was a long time ago."

Kate nodded, the silence falling gently between them. "If you could dream," she whispered, "what would it be about now?" She held her breath as she watched him wrestle with her question.

"I don't deserve to dream, Kate."

Reaching out, she touched his arm, her fingers curling across the sheepskin coat. "Yes, you do."

Her touch was galvanizing. In that moment, Sam was ready to risk it all. The words came out choked and low. "Then I'd dream of having you back in my life again."

The emotion behind his admission embraced her. Kate saw hope burning in the depths of his gray eyes. "You—would dream of me back in your life?" She found that impossible to believe.

With his thumb, Sam pushed the brim of his hat upward an inch or two on his brow. The startled look on Kate's face said it all. "Am I a nightmare to you, instead?" He held his breath even though he'd asked the question teasingly. What if she said yes? Then the rest of his hope would be destroyed—forever.

Tears burned in Kate's eyes. Wordlessly, she leaned upward and placed her hands flat against his chest. She saw surprise, then joy followed quickly by desire, in his widening gray eyes. Her heart cried out for him, despite all the pain, the past mistakes they'd made that had convoluted and stained their individual lives. Parting her lips, she pressed them against the hard line of his.

Instantly, she felt Sam's returning hunger, his mouth shamelessly taking hers, molding, melding her tightly against him. This time the kiss was not tender or gentle. It was taking, giving, sharing a desire whose flame had never died out over time. Her breath became short as he took her, his hands sliding behind her, pressing her solidly against his hard, trembling body.

The coldness of the air, the moisture of their breath, the moan that came up from her throat, all combined in a whirlwind of sensation. She slid her fingers along his freshly shaved cheeks, felt the warmth and sandpapery texture that was Sam. He smelled of pine and snow and that very special scent of him, only him.

This time there was no holding back with Kate. She had her answer. Whatever was left of their old love was still alive. Her arms slid around his thickly corded neck and she ached to feel his skin against her own. As his hand moved and caressed the side of her breast, she trembled violently. Oh, how long had she gone without his touch? His exploring, searching hands slid down her body, eliciting fire she longed to share with him.

The soft snort of the horses moving restlessly nearby brought Kate back to her senses. In a daze, she felt Sam's mouth leave her own wet, throbbing lips. As she lifted her lashes, she saw the burning, molten desire in his eyes, his face inches from her own. His breath was warm against her face. Weakly, she curled her fingers into the sheepskin collar of his coat to keep from swaying. Her senses reeled, awakened from some deep slumber. An ache between her legs told her how badly she wanted Sam.

"I..." she began unsteadily. "Sam..."

"I know," he rasped, drawing her against him again. His heart thundered like a freight train in his chest. He felt tied in a burning, painful knot of need for Kate. His mouth tingled with her softness, her womanliness. She was as eager and starved for him as he was for her, he discovered. That was heady knowledge. Sam had never expected such a gift from Kate, and he was stunned. He didn't deserve it—at all. Yet the generosity of her heart was overwhelming, and this time, there was no mistaking her intent. She had kissed him. It had been mutual. Sizzling. Needed.

Wryly, he looked down at her, one corner of his mouth lifted. With his fingers, he smoothed some strands of hair from Kate's flushed cheek. "I think we're upsetting our horses, don't you?"

Laughing self-consciously, Kate felt a fierce welling of love tunnel up through her. In that moment, Sam look twenty years younger, like the football star she'd fallen hopelessly in love with so long ago. His gray eyes were lighter and the joy in them thrilled her. Giddy, she said in a softened voice, "I think we've embarrassed them by our unexpected behavior."

Chuckling, Sam was delighted to see Kate return his touch as she grazed his hard jaw with her fingertips. The intimacy was nearly his undoing. He wanted to love her so damn badly he could taste it. He wanted to make up for all the years of pain he'd given her. Yet he was older and wiser now, and he also knew that waiting was not their enemy, but their friend. If Kate loved him anyway near as much as he did her, they had all the time in the world to discover and then explore it—together. To blindly rush in, driven by guilt or hormones, wasn't what he needed right now—he'd done that once and paid dearly and he wasn't about to do it again. That knowledge and experience gave him the ability to smile warmly down at Kate.

"The horses might be embarrassed, but I don't think we are. Are we?" He said it lightly, teasingly. There was no way Sam wanted to burden Kate or make her feel angst over their unexpected kiss.

Heat stung Kate's cheeks as she absorbed Sam's warm, caring look. It passed right on through her to her wildly beating heart, thrumming with untrammeled joy. Just getting to touch Sam was such a gift to her.

"No," she whispered, meeting his smile with one of her own. "I don't think we are."

Sam tore his gaze from her upturned features. Kate's eyes were alive with happiness. No longer was there wariness in them, or that darkness he'd seen so often since she'd gotten out of jail. Still holding her, he moved out from between the horses. "Look up there," he said, pointing to a good-looking spruce about two hundred feet up the snow-covered hill. "What do you think about that one as a Christmas tree?"

Kate was grateful for his return to less significant things. She needed time to feel her way through what had just occurred between them. Right now, her knees still felt a little like jelly. It was wonderful to just lean against Sam, to have his arm protectively wrapped around her shoulders.

"Yes, that looks like a good tree," she agreed a bit breathlessly.

"Good," he said, slowly releasing her and moving to the packhorse to retrieve the ax. "Let's get on with this Christmas celebration, shall we?"

Chapter Nine

Kate couldn't still her excitement as the five-foot-tall blue spruce was set upright in the living room of the ranch house. They had gotten home by two in the afternoon, and by three the tree was up in the corner. A fire burned brightly in the red sandstone fireplace on the other side of the room.

"This is just like in the past," Kate said breathlessly as she brought out the Christmas ornaments from a closet in the hall. How familiar it felt to go to that closet and find the decorations there. Odula had taught them all organization, and everything in the house had a nook or cranny of its own. Placing the boxes on the davenport, she smiled up at Sam who was brushing off his hands.

Her body tingled in memory of his hands, his form, pressed against hers up on the mountain. Something magical had happened in those moments. Something that had set her heart singing.

"There are traditions that ought to be faithfully kept," Sam agreed. He peered into one of the boxes, where colorful ornaments sparkled back at him. "I wonder how many years these bulbs have been unused? The five years I was here at the ranch, Kelly never celebrated Christmas once."

Surprised, Kate began to string the lights on the tree, after trying them out and finding they still worked. "He didn't?" Sam came over to help her, picking up the other end of the lights.

"No, he'd get roaring drunk, sit on this couch and stare moodily into the fire." Sam wound the lights around the tree while Kate attached them here and there. The two of them worked in close proximity, their hips or arms touching occasionally. He savored each grazing touch.

"Probably remembering," Kate said sadly.

"If I were in his shoes, I'd be doing that," Sam murmured. He stood back while Kate plugged in the lights, illuminating the tree with colors. Nodding, he said, "Perfect."

Kate handed him a box of ornaments. Everything was perfect because she and Sam were spending time together once again. Over the past six weeks, they'd rarely seen one another except at work. "Did Kelly ever talk about us?" she ventured softly.

Sam set the box on a nearby chair. His hands were so large, the ornaments so small and fragile in comparison. Carefully, he began to hang them, one by one. "After Odula died, he went into a deep depression that lasted a year, from what I heard. He lost most of his wranglers in that time, staying drunk and firing them for no good reason. I was still working up at the Maitland Ranch near Flag, so I heard this stuff secondhand.''

Sam picked up the silver star. "Kelly kept hiring and firing wranglers. He got a real reputation for drinking, exploding like an angry old peccary and firing the next poor cowboy that happened to have the bad luck of crossing his path.'' Sam frowned and placed the star carefully on top of the tree. When it slipped, he caught it and gently affixed it so that it remained upright.

"When he hired me about four years later, the ranch was a disaster site. I made a deal with Kelly—I would handle hiring and firing wranglers and he would stay out of my territory and keep the books.'' Sam grimaced. "That was a big mistake, but there was nothing I could do about that. He owned this place, I didn't.''

"And so, at Christmastime, he'd just drink?''

"He'd never put up a tree and yes, he'd hit the bottle. He was lonely, though. After the chores were done, he'd invite me over for a drink.''

Kate watched as Sam carefully placed another ornament on the spruce. "Did he—did he ever talk about any of us? My sisters?'' she asked again.

Sam met and held her gaze. He saw the pain in Kate's eyes. "Plenty. Kelly was a storyteller. You know that. I'd sit here with him drinking my beer in front of the fireplace while he bragged on about you three girls.''

Gawking, Kate whispered, "Bragged on us?''

"Yes.'' Sam stood back, appraising the tree. Slanting a glance at Kate, who looked stunned, he murmured, "Especially you. He loved you in his own way, Kate. I know you don't believe that, but he did."

She bridled. "A twisted love," she muttered, retrieving the boxes of bright silver icicles to hang on the branches. Handing Sam a package and taking one herself, she sat down to open it.

"He loved you the best he knew how," Sam said, sitting on the couch next to her. When Kate's mouth became fixed in a hard line, he added, "I'm not defending him. He had no right to strike you like he did, Kate. If I'd been around, I'd have decked him, drunk or not."

"It was the last time he ever touched me."

"Well, he'd done enough damage by badgering, manipulating and taunting you girls as you grew up."

"He thought we were boys, not girls. He didn't want little girls running around. He'd wanted four strapping sons instead."

"That was Kelly's loss," Sam growled. "The three of you are pretty special in my book."

"Rachel and Jessica are. I've managed to screw up my life every step of the way."

"Kelly rode you the hardest," Sam countered quietly. "He used to sit here and talk about how hard he'd been on you. How he had to be hard on you to make you into a strong woman so you could run this ranch someday after he died."

Kate's hands stilled on the icicles. "I was Peter's replacement?"

"Yes. I think Kelly thought he had to be brutal and tough toward you all the time in order to teach you how to run this place." Sam sighed. "He was wrong.

You don't train children by beating them. All that does is scare the living daylights out of them and they do one of two things—rebel or run.''

Kate stood up and began placing the icicles on the tree. Her gut was tight with nausea and grief. "I did both.''

"You could have done worse,'' Sam chided, slowly easing to his feet. He held her angry gaze as he walked over to the tree in turn.

"Like what? I rebelled against him from the time I was old enough to know that how he was treating me was wrong. And when I could, I ran as fast and hard as I could away from him.'' She looked around the room, her voice softening. "Away from here.''

"What happens when you continuously beat a horse, Kate?''

"It'll either cave in, its spirit broken, or it'll fight back.''

Sam hung some tinsel near the top of the tree. "I've always seen you as a wild, free mustang.'' His mouth pulled into a slight smile and he slanted a glance in her direction. "Right or wrong, I still do. Kelly beat you verbally and whipped you emotionally all your young life. You had those two choices staring you in the face. Somewhere in your heart, you knew Kelly wasn't going to ease up on you and treat you like an adult when you were eighteen. Maybe you sensed it. After he broke your nose in that fight, you knew you had to run. If you'd have stayed, it would have gotten worse.''

"That I did know,'' Kate confided, slowly hanging the last of her tinsel on the tree. "I knew if he could hit me once or twice, he'd hit me again. I got tired of feeling like a target.''

"He didn't see what he was doing to you. He thought he was grooming you to take over the ranch someday.''

"He never told me that, Sam.'' She stood in the center of the room, feeling frustration and anger.

"Kelly didn't know how.'' Sam walked up to her. Kate's cheeks were flushed from the warmth of the fire. Several errant locks of hair dipped across her worried brow. "He sat here telling me how good a rider you were. How smart you were with the accounting books. He was proud of your straight A average in school, Kate. He dreamed of you going on to college and then coming back here after graduation, when he was going to hand over the daily running of the ranch to you.''

Startled, she stared up at Sam's features. "If that's so, then why didn't he ever call me or write to me and tell me that? I kept in touch with Mom by phone and letter all those years. He knew where I was, what I was doing.''

Reaching out, Sam tamed those unruly tendrils back into place. How badly he wanted to slide his fingers through her thick, silky hair. But he resisted. Barely.

"Pride, I think, stopped him. Stiff-necked pride,'' he told her, watching her eyes grow velvet with his touch.

"Damn him!'' Kate whispered, tears flooding into her eyes. "It was his way of getting even with me for running away.''

"No, I don't think so. In the later years, when

Kelly had time to reflect on how he'd ridden you into the ground, I think he was feeling pretty guilty. And I don't think he knew how to tell you that or to say he was sorry." Sam reached out and placed a hand on her slumping shoulder. "If you had been here those five years like I was, you'd have seen photos of all you ladies on the television set. If anyone came to the ranch, Kelly bragged on about the three of you any chance he got. Some of the neighbors got tired of him saying the same things over and over again."

Sam smiled fondly in remembrance. "Believe me, Kelly was proud of you, Kate. He kept a shoe box in his bedroom that had all you girls' report cards in it. On some nights when I was in the office working on the books, he'd bring the box in, sit down and start pulling up different report cards, talking in amazement about all the subjects you three had taken and how smart you were."

Sam's hand felt steadying to Kate. She hung her head and ached to step into the circle of his arms once again. Somehow, she knew he'd hold her if she wanted. Her stomach hurt with pain and unrelieved grief and anger. "It was all so senseless," she whispered brokenly. "Damn him for not telling us these things."

Gently, Sam rubbed her shoulders, feeling the tension gathered in them. "Kate, give yourself some time. A lot's happened since you left. There's more to tell, but I don't think you're up to hearing it yet."

Sadly, Kate nodded. "Probably not, Sam. So Kelly loved us, but he didn't have the guts to tell us that to our faces. Wonderful. So the three of us have suffered half our lives because he was a coward and couldn't reach out to give us a hug or kiss us on the head.'' She pulled away, afraid that she was going to raise her arms and throw them around Sam's neck, seeking refuge with him. ''You're right, Sam,'' she whispered bitterly, ''I'm not ready to hear much more about Kelly and his drunken exploits.'' She turned and looked at the tree, her voice raw and unsteady. ''All I want—need—is my family back. I can hardly wait for Rachel and Jessica to get home. I want things the way they used to be, only better this time. Much better.''

Sam studied her profile and the anguished set of her lips. ''The past can't be changed, Kate. But you can change the present and plan for the future.'' He managed a slight smile. ''You three ladies have a hard road ahead, but my money's on you to save this ranch and rediscover your roots.''

Kate wasn't so sure of victory, but she didn't say so. Resting her hands on her hips, she looked over at him.

''I'm planning a turkey dinner with all the trimmings tomorrow evening, Sam McGuire. And then I'm going to open the gifts my sisters sent me. Just like we did every Christmas night. Would you like to join me? I'm not going to be like Kelly. I won't tell you I like being alone on holiday. And I'm sure as hell not going to hit the bottle to make up the difference. What do you say?''

He saw the defiance burning in her eyes. Here was the Kate he knew from long ago, the mustang, wild and free. Her spirit might be badly beaten, but Kelly had never broken her. He grinned. ''I wouldn't miss it for the world, Ms. Donovan. What time is dinner?''

"Right after we get the animals bedded down and fed for the night."

"Six p.m. I'll be there," Sam said, picking up his hat and shrugging into his sheepskin coat. "With bells on," he promised huskily.

Sam followed Kate into the living room after the tasty homemade meal of turkey and trimmings. He wore his Sunday-go-to-meeting clothes—dark brown slacks, a dark suede blazer, a freshly pressed, white cotton shirt and a bolo tie. Having taken extra pains to shave closely before coming over for dinner, he'd nicked himself once or twice. But the extra care had been worth it. Especially now that he was alone with Kate once more. He held a wineglass that she had just filled with sparkling grape juice. Unlike her father, she never touched alcohol. Odula had raised them to realize being Native American meant they would never be able to drink.

As he moved toward the tree, he noticed the dancing firelight reflected around the darkened living room. The lights on the tree were festive, and he felt happier than he could ever recall. The dinner had been intimate. And Kate looked beautiful in a dark pink corduroy skirt that fell to her ankles. A fancy white blouse with lace at the throat brought out her natural color, and the red velvet vest she wore over it heightened the bright color in her cheeks. He saw her frown and stop midway to the tree, where she was going to open the presents from her sisters.

"What's this?" Kate demanded, pointing beneath the tree. There was a third present there—one she did not recognize. And then she realized Sam must have put it there when she wasn't looking. She glanced over at him. He was smiling at her with his dark gray eyes.

"You're pretty sneaky, Sam," she accused, setting her wineglass on the mantel and moving to kneel on the red-and-green material that served as a colorful skirt beneath the tree.

"Now, I wouldn't say coyote sneaky," he remonstrated. "Clever, maybe?" In many Southwestern tales, the coyote was known as the ultimate trickster. Most ranchers saw them as sneaky. The Native Americans, however, saw the coyote as sacred and felt that tricks needed to be played on humans sometimes to teach them invaluable lessons.

Familiar with the tales, Kate chuckled, settling down and rearranging her skirt around her. Leaning toward the back of the tree, she pulled out another gift. "Maybe you're right. Here, come and join me. Santa Claus left something for you, too, I think...." She pretended to be studying the card on the long, rectangular gift.

Sam crouched down nearby, his body almost touching hers. He reached out and took the red foil package with a glittering gold ribbon. "Talk about sneaky," he exclaimed, his fingers touching hers in the exchange.

Chortling, Kate smiled up at him. "Once a coyote, always a coyote."

"Now you're a coyote," Sam drawled, studying the gift with obvious pleasure.

How close he was. And how incredibly handsome! Her gaze dropped, as it always did, to his strong, powerful mouth. Catching herself, Kate pretended to be

interested in the gifts. She wanted to tear into Sam's
gift first, but that wouldn't be right. So she picked up
Rachel's large present and drew it into her lap. Not
bothering with protocol, Kate eagerly tore into the
gift, the lively green foil flying around her.

Sam watched Kate's animated features. She was
like a kid again—exuberant, enthusiastic and completely spontaneous. This was the old Kate he knew
and loved. He saw her smile blossom as she opened
up the box to view the contents.

"I figured as much," Kate said, "a *big* homeopathic kit." She pulled out a huge white plastic container about the size of a bread box. Opening it carefully, she pulled out one of the five shelves. At least
thirty small amber bottles, all with Latin names on
them, stared back at her. "I think Rachel wants to
make sure I have enough homeopathic remedies on
hand to treat the whole world," she said with a laugh.
Fingering some of the bottles, she added, "Rachel
said we could use the remedies on animals, too. She
said in a letter that we could save a lot on vetting
bills if we switched to this type of medicine instead."

"Why not? If it's cheaper and it works, it's a good
idea," Sam agreed. He leaned over and gave Kate the
next gift. This one was from Jessica.

Opening it quickly, Kate smiled with pleasure. Inside the box were several colorful packages. One was
a bath salt made from purple cone flower, another was
bergamot bath oil. As well as a sponge, there were
four bars of handmade soap that had the scent of jas-
mine. Kate read the card out loud. "You're going to
need long, hot soaks in the bathtub at night after those
hard days you're putting in. I make all these things

by hand and sell them through my company. Enjoy them. Let them heal you after a tough day. Love, Jessica.''

''How about that?'' Sam said, looking through the many gifts. ''Your sister is really creative.''

''Yes, she is,'' Kate murmured, proud of her little sister. She picked up the bath salts and looked at the design on the front of it. ''Mother Earth Flower Essences. That must be the name of her company.'' She laughed a little and fingered the blue turtle with a colorful array of wildflowers sprouting out of its back, a smile on its face. ''This is just like Jessica. She *loves* turtles! Growing up, she always had one as a pet—an old desert tortoise that used to hang out near the watering trough in the north pasture. I remember she would take cut-up fruit and lettuce leaves to it every day or so without fail.'' Shaking her head, Kate whispered in a choked tone, ''Isn't it funny how all the things we did as kids can later turn into something beautiful and meaningful like this? It's just amazing to me.''

Reaching out, Sam picked up his gift for her. ''I think you're right,'' he murmured. ''Here, this isn't much, but I hope it brings a lot of the past back to the present, Gal.''

Curious, Kate accepted the gift. It was a very small box. Sam had tried to wrap it the best he could, the ribbon slightly askew, the corners of the paper sticking out here and there, as if the gift was put together at the last minute. ''You didn't have to do this, Sam.''

He smiled enigmatically, his arms resting on his knees as he watched her face. ''I've been wanting to give you this gift for a long time, Gal....''

Mystified, Kate opened the tiny box with trembling fingers. "What on earth could it be?" she wondered aloud.

He chuckled indulgently. "Open it and find out."

Tossing the paper aside, Kate slowly removed the lid. Her brows knitted. Inside was a piece of lined paper, cut lopsidedly and then folded. "What are you up to, Sam McGuire?" She picked up the paper and put the box aside. In the dim, dancing light, she could barely make out his scrawl. Holding the note closer, she read, "Go to the truck?"

"Yup."

Stymied, Kate tried to read the second line. "Sam, your handwriting is the pits. What on *earth* does this next line say?"

Placing his hand beneath hers, he helped her stand. "It says," he continued, as he steered her toward the door, "to go to my pickup, to the front seat. There's something waiting there for you."

The coldness of the night air hit Kate as she followed Sam out onto the damp, dark porch. It had quit snowing hours ago and she could smell the pungent fragrance of the juniper wrapped in snow blankets as they stepped off the porch. Sam's big red Dodge Ram pickup sat a few feet away.

"You're being a coyote again, Sam." Her heart sped up as he kept his hand on her arm and led her to the door of the truck.

"Don't get all upset, Gal. Just open the door. Your Christmas gift is in there."

In the dim light from the ranch house window, Kate opened the door. She heard a little yap and her breath snagged. From the floor of the pickup, which was covered with newspapers, a little black-and-white form leaped right at her. She heard Sam's indulgent chuckle as the puppy, a New Zealand collie, jumped up on the front seat.

"Oh!" Kate breathed. The puppy wasn't more than eight weeks old, her black, shiny eyes like buttons, her mouth open and already gnawing on Kate's outstretched fingers. "A dog!"

"Not just any dog," Sam said, leaning over her shoulders as she scooped the puppy up into her arms and held it against her breast. "Remember how Zeke, your cattle-heeling dog, died when you were eighteen? He was New Zealand bred, and your mother had bought him fifteen years earlier. Zeke was the best cattle-heeling dog I'd ever seen." Sam smiled as Kate gazed up at him, tears in her eyes. "Right now, we can use every able body we've got, Kate. Having a collie will help a lot, especially moving those cattle from pasture to pasture. Of course, she's got to grow a little first."

Kate stroked the puppy's black-and-white-peppered fur. "She's cute, Sam."

He was so close. So wonderfully close. Kate felt comforted even as she recalled Zeke's death. At fifteen, the old dog had been a little too slow when one of the Hereford bulls got nasty. Zeke had been nipping at the animal's hind legs when one good kick had sent him to his death.

Kate closed her eyes, tears matting her lashes. She felt the warmth of the little puppy wriggling happily against her, felt her tiny pink tongue licking her fingers. "Oh, Sam," she whispered. Blindly, she turned and threw her free arm around his broad shoulder.

Being careful not to crush the puppy, she leaned up to kiss his cheek.

In that instant, she felt Sam tremble. Without warning, his arms came around her, pulling her even closer, though he, too, was careful not to hurt the puppy. Leaning down, he intercepted Kate's kiss. Instead of finding his cheek, she found his mouth instead. Her world exploded. His mouth took hers, molded her to him. A soft moan came from her as she placed one hand against his chest. She felt his arms leave her, his hands settle on the sides of her face to angle her to better advantage and continue the breath-stealing kiss.

His mouth was cajoling, strong and consuming. A fire sparked and ignited hotly between them as he slid his lips along hers. Kate felt his warm, moist breath against her face. Her fingers curled against his chest as she returned the power of Sam's kiss. Instantly, she felt him tremble again. A groan, or maybe it was a growl, came from deep within him. She felt his fingers slide through her hair, cherishing her, stroking her as if she was some beautiful, fragile thing. Each stroke of his fingers against her scalp incited more heat within her. The beat of his heart felt sledgehammer hard beneath her palm. His breathing was erratic. So was hers. His mouth was commanding, her response hungry.

It felt as if a volcano, simmering deep inside her, had suddenly exploded. A hot, scalding heat flared upward through her, making her acutely aware of every inch of her skin beneath the clothes she wore. Her breasts tightened as his hands moved restlessly from her hair down her face, following the line of her neck and shoulders. She moaned as his hands brushed the sides of her taut breasts, which screamed out for his touch.

"Kate," he groaned. He couldn't get enough of her mouth, of her. She tasted sweet and tart to him. The eagerness of her response tore at his disintegrating control. Sam slid his hand around her hip, pinning her lower body to his. He let her feel the hardness there, the desire that raged within him. "I need you," he rasped against her mouth. Her lips were wet, soft and pliant beneath his, begging him to go deeper, to explore more of her. "I need you...." His words were lost as she returned his kiss, her tongue tangling with his.

The world closed in on them, the only sound their ragged breathing, the only sensation their hands touching, exploring one another. Kate was consumed by an inner fire Sam had ignited. His mouth was as she remembered from that morning up on the Rim—strong yet tender, directing without controlling. Each time he slid his lips against hers, a little more of her crumbled. Each trembling touch of his hands upon her face, her breasts, her hair, made her knees grow weaker and weaker beneath the onslaught. For that instant, Kate felt as she had when they were teenagers. She remembered that same hungry, exciting exploration of their bodies with their hands, their mouths....

The puppy whined and struggled, caught between them.

As if drugged, Kate pulled away from Sam, her other hand holding the puppy close. The tingle of her lips told her how powerfully Sam had taken her.

Dazed, she stepped back, her knees wobbly. They were both breathing hard. His eyes were like glittering ice shards as he studied her in the intervening moments after their unexpected kiss.

"Time...." Kate whispered unsteadily, reaching up and touching his lips. "I need some time, Sam...."

Chapter Ten

Kate sat on her bay mare, Cinnamon, overlooking a herd of Herefords recently moved to a new pasture that butted up against the Mogollon Rim. The towering ridge, a wedge of red sandstone topped with white limestone formed a watershed of sorts. Luckily, the high country on the rim got enough snow to fill the lakes and reservoirs there. However, rains that were supposed to come and feed the parched desert lands thousands of feet below it had never arrived that year.

Cinnamon snorted softly and switched her tail. The mid-March sun was bright and warm. Kate reveled in it. Down below, she saw Sam urging the stragglers into the pasture area. *Sam*. Her heart contracted as the memory of his branding kisses seared through her— just as it did every time the recollection came unbidden to her. Automatically, her fingers tightened around the leather reins.

She smiled a little, watching Pepper, the New Zealand collie that Sam had given her for Christmas, race around, nipping at the heels of cows that were lagging behind and calling for their wandering, errant calves. Not quite five months old, Pepper was already being faithful to her genetic background. In Australia and New Zealand, the dogs were prized for their ability to herd and keep sheep together. Here in the U.S., they were excellent at helping a cowboy move a herd of cattle.

Dismounting, Kate checked the cinch on her saddle. It felt looser than normal. Maybe because she'd tossed and turned so much last night, she hadn't been as careful or thorough as she should have been with her equipment this morning. Nudging aside the rope that hung from the leather-covered horn, she lifted the stirrup back over the saddle to take a better look. Sliding two gloved fingers under the soft cotton strands of the cinch, she decided it seemed tight enough. Oh, well, it must be her imagination.

Dropping the stirrup down against Cinnamon's barrel, Kate remounted. She heard an approaching horse and knew it was Sam on his big chestnut gelding, Bolt. Inevitably, her heart started skipping beats in anticipation of his nearness. Because the demands of the ranch were widespread, they rarely saw each other. This morning was especially wonderful because for a few hours they got to work together.

Sam pulled his Arabian gelding to a halt. Even though it was only ten a.m., he was sweating from the work. Taking off his hat, he wiped his brow with the back of his sleeve and studied Kate, who smiled at him in silent greeting. Her hair nearly touched her shoulders at the back now, soft and slightly curled. It didn't matter if she wore a Stetson, jeans and a long-sleeved shirt, she couldn't hide the fact that she was all-woman. Every now and again, the memory of their stolen kisses burned brightly within him. It had kept his hope alive these past three months. Did he really dare to dream the impossible—that someday Kate might love him as he had always loved her? Over the past few months, Sam had watched as Kate slowly began to shed her shell. She was not only opening up to him a little at a time, she was also much surer of her role on the ranch and more confident that she could save it. Yes, time was on their side, there was no doubt.

"We're done, Boss. Mamas and babies will be glad to munch on that green grass down below." He twisted around in the saddle and watched the herd of three hundred Herefords. Half the cows had already birthed their calves. The other half would be dropping their babies in the next month. It was a demanding time on the ranch right now. Usually, cows could calve without problems. But when there were problems, someone had to be nearby. The pasture was an hour north of the ranch, which meant one of them would have to drive out during the daylight hours at least two to three times a day to check the herd. Losing a calf meant losing a lot of money, and right now, Sam knew they were hitting bottom again financially.

Kate studied Sam's darkly tanned, glistening features as he settled his hat back on his head, his eyes glittering with some unknown emotion. She felt her body respond hotly to his gaze and she could practically taste her hunger for him. Only this time, she wanted to go all the way. To love him with all the fierce passion that clamored restlessly within her. Maybe that's why she wasn't sleeping well at night. How could she with the memory of the searing kisses they'd shared burning in her heart and mind?

Sam gestured to her horse. "Cinch problems?"

"It felt a little loose was all," Kate said. "Must have been my imagination." She gloried in the warmth of the sun on her back. With a sigh, she whispered, "Isn't this beautiful, Sam? A bright blue sky, temperature in the high sixties, green grass like a carpet under our feet and the smell of the pine nearby..." She closed her eyes and then laughed. "I sure wish I could bottle all of this up and wear it!"

Grinning, he moved his horse to parallel hers, their cowboy boots occasionally touching as the animals shifted. What he was looking at was beautiful: Kate Donovan on horseback. Since their stolen kisses, she'd been far more expressive with how she felt. Maybe she was beginning to trust him a little. He hoped so.

"Days like this ought to be bottled and sent east," he agreed, lifting his leg up and over the saddle horn. Leaning his elbow on that leg, he looked down to see Pepper panting happily between them. The dog was small, maybe all of twenty pounds, and Sam didn't know many creatures brave enough to plop down between huge horses with such trust.

"That dog of yours is turning into a good heeler," he told Kate, catching the dancing warmth in her blue eyes. He drank in the soft, upturned corners of her mouth. There was no question that Kate belonged out here, on the ranch. Somehow, being home was helping her to heal a lot of open wounds from her past, too. For that, Sam was grateful.

"Pepper's going to be great," Kate agreed. She leaned over the saddle, her hands outstretched. "Come on, Pepper," she called.

Instantly, the puppy leaped upward.

Kate caught her dog and hefted her up into her lap. She positioned the puppy carefully between her thighs so that she had a safe place to sit. Chuckling, Kate avoided Pepper's pink tongue and patted her head.

Kate and her dog and her horse. It was all so natural, Sam thought as he watched her laugh and play with Pepper. The dog adored her. Who wouldn't? He sure as hell did. As a matter of fact, he envied Pepper—at least Kate allowed the dog to get close to her. He turned away and momentarily scowled. Although his gaze was on the red-and-white Herefords that dotted the green pasture below, his mind and heart were elsewhere.

How many times had he awakened at night from torrid dreams of making love to Kate? He wasn't sorry at all for those rare moments when they could share an intimate kiss. Each was leading to more exploration, more trust and deepening intimacy between them. He *wanted* to taste her, feel her, share her breath, her caresses. In some ways, the kisses were softening Kate and making her more accessible. In other ways, she avoided him like the proverbial plague. Sometimes, without thinking, he'd get too close to her and she'd automatically step away from him. Sam didn't blame her. After all, he'd betrayed her once and he knew that the hurt was a tough wall to dissolve between them. Kate had to learn she could trust him not to leave her in the lurch again—that he would always be there for her.

Wiping the sweat collecting on his upper lip with his gloved hand, he furrowed his brow more heavily as he watched the cattle below. Sam released a long, ragged sigh, then he straightened in the saddle and lowered his leg. Picking up the reins, he looked over at Kate and Pepper. There was such life shining in Kate's sky blue eyes, in her smiling, parted lips as she stroked the puppy's head. "I've got to get back. Need to pick up sweet feed at the mill. Charley's got the order ready for us."

"Oh..." Kate quickly let Pepper slip gently back to the ground. "You're right. We can't take breaks like this too often." Picking up the reins, she clucked to Cinnamon, who headed back down the knoll at a brisk walk.

Sam joined her, keeping his horse a few feet from hers so that their boots or legs wouldn't accidentally touch. They headed for the big aluminum gate at the south end of the pasture. "Is there anything you want in Sedona while I'm there?"

Since Chet Cunningham had embarrassed her at the restaurant, Kate had not gone back to town. Sam understood why, but he also knew Kate couldn't keep herself locked up like a prisoner at the ranch for the rest of her life, either. If she wanted anything, she handed him a list and he picked up the items for her. Shopping for groceries wasn't one of his favorite things, but he did it anyway. He knew Kate was afraid to meet too many accusing looks if she ran into townsfolk in the aisles. Someday, that wound would scab over, too.

Stealing a glance at him, Kate said, "I thought I might ride into town with you. There're some things I'd like to pick up at the saddler in West Sedona."

Unable to hide his surprise, he stared at her.

"It's about time, don't you think?" Kate asked wryly.

"The time is right when you feel ready to tackle it, Gal." At least he was able to call her by this endearment. And every time he did, he saw Kate's tender reaction. That was all he could do right now. He couldn't touch her or kiss her anytime he wanted—at least, not yet. But the friendship and trust they were establishing was a good foundation.

"I'm such a coward at heart, Sam," Kate said with a sigh, waving her hand helplessly. "I know I've been hiding out here, using the ranch chores as a convenient excuse. Jessica read me the riot act on the phone the other night. She made me mad, but she was right."

"About what?"

"How I was letting Chet Cunningham, one person in ten thousand in Sedona, stop me from living my life fully."

Sam grinned sourly. "That little space-cadet sister of yours has her head screwed on straight."

With a laugh, Kate leaned down and patted Cinnamon's sleek neck. The horse automatically arched a little more in response. "Jessica *seems* to be spacy and ungrounded, but she's not."

"She reminds me of a leaf falling off a tree at the whimsy of the wind."

"Yes, but every leaf knows where it's going—to the ground." Kate grinned. "My little sister is flighty, but she's practical."

"Part of your mother's gift to all of you," Sam agreed congenially. The aluminum gate was double locked, so he dismounted and walked up to it. "You three ladies all have the genius of common sense," he told her, opening the gate and moving him and his horse through it.

"Mom could make a silk purse out of a sow's ear," Kate agreed with a laugh. She clucked to Cinnamon and moved through the open gate, with Pepper at the mare's heels. Kate watched as Sam carefully double-checked the gate to make sure it was secure. If the cows and calves got out, they could wander over nearly five thousand acres of desert unattended, and that wasn't such a good idea right now.

Kate enjoyed watching Sam as he mounted again, his actions graceful and confident. Giving her a significant look, he brought his horse into a walk next to hers. "So Jessica badgered you into coming to town with me today?" He would have wished Kate wanted to ride in the truck with him on her own accord, but that was pretty selfish of him. Wounds from the past took time to heal and he just had to dig down deeper in himself to find patience.

"Mmm, maybe not badgered. She sent me one of the natural essences she makes for her company. Matter of fact, it comes from broom snakeweed," Kate said, gesturing toward the desert. "It comes from right here. All that yellow-flowering brush."

Raising his brows, Sam said, "That's a pasture weed out here." Snakeweed was a prolific plant that during the spring rain would burst into life, with hundreds of tall, green arms and a cloud of little yellow flowers on top. The wind would pick up the fragrant scent, one of Mother Nature's perfumes. It smelled nice, but it also discouraged grass growth, so it wasn't a favorite of ranchers. But there was no stopping snakeweed, so one learned to live with it.

"I know," Kate said with a laugh. "Jessica said she made that essence several years ago when she was visiting a friend in Tucson. She told me it was a medicine that helped a person confront his or her fears. I've been taking four drops four times a day for the last couple of days and I have noticed I'm not as scared as I used to be when I thought about going into town."

"So, it helps with a person's fears, whatever they might be?"

"That's what Jessica said." Kate shrugged. "Seems to be working. My stomach doesn't clench into a knot when I think about going into town."

Impressed, Sam said, "She's really got something with that stuff of hers, doesn't she?"

"Listen, Jessica's natural essences are used around the world by people who don't want to use drugs. They're natural, and they work. At first, I was like you—unconvinced. But she's so enthusiastic about them and what they can do to help that I had to try them. She says she has another natural essence that cures depression."

"That's pretty heady stuff," Sam agreed. "Trade in your antidepressants for a little one-ounce bottle of a flower essence, instead. I'd do it, too."

"Besides, it's cheaper, safe and has no side effects," Kate added. "Drugs can't compete with that, and that's why her products are just flying off the shelf."

"And Jessica's money is helping to sustain the ranch," Sam noted. Faithfully, every month, the two sisters sent checks. Without those life-giving infusions, the Donovan Ranch would again fall behind in mortgage payments, and the bank, this time, wasn't going to be lenient. In Sam's opinion, the bank would foreclose without a bat of an eyelash. The banker, Fred Smith, was a good friend of Cunningham's, and over the years, the grizzled old rancher had made no bones about wanting to scoop up the Donovan ranch if the bank did foreclose. Then the Bar C would be the largest ranch in the State of Arizona.

"Yes," Kate said with a sigh, "thank goodness for their checks." And their weekly phone calls to her. How she looked forward to Sunday, when telephone rates were cheapest. She would spend at least half an hour talking with each of them, catching them up on ranch news, where they stood financially, and sharing how their personal lives were going. Next to being with Sam, Kate looked forward most to those life-giving phone calls from her sisters.

As the ranch house appeared in the distance, Sam gazed over at Kate, who had lapsed into deep thought, her face serene. "Why don't we take lunch in town?" He looked at the watch on his dark, hairy wrist. "It's nearly eleven a.m."

Startled by the suggestion, Kate felt heat rush to her face. "Where?"

"The Muse Restaurant?" he drawled good-naturedly.

Laughing, Kate said, "The way I feel right now, the Muse would be fine, too."

"The Muse has the best barbecued pork ribs in town...."

Matching his grin, she said, "Why not? I'm like a starvin' wolf." Then she patted her lean rib cage with her gloved hand.

"You got a deal. We'll pick up the feed and then stop at the Muse for lunch and go to the saddle maker afterward." Sam could barely keep the joy out of his voice. At last! Kate was moving forward again, growing and reaching out. This time he hoped like hell Chet Cunningham was nowhere to be seen. Usually the cowboy frequented Bailey's Bar in West Sedona. His appearance at the more posh establishment months ago had been a real fluke. Chet got into his share of brawls down at Bailey's, had seen the inside of Sedona's jail a number of times and had gotten out only because of Old Man Cunningham's power in the community. Well, it was noon, and Chet and his brother were probably riding the range, nowhere near Sedona, Sam hoped fervently.

Kate wiped her fingers on a linen napkin and grinned across the table at Sam. "This was a great idea. These ribs were good. I made a real pig out of myself." She looked at the scattered bones left on her plate. She'd eaten as if starved, but she knew that was because when Sam was with her, she relaxed. Since prison, her appetite wasn't consistent, but when Sam was around, she ate well. When he wasn't, she picked at food, not really hungry at all. And having lost

twenty pounds in prison, she needed to gain them
back in order to do the heavy, demanding ranch work.

Sam set their plates aside. The Muse was full of
patrons, the waitresses hurriedly making trips between
the tables and the kitchen. He and Kate had gotten a
table for two against one wall, near a hat stand covered with cowboy hats. Earlier, when they'd arrived,
Sam had cruised the bar area to make sure Chet Cunningham or his more obnoxious older brother, Bo,
weren't in there drinking. Fortunately, they weren't.

"Let's head down to the leather shop," Sam said.

Scooping up the bones into a doggy bag for Pepper,
Kate nodded and stood. "I'm ready." She was aware
of several locals looking at her from time to time, but
the broom snakeweed essence she was taking—and
Sam's reassuring presence—took the edge off her
normally nervous response to such curious stares.
How proud Jessica would be of her progress. Coming
into Sedona for the first time in nearly four months
left Kate feeling really free. As she walked with Sam
out the front door onto the patio filled with bright-
colored flowers in terra-cotta pots, she realized how
much she had been a prisoner of a different sort. And
worst of all, she'd sentenced herself this time to hiding on the ranch.

Sunlight glanced down through the branches of the
fernlike mimosa trees that bordered the patio outside
the restaurant. She felt Sam's hand on her arm, and
inwardly she tensed, but only for a moment. More
than anything, she ached for his unexpected touches
and those times when they could be together and
share a warm, escalating kiss.

Kate wished she had the courage to tell Sam that

she was dangerously close to surrendering completely to her emotions and letting go, that she was longing to love him completely. His kisses were like a teasing dessert, a promise of sweeter things to come. As he slipped his hand under her elbow, her skin tingled pleasantly, and she looked up at him. The dark gray of his eyes gave no hint of emotion, but his fingers tightened briefly around her elbow. How could she tell him she wanted more of his touches? That she wanted the kisses to move to a new, exploratory level? Sometimes she chastised herself for being such a coward. But at least this time she wasn't running. She was making a stand and a commitment to the ranch—and to herself. Kate knew that Sam's presence was very much a part of her being able to do that. He fed her strength and belief in herself.

Kate stepped off the red flagstone steps to the asphalt parking lot. Perhaps she needed to sit down and talk to him of her fears, her assumptions and her dreams. Maybe it was time. He deserved her honesty, not her cowardice.

Fay Seward was at a sewing machine when Sam and Kate entered the small leather store where everyone in town got their saddles, bridles and harnesses repaired.

"Howdy, Sam," she called as they entered. "Well, hello there, Kate. I'll be with you in just a sec…"

"Thanks, Fay," Sam murmured, tipping his hat toward her.

Kate smiled a greeting at the shop owner. Wearing wire-rimmed glasses that gave her a school-marm look, Fay was in her early fifties, her short, ginger-colored hair in tight curls around her oval face. Kate admired Fay's neat appearance despite the fact she worked at a man's job. As Kate wandered through the small shop, breathing in the wonderful smell of clean and rubbed leather, she gazed at all the new horse headstalls hanging on one wall, the new and used saddles sitting around on pine boxes with wheels. Fay's creativity could be seen everywhere. Some of the headstalls had brow bands of woven horsehair, black and white against the tobacco brown or chocolate color of the leather. She stroked several gently and relished the soft suppleness of the leather.

"Take a look at this," Sam called from the other side of the room. He pointed to a black saddle that had the center of it cut out.

Sauntering across the old, creaking wooden floor, Kate eyed the unusual saddle. "What kind is it?" she asked, running her fingers lightly across the polished black leather.

"It's a U.S. Army make—the McClellan cavalry saddle," Sam told her, examining the brass fittings mounted on the front of it. "And look at this—it was made in 1918. Fay must have sewn new leather straps on it."

"Who would ride such a thing?" Kate wondered. The saddle had a high pommel and cantle, but no horn. It would be useless to ranchers. There would be nothing to twist a rope around when they'd lassoed a steer.

Chuckling, Sam knelt down and closely examined the fine workmanship Fay had put into it. "Probably belongs to one of the Civil War reenactors from Camp Verde." He glanced up at her. "They've got an entire unit of men who wear Civil War outfits, go through the old cavalry drills. And,'' he continued, easing upward and patting the saddle affectionately, ''they use equipment from that era on their horses. The McClellan was made during the Civil War and used up until the army traded tanks for horses after World War One.''

Kate admired the saddle. ''A lot of history here, isn't there?''

Sam was going to say yes when he heard the door open. Looking up, he instantly narrowed his eyes. In walked Chet and Bo Cunningham. Damn! Baby-faced Chet, his cheeks always red so that he looked like he was blushing, broke into a gleeful grin.

''Well, lookit what the cats dragged in, Bo....''

Kate froze. Her heart shattered. Chet Cunningham! She'd recognize that high nasal twang of his anywhere. Looking over at Sam, she saw his face become a thundercloud of anger, his gray eyes slitted and menacing. Slowly she turned to face her torturer. To her dismay, she saw Bo Cunningham standing beside the short, wiry Chet. Bo was around thirty-one, ruggedly handsome with dark hair like his father, and flashing black eyes he got from his Apache mother. Kate had never liked these two while growing up, though they all went to the same school together. The only Cunningham she liked was Jim, though she rarely saw the son who had gone on to work for the EMT. The other two brothers were nothing but trouble looking for a place to happen.

Kate felt Sam move closer to him. Much closer. She felt protected though she could feel the tension radiating around him. A chair scraped along the wooden floor and Kate's attention wavered. She saw Fay Seward frowning as she moved to the oak counter.

"You boys don't have anything in here to pick up, as I recall."

Chet grinned and swaggered over to the counter. "Miss Fay, how are you this fine day?" He tipped his hat to her in a dramatic motion.

Bo, who was built like his father at six foot three inches tall and more than two hundred pounds, kept his black gaze on Kate. "We're just passin' through, Miss Fay," he said in a low, soothing voice. His mouth twisted like barbed wire as he turned to Sam. "Saw your Ram pickup out front, McGuire. Thought we'd drop by and see how things were goin' at the Donovan Ranch." His smile hardened as his gaze pinned Kate viciously. "Looks like you got what you always wanted, Sam—the Donovan Ranch and that wild ex-con of a girl you were always moonin' over ever since she ran away in high school." He chuckled and moved over to the counter next to his brother.

Kate swallowed hard. From somewhere deep within her, she found her voice. It was low and husky when she spoke. "Bo, you and Chet are nothing but rattlers with nothing good to say about anyone. Time hasn't changed either of you in the least."

Bo spread his arms on the counter, staring at her from beneath the low brim of his dark brown, dusty Stetson. His mouth worked into a sneer. "Hey, Chet, listen to her crowin', will you? Now, neither of us have spent any time in a prison and yet here she is, chiding us." He chuckled.

Chet laughed, too. He raised his beat-up, sweat-stained straw hat off his head and scratched his black hair. "Katie Donovan always thought she was better than us. Always had her nose stickin' in the air at high school. Remember that?"

"Sure do," Bo drawled. "Miss Nose-in-the-Air. That's what we called her." His mouth twisted more. "Eighteen months in the pen didn't change her at all, did it?"

Kate was ready to take them on verbally, her anger soaring. Before she could, she felt Sam brush by her shoulder, his rage barely contained as he strode toward the two younger men. Worried that a fight might break out, Kate moved quickly in turn. Then she saw Fay pick up a baseball bat from beneath the counter.

"No," Fay growled at the Cunningham men, "if you two think you can come in here and bad-mouth payin' customers in *my* establishment, you got another think comin'. As if you two have any room to talk! Both of you boys have been in and out of Coconino County Jail more times than I've got fingers and toes. You quit pickin' on Kate. She served her time. It's done. It's the past, so you let it lie." She laid the baseball bat circumspectly on the counter between them, her hand over it, staring down the Cunningham men. "What'll it be, boys? A lump or two on your head if you keep shootin' off your mouths, or leavin' while your heads are still attached to your shoulders?"

Sam halted halfway to the counter. Automatically, he put his arm out to stop Kate from moving around him. His fingers bit deeply into her arm and he felt her trembling with rage, and he waited. This was Fay's establishment and her territory. She was tough but fair, and if she could handle the Cunninghams, he wouldn't step into the fray. But if they continued calling Kate names, he was going to settle the score with them outside—once and for all.

Bo eased into a standing position. He threw back his broad shoulders and chuckled. "Now, Miss Fay, we don't mean you no harm." He gestured toward Sam. "Nah, we're just droppin' by to say howdy-do, is all." He tipped his hat to the older woman. "We'll be leavin' now, nice and peaceful like. Chet?"

Chet grinned and followed his older brother out of the store. "Sure thing, big brother. We got some hay to pick up at the feed store." He tipped his hat respectfully in Fay's direction. "Ma'am? Have a nice day."

The door shut with a slam.

Kate released a broken sigh of relief.

"Those damned boys never grew up," Fay snarled, putting the baseball bat beneath the counter once again. "Old Man Cunningham spoilt those two varmints but good. Bad milk gone to sour if you ask me." She looked over at them. "I'm awful sorry, Kate and Sam. Try and consider the source and let it be like water runnin' off a duck's back, will you?"

Easing her fingers from Sam's upper arm, Kate felt his thick, hard muscles. He was as solid as the Mogollon Rim. Managing a weak smile, she said, "Thanks, Fay. This wasn't your fight. Chet has been gunning for me ever since I got out of...well, since I came home."

Snorting, Fay flashed an angry look toward the door. "Those two need their heads banged every once in a while to keep 'em in line. Chet hasn't a brain in that empty skull of his and Bo's more dangerous than a rattler." She walked briskly over to the wall of headstalls. "Come on, I've got those two bridles fixed for you, Sam. Here they are."

Relief washed through Kate as Fay went about the business at hand. Gratefully, she paid for the headstalls, glad that Fay didn't mention her prison past. The older woman treated her like she would anyone. And best of all, she had stood up and defended her. Kate hadn't known Fay well growing up, but she was coming to appreciate her forthright manner.

"Thank you," Kate murmured as she handed her the cash. "For everything...."

Fay placed the headstalls in some brown wrapping paper and tied it up with string. "Teenagers in men's bodies if you ask me. Testosterone for brains. They don't think with their heads, they think with what's between their legs." She handed Kate the package. Squinting her blue eyes, she jabbed her brown, stained index finger at Kate. "Don't let a few snakes in the grass make you feel badly, young lady. Hell, no one has a clean past. I spent time in a local jail once for beating up my husband because he was beating up my daughter. And I've made a lot of decisions I ain't proud of, either. We've all got pasts. What you need to do is let it go. Walk proud, with no apologies." Her glance cut to the door. "Especially to the likes of those two troublemakers. Folks around here will judge you on what you do now, on a daily basis, if they've got any brains."

Barely able to stop from chuckling, Kate kept a respectful and somber look on her face. "Thank you, Fay. You're a wonderful teacher."

Taking off her glasses, Fay tenderly rubbed the bridge of her nose with her fingers. "Then take it to heart, missy." She put her glasses back on and looked over at Sam. "And you stop being so defensive about Kate, here."

Chastened, Sam had the good grace to blush under Fay's squinty-eyed look of censure. "I got a little tense," he admitted.

"I saw you cock your fist. That's why I went for the baseball bat. It makes for a real balance in a fight. I was countin' on you being smarter than those two rocks-for-brains, and holding your ground."

His mouth pulled into a sour grin. "Miss Fay, I would *never* think of starting a fight in your establishment." And he wouldn't. Fay Seward was known to be crusty, combative and downright cantankerous if she was unfairly disturbed. Every rancher in the territory knew that. And she was famous for her baseball bat. More than a couple of cowboys had tasted the bat's infamous reputation.

"Humph, you'd better now. Kate's got two legs and a brain in her head. She can speak up and defend herself." Fay's eyes flashed. "You're behavin' like a mongrel dog that's found his lifelong mate. Don't be like those two boys and let your brain turn to mush just 'cause you're emotionally in over your head."

Kate bit back laughter. She saw Sam's brow draw down in displeasure, but he didn't get defensive.

"Yes, Miss Fay," he murmured politely, and tipped his hat to her. "I'll come by for that saddle sometime next week?"

Fay twisted around, searching for the saddle that needed repair. "Yessir, you can come by next Friday.

I'll have new straps and a cinch for it by that time. Good day to you both.''

On the way home, Kate mulled over the entire sequence of what had happened in Fay's saddle shop. What had Fay meant when she said Sam was acting like a mongrel dog who had found his lifelong mate? She risked a glance at his harsh profile as he drove up 89A out of Sedona. Just as quickly, she moved her gaze out the window to drink in the juniper and desert pine that dotted the red sand earth. Wasn't his protective stance a normal, natural thing? Fay didn't think so. And what about Bo Cunningham's comment that Sam had what he'd always wanted—the ranch and her? That comment didn't make sense, either. Or did it?

Chapter Eleven

Early, unexpected April heat swept across the desert expanse, parching everything in its path. Kate felt a fine tremble of tension run through her as she sat on her Arabian mare, eyes squinted against the strong noon sunlight. She pressed her calves to the bay, and instantly, Cinnamon broke into a slow, controlled lope. Ahead of her, moving up a sandy slope littered with multicolored pebbles, Mormon tea plants that towered eight to ten feet tall and prickly pear cactus, was Sam. He, too, urged his rangy gelding, Bolt, into a lope.

Today they were gathering the three Hereford bulls from their collective pasture, to move them to three new pastures where they would each have a harem of cows to impregnate for the next year's calf crop. They'd decided to leave Pepper home for this job, as it was much too dangerous for a young puppy. Handling bulls was never easy work. It was hard, dirty and dangerous. Worse, neither Sam nor herself knew these bulls. Kelly had bought them after Sam had left the ranch. One of the things a rancher needed to pay attention to was the personality of a two-thousand-pound bull, which weighed twice as much as a horse. Sam and she had watched the bulls and gotten an idea of their temperament, so that when it came time to herd them, they could be prepared as much as possible for any exigency plans.

Even so, Kate had had a bad feeling when she woke up at four a.m. that morning. The moving of the bulls had been put off until it could no longer be ignored. Two people on horseback handling three bulls wasn't enough to get the job done safely. But they had no choice. These bulls were restless. They could smell the cows in season and were frustrated because they hadn't been able to breed. Bulls were not oriented by herd instinct. Once a bull smelled the scent of cows, he could break off at a moment's notice, hurtle his massive body right through a startled horse and rider and kill them in order to get to the cows.

Today, Kate wore leather chaps, as Sam did. The chaps were wide and flared at the bottom, covering part of her dusty, cracked cowboy boots. If a bull decided to take off, she or Sam could be brush popped through thickets of cutting chaparral, slammed into the long, crochet-needle-size spines of a Mormon tea bush or worse, be run into a five- to eight-foot patch of prickly pear cactus. The leather would be a good guard against abrasion, up to a point.

Flexing her gloved fingers on the reins, Kate felt Cinnamon move nervously beneath her, picking up on her tension. The sun beat directly down on them as they spotted the bulls just below the base of the hill, foraging for almost nonexistent grass. Spring was supposed to yield several inches of rain to feed the dry, arid land, but so far it hadn't. Now food was more sparse than ever and the bulls had ranged over a much larger area in order to survive. It would make herding them even longer and more difficult.

"There they are," Sam said, glancing at Kate as she pulled up beside him. He saw the grim set of her lips. She wore a red bandanna around her throat, protective chaps and gloves, plus a special long-sleeved, heavy twill shirt that would to a degree protect her flesh from brutal contact with Mormon tea and chaparral. Her face glistened; her sky blue eyes narrowed, intent upon the bulls.

He wasn't feeling too easy, either. Today they both wore pistols—Colts—around their waists. If a bull got mean and charged, it might have to be shot in order to save their lives. When blinded by the mating lust, a bull was a ton of raw testosterone and adrenaline on the hoof.

Sam rested his hand on the low-slung holster that held the Colt. Earlier, they'd put bullets in the chambers, locked and loaded them and put the safety on. Riding around with a bullet in the barrel of a pistol wasn't something he liked to do, but there wasn't much choice. If he knew the personalities of the bulls better, he might be feeling less tense. Therefore, out of a lifetime of experience, Sam treated the bulls like C-4 plastic explosives just waiting to go off at him.

Or worse, at Kate. Worriedly, he assessed her. She seemed easy and relaxed in the saddle, but he saw tension in the line of her mouth.

"You sure you want to do this?"

She quirked her lips. "No, but I didn't see anybody else volunteering." Patting the bulging saddlebags behind her, she added, "I've brought two first-aid kits—one with dressing and bandages, the other that homeopathic kit Rachel sent—just in case."

Scratching away the sweat trickling down his cheek, Sam nodded. "Good." He sincerely hoped they wouldn't need either one of them. "We'll probably look like a couple of pin cushions before this little dance is over."

"Chaps will help."

"Help, but not stop all of those cactus spines." He motioned to the landscape stretching before them. Thousands of Mormon tea bushes stood with their arms full of greenish yellow needles. They reminded him of long crochet or knitting needles, sticking out all over the bush as if it were a giant pin cushion. "This is a bad area. Keep your face protected, Kate. I don't want you to lose an eye to one of those damn bushes." He hated Mormon tea. It was far more dangerous to a human and horse than the prickly pear patches that proliferated on the red, sandy desert.

Except for protective wrappings on their vulnerable lower legs, the horses had little way to defend themselves against hostile plants and bushes. The gelding Sam rode was long-legged, rangy and savvy. From years of experience, Bolt knew how to avoid these dangers. And the Arabian Kate rode was trail trained, also. These horses were smart and they knew how to read cattle. Sam knew his horse had plenty of experience with testy, dangerous bulls. He wasn't sure that Cinnamon had any such experience—and that put Kate at great risk. A horse not expecting to get charged by a bull could freeze—and leave it and its rider a handy target. If Cinnamon was used to docile Herefords and had no experience with the cantankerous behemoths, that was a high risk. But what else could Sam do?

He had known Donovan horses that had bull-herding experience, but when he returned to the ranch, they were all gone. And Cinnamon was new. He'd watched the mare and knew she had a good head on her shoulders. Her response in other situations had been steady and controlled. But bulls could scare even the most levelheaded of horses if they made a split-second charge. A horse could freeze or could leap to one side to avoid being struck. Worse, if Kate asked Cinnamon to make a swift countermove, and the mare, because of inexperience, didn't trust her mistress in the dangerous situation, they could be injured or killed.

It was very important that a ranch horse trust its rider completely. One wrong move, one misstep, could get them killed. There were places on the Donovan Ranch that could only be reached by taking the canyon walls. If a horse did not watch where it was placing its feet or heed the signals of the rider's legs or the reins, they could both slip to their death.

Scowling, Sam studied the three red-and-white Hereford bulls. Luckily, they'd found some pretty good patches of yellowing grass beneath a large stand of Mormon tea and they were closely grouped. That was unusual, but he hoped it was a sign of good things to come. He pointed his gloved finger at the bull nearest them, the largest one with the red ear tag hanging off his left ear. The bull lazily flicked at the flies buzzing around his massive head. "Let's call him One Horn. He's the biggest. I'll take him on. That next one, the middle-sized one, will be Red. The smallest over there we'll call Whitey."

Names would help them when they called out instructions or orders to one another. Red was a muscular powerhouse, his small eyes regarding them suspiciously even now. Sam didn't trust that son of a bitch, either. Whitey was the smallest of the three bulls, and looked the least interested in their approach. One Horn had one of his horns missing, and the other was deformed and thrust upward like a twisted dagger waiting to impale some unlucky soul. Sam didn't like horned Herefords. He'd argued against purchasing them, but Kelly had liked the old traditional Hereford breed with horns.

A Hereford's horns normally were small and curved inward toward the bull's face, which made them a lot less dangerous than other breeds of cattle to a cowboy who had to herd them. One Horn's straggly appendage was like a razor-sharp knife. A savage head toss by One Horn would be like experiencing the cut of a saber. The bull, if angered, could slice and gut open a horse chest to flank in one horrifying motion. It wasn't a very pleasant thought.

Kate's Arabian mare weighed only eight hundred pounds. Sam's gelding was a good four hundred pounds heavier—not to mention a lot taller. Herding bulls with heavier horses was smart because a bull

could bump a horse and the horse could stand its
ground and not get tossed around like a tumbleweed.
Bolt was built like a proverbial tank, with a lot of
width across his chest, heavy hindquarters for getting
his rear legs solidly beneath him, enabling him to turn
on a dime, and a long barrel that gave him the ability
to reach a long, ground-eating stride very swiftly.

"None of them look very pleasant, do they?" Kate
asked wryly, sitting up in the saddle and stretching
her legs. In a few moments they'd be working hard.
Once they got the bulls together and moving in the
same direction, there could be no stopping or resting—or the bulls would scatter like leaves on the
wind, and the herding process would have to begin
all over.

"No," Sam growled. He gestured toward the bulls.
"Watch One Horn. He's eyeing us. I looked at the
breeding records in your office on these three bulls
and he's the oldest. That means he's got more experience."

"Translated," Kate said grimly, "it means he
knows how to down a horse and rider if he gets a
mind to."

"Yes," Sam agreed unhappily. Reaching out, he
gripped her upper arm momentarily. "If I yell an order to you, Kate, just do it. Don't wait, don't analyze,
all right? You've got to trust me enough to know that
I know what's right if these bulls get riled."

She smiled a little and reveled in the firmness of
his hand on her arm. "I trust you with my life, Sam
McGuire." The tenor of their relationship was continuing to evolve, their exchanges more open, filled
with personal warmth. In the last month, Kate had

initiated a touch now and then—not often, but it let him know that she was reaching out to him. He'd gotten the message. Now and then, in return, he would touch her. Usually in moments when he was worried for her safety. Like now.

Sam released Kate's arm, his gaze resting on her blue eyes flecked with gold. Yes, things were moving the right direction with her as far as he was concerned. The energy between them was one of friendship now and ripe with sexual tension. The next step would be a heady one to take, Sam thought as he pulled his hat down tightly so it wouldn't fly off once they got started herding these contrary bastards. In time, if everything went right, he knew Kate would let down her guard and trust him. In time, she might trust him enough to learn to love him once again—as he loved her.

"Let's move nice and easy toward them," he said from between tight lips.

Kate nodded tensely and rode at his side. Her heart skipped a beat as One Horn snapped his large head up toward them. He had small, beady eyes. Evil eyes, in Kate's opinion. There was an old horseman's saying that the smaller the eyes on a horse or steer, the less brains it had and the more dangerous it could be. The larger the eyes, the more intelligent it was and therefore easier to work with.

Upon Sam's command, they separated and quietly moved around the three bulls. Kate saw massive amounts of drool hanging in long, glistening strings from One Horn's white muzzle as he studied her. A chill crawled up her spine. Her hands automatically tightened on the reins and she gripped the barrel of her horse more securely with her long legs. Cinnamon sensed her tension and snorted, her own attention on One Horn.

To Kate's relief, One Horn grudgingly turned as Sam approached him, just like a docile steer or cow would. Cinnamon was trained for leg commands, and Kate pressed her right leg against the animal's side, turning left to cut off the other two bulls, which were beginning to go in different directions, away from One Horn.

Instantly, the bay responded and pebbles flew from beneath her rear hooves as she made the cut. Good. Red and Whitey stopped their escape plan and moved back toward Sam and One Horn. Releasing a breath of air, Kate kept her horse reined in. If one of those bulls decided to charge, she knew it could turn its massive body and come hurtling at her in a split second. She needed to keep her distance in order to react in time and get the hell out of the way.

In her gloved right hand, she held her coiled rope. Not that they would ever try to lasso a bull—that would be foolhardy. With a bull's power and weight, he'd yank a cowboy straight out of the saddle. If the saddle cinch didn't break and shred under the bull's strength, the horse could be pulled off its feet and dragged along, too. No, the rope was for making occasional slapping sounds against her leather chaps, but that was about all.

For two hours they kept the bulls in a slow-moving, loose-knit herd. The rocky, cactus-strewn hills came and went. Kate was beginning to relax. Soon the breeding pastures would be coming up. She noticed that the bulls were lifting their noses more often to

the air, testing it for the odor of cows in season and
that they had picked up their pace to almost a trot.
This was where it could get dangerous. No fence on
earth could stop a bull if he chose to plow through it
to get to the cows. The breeding pastures were
smaller, the posts eight feet high with six strands of
barbed wire, designed to detour a bull. But that's all
the fence would do.

"Kate!"

Sam's voice thundered at her, interrupting her errant thoughts. Startled, she jerked her head and saw
him pointing up to the right of him. A Hereford cow
was loose. "Oh, damn," she whispered in a strained
voice. Automatically, her hands tightened on the
reins. Cinnamon tensed, waiting for a command.

The cow mooed plaintively toward the three approaching bulls. Kate knew without a doubt that the
animal was in season. And she also knew that all three
bulls had caught the hormonal scent on the air and
were going to try and race one another to get to her
first in order to breed with her. Double damn! Of all
the things Kate imagined could happen, a loose cow
wasn't one of them. She saw Sam swing Bolt
abruptly. One Horn made a bid to veer off to the right
toward the cow.

"Get to the cow!" Sam shouted. "Get her herded
back to the pasture!"

It was a brilliant plan, Kate thought. Sam's experience over her own lack of it was obvious. Yes, get
the cow herded up ahead of the bulls and they'd follow like mesmerized kids behind the Pied Piper. Sinking her heels into Cinnamon, she made the mare leap
to the right. Dirt and stones flew as Kate galloped

hard toward the cow half a mile away. Out of the corner of her eye, she saw One Horn toss his head ominously as Sam slapped his coiled rope against his chaps, warning the bull to go back and join the other two.

Kate had no time to watch. Hunching low, her hands against Cinnamon's sweaty neck, she rode at a dizzying pace toward the cow. The Arabian's small size allowed her to weave around the Mormon tea and cactus with finesse and ease. Cinnamon's ground-eating stride thundered beneath Kate. The wind whipped past her, the horse's black mane stinging her face as the mare ran. Up ahead, Kate saw the cow move toward the breeding pastures. Good! This was going to be easier than she'd thought. The cow could've turned contrary and headed straight to the bulls instead, causing all kinds of hell to break loose. If that had happened, the bulls would begin to fight one another, causing serious injury and maybe death to one or more of them. Tens of thousands of dollars spent on a good breeding bull could be lost in a moment like this. Kate didn't want that to happen.

Just as she crested the hill, she heard a bawling and bellowing behind her. The cow was trotting quickly toward the breeding pastures, no more than half a mile away at this point. Jerking her head to the left, Kate pulled her horse to a skidding stop.

"Sam!" Her cry careened down into the gully area between two hills, where he rode with the three restless bulls. "*Nooo!*" She saw One Horn toss his head and charge Sam. Without thinking, Kate sank her heels into Cinnamon. The mare hurtled back down the slope. Kate's heart slammed into her chest as One Horn bore down on Sam.

With a grunt, Sam jerked Bolt to the left as One Horn lifted his massive, drooling head and charged. Despite his heft and size, the bull moved like lightning. Bolt dug in his hind legs, throwing all his weight to the right. Sam stayed with the big gelding, his gaze pinned on the swiftly moving bull. Spittle flew up around One Horn's face and caught on the twisted horn, which glittered like a deadly knife.

Bolt knew what to do—he headed away from the bull at full speed. Sam felt his horse using every ounce of strength to create distance between them.

One Horn bawled angrily and made a sharp move to the right, to head them off.

Damn!

A small gully, cut deep and wide by thunderstorms and flash floods year after year, loomed before them. It lay at the bottom of two bracketing hills. Sam heard Kate's cry but he had no time to look up. A huge stand of Mormon tea appeared to the left of them, just before the gully. On the right was a five-foot-tall patch of prickly pear. The gulch walls were too steep for them to cross it at a dead run. If Bolt tried to leap across and scramble up the steep, rocky hill, he'd never make it.

The choices were few. Sam twisted his head. One Horn had read the situation correctly. Determined to cut them off, he was hurtling toward them, bawling, the spittle streaming out of his open mouth, his eyes red with rage. Sam began to pull back on the reins to signal Bolt not to try and make that deadly leap. The horse could break his neck, and so could Sam once

Bolt, who was going too fast to negotiate the rocky hill properly, smashed into the other side.

Again Sam heard Kate's cry, this time closer. Where was she? No time to look. Where to go? The gulch and hill loomed before him.

Without warning, Sam hauled the reins against Bolt's thick, sweaty neck.

Instantly, the big gelding responded. The action threw them into the stand of Mormon tea. Sam tried to protect his face as the horse slammed full speed into the thick, tough greenery. The heavy branches scraped against him but that was the lesser of two evils. He heard Bolt grunt and stagger to the right as the horse lost his footing and they slid into the stand. One Horn bawled. The sound was right on top of them.

Bolt grunted, his hindquarters skidding across the sandy desert and sharp rocks. Sam hung on with his legs while trying to unstrap the Colt from his left hip. They had slid completely, like a baseball runner into home plate, into the thick stand of Mormon tea. The long, stabbing needles mercilessly gouged at horse and rider. Sam felt the jabs, but there wasn't time to focus on the pain. He heard the crash of One Horn following closely behind them.

Bolt, his hind legs beneath him now, was breathing hard. There were at least a dozen puncture wounds in the horse from the Mormon tea and the gelding's chest ran red with trickles of blood. As he directed Bolt to move swiftly out of the grove, Sam glanced behind them. One Horn was coming through the Mormon tea like it was a Sunday walk in the park, plowing the ten-foot bushes aside with his massive weight.

Sam saw the killing rage in the bull's eyes, and in that second he knew that one of them was going to die very shortly.

Bolt also seemed to realized that this was a life-and-death confrontation. The horse spun to the left, the shortest way out of the grove. Dirt flew in all directions beneath the powerful, hammering strides of the animal. Once they cleared the bushes, Sam caught sight of Kate, her face white with terror. She was heading right toward One Horn, her coil of rope lifted toward him.

"No!" Sam shouted hoarsely. *No good! Damn!* Bolt weaved to the right in one smooth motion, his long legs eating up the distance between them. Kate couldn't take on that bull! But that's exactly what she was doing. She was trying to get One Horn's attention away from him and transferred to her. Damn her courage! Sam's lips lifted away from his teeth as he leaned forward, asking for every ounce of Bolt's power in order to close the distance. One Horn was torn between his moving targets. He slowed a little, looking first at Kate, then at Sam. But it was Kate's shrill scream that enraged the bull the most. In one lightning move, One Horn twisted to the right, bawling out his challenge and bearing down on Kate.

The ground was uneven—soft here, hard there. Bolt negotiated the terrain as he carried Sam closer. Cursing, Sam managed to get the Colt out of the holster. Trying to unsnap the safety while his horse was barreling down the side of the slope was nearly impossible. He kept missing the catch again and again. There was no way to stop One Horn now. They were trapped in a small area, the rocky hills acting like

prison walls that refused them the room they needed
to get away from the infuriated bull. The only way
out of the situation was to kill One Horn before he
killed one of them.

Kate sucked in a breath as One Horn suddenly spun
around and bore directly down on her. Cinnamon reacted first, leaping to the right, her feet sliding down
toward the narrow gulch. *No!* Instantly, Kate threw
her weight to the left, and the horse steadied. Kate
could hear the grunting, sucking sounds One Horn
made with each galloping stride he took closer to
them. Sam's voice thundered, but Kate couldn't make
out what he was yelling. The bull was less than fifty
feet away, his small, red eyes fixed on her. Drool
streamed out of both sides of his mouth as he lowered
his head to charge. The wicked horn glinted in the
sunlight.

With a cry, Kate slapped her rope against the
horse's rump. Cinnamon leaped forward, startled, and
they galloped parallel to the gulch. Up ahead, a large
patch of prickly pear loomed. She suddenly saw One
Horn change course. He was trying to force her and
the horse into the cactus patch or down into the narrow gully. The bastard! The bull was determined to
kill them. And that realization startled Kate as nothing
else.

Cinnamon realized the bull's intent, too. The mare
was breathing hard, trying to outdistance the accel-
erating beast. Kate knew that the hill, covered with
black lava and cactus, could be negotiated, but not at
this speed or angle. She might take a horse up that
steep face at a slow walk, but not at a wild, headlong

gallop. Her choices were few. If she tried to go left, One Horn would intercept her.

For Kate, the only choice was the huge prickly pear patch looming before them. It was a good five feet high at the lowest point, and at least fifty feet deep. She knew now that One Horn was counting on the fact that she wasn't going to run her horse through that patch. But he was wrong. Gathering up the reins, Kate synchronized each movement of her body with Cinnamon's stride. In seconds, they were riding as if they were literally a part of one another. The mare steadied under Kate's hands and guidance.

Gripping her legs tight against the horse's barrel, Kate heard One Horn's breathing coming up fast behind her. She knew there was less than five feet separating them. She would have to jump the patch. Or try at least. Kate was hoping that the bull wouldn't plow through the cactus, being too old and wise to the pain the sharp spines caused. Would he stop? Would Cinnamon trust her and make the jump? The horse could refuse and skid to a halt, trying to escape to the right or left instead. If she did that, Kate knew, One Horn would kill them.

Everything slowed down for Kate. She felt each jolting, thundering movement of the horse, felt the hot sun beating down on her, tasted fear in her mouth and felt sweat stinging her eyes. Prickly pear branches grew at all heights, some five to six feet in the air. Would her small mare be able to jump not only far enough, but high enough? Kate didn't know. But she had to ask for a life-and-death effort from the mare. She placed her gloved hands on the sides of the animal's slick neck, the reins tight as she aimed for the narrowest point of the cactus patch. Applying pressure to the animal's sweaty, heaving sides, Kate signaled the horse to pick up speed in preparation to jump.

The wet mane stung Kate's face as she lifted her butt off the saddle, trying to give Cinnamon every chance to use her hindquarters to power them up and over the patch. Kate felt a moment's hesitation in the mare. Instantly, she pressed Cinnamon with her legs. The mare responded. If the Arabian didn't clear the patch, Kate knew it could badly injure them. Depending upon how the horse fell, Kate might be killed, too. In those slow-motion moments before she asked the Arabian to leap, Kate's heart centered on Sam. How she loved him! She swore that if she got through this alive, she'd tell him that.

Kate felt Cinnamon lifting her front legs as the horse began to leap. Everything began to swirl like a surreal picture in front of Kate's eyes and she pinned her gaze on the landing point. She heard Cinnamon grunt as she powered off the desert ground. They were airborne! Never had Kate sat so still. She felt her horse stretching, stretching forward. Then Cinnamon's legs and hooves tucked deep beneath her belly. Kate knew that if she moved in any way, she could throw the horse off and they could die. She saw the five-foot-tall cactus flash beneath them. The Arabian grunted as it grazed her, her tender belly scraped by the needles.

The bawling of One Horn shattered Kate's concentration. She had no way of knowing whether the bull was following them across the patch or not. Her eyes widened. Her lips parted in a cry. Cinnamon suddenly stretched her legs forward, her black hooves aimed toward that clear patch of ground. Were they going to make it? Her breath jammed in her throat.

Yes! Cinnamon cleared the patch by half a foot! The horse landed hard and Kate was thrown violently forward. Instantly, she threw the reins away to give the horse its head so that she might come out of the ungainly, off-balance landing. Too late! Kate knew Cinnamon had overstretched herself, giving all she had to save them. The mare's front knees buckled. Kate leaned way back, her spine touching the horse's rising hindquarters. Cinnamon was going to flip end over end! Fear engulfed Kate. With a cry of surprise, she allowed the forward momentum to rip her out of the saddle. Instead of hurtling over the horse's head, which would leave her in the path of Cinnamon's hooves, Kate pushed away with her legs. She tucked her head against her body as she flew through the air.

In seconds, Kate slammed into the hard, unforgiving ground. She heard Cinnamon grunt heavily off to her right and felt the ground shake as the horse landed in turn. Rolling to distribute the shock of the fall, Kate kept her arms tight around her knees. She heard several gunshots fired in rapid succession as she landed in a Mormon tea bush. Pain shot up into her back and she suddenly stopped rolling.

Straightening her arms and legs, Kate scrambled to her feet and anxiously looked toward the patch. Her eyes widened enormously when she saw One Horn staggering around in the middle of the cactus, his head bloodied. Sam was astride Bolt, his Colt aimed at the crazed bull. On wobbling legs, Kate watched the bull resist the bullets placed in his brain. Then

One Horn's red-eyed gaze settled on her. Foam and spittle mixed with pink and red bubbles of blood running out of his mouth. He bawled in fury. Flailing, he fought to move toward her. Kate froze with shock. The bull was dying, but still trying to reach her!

She heard the Colt bark two more times in quick succession and saw One Horn's head jerk upward at the first shot. His forward progress stopped. The second shot felled him. He grunted, flung his head up in a twisting motion and crashed to the ground, only ten feet away from where Kate stood.

Chapter Twelve

Kate turned drunkenly to check on her horse. Cinnamon stood alertly, shaking off the excess sand after her fall. The mare seemed fine despite the almost deadly leap she'd made.

"Kate!"

Dazedly, Kate turned back toward Sam's voice. She watched him ride the gelding around the cactus patch, his face stony, his flesh glistening with sweat, his eyes dark and fathomless. Bolt's hindquarters lowered as the gelding slid to a stop, and sand flew up in sheets around them. Sam dismounted, his gaze pinned savagely upon her.

"I—I'm all right." Kate wobbled as he ran up to her, his hand outstretched. But she wasn't, and she knew it. She had nearly died. One Horn had plowed through the cactus patch after her. And Cinnamon had fallen. The bull would have gored her to death in the sand right where she stood if Sam hadn't shot him.

Sam reached out, his fingers closing over her shoulder. "Kate…you're white as a sheet," he muttered tightly. "Broken bones?"

"No…" Kate closed her eyes, a ragged sigh escaping her lips. "Oh, Sam…" She leaned forward, lifting her arms and sliding them around his neck. He was hot, sweaty and dirty, but she didn't care. At this moment, all she wanted was him and the sense of safety he'd always given her. She wanted to sob out her love for him, and the words were nearly torn from her as she collapsed into his arms.

"Come here," he rasped hoarsely, wrapping his arms around her. Crushing Kate against him, Sam steadied her against the hard angles of his body. She fit perfectly and he groaned as her head rested against his jaw. He felt Kate trembling, and it got worse the longer he held her.

"It's all right," he breathed huskily, turning his head and pressing his mouth against her damp, gritty hair. "Everything's going to be all right, Gal. I promise you.…" He felt Kate moan as he pressed a not-so-innocent kiss to her temple. She shifted and lifted her face to him. He saw tears swimming in her dark blue eyes, saw the terror in them—and something else.… For those few seconds, Sam couldn't believe what he thought he was seeing. He remembered that look from so long ago. Did he dare hope?

"I almost died," Kate murmured, holding his stormy gray gaze. "I could've died and never told you, Sam.…" She choked on a sob and moved her hands to his face. "I love you…I never stopped loving you! I could have died just now and you'd never have known—''

Her words were caught by his descending mouth. He captured her lips fully, his mouth hot, hungry and seeking. Sinking fully against him and allowing Sam to take all her weight, Kate surrendered to him. Tears streaked down her cheeks, met and melted into the line of their mouths as they devoured one another. She'd almost died! Eagerly, she returned his powerful, molding kiss with equal need and fiery hunger. She could smell his masculine scent, taste his fear, feel the roughness of his beard scraping against her face. She suddenly remembered all those wonderful things about Sam that she could have never have experienced again if One Horn had gotten to her before Sam had killed him.

Knees wobbly, Kate tore her mouth from his, breathing hard. She gripped his arms to steady herself. Apologetically, she met his stormy, silvery eyes. She'd known this man before—the raw hunger in his eyes, the cajoling strength of his mouth upon hers, the roughened tenderness of his hands upon her body. ''Sam,'' she whispered, ''I—I think I'm going to faint....''

Kate awoke slowly. She felt the heat of the sun on her body, heard the soft snort of horses nearby. More than anything, she felt a damp cloth being gently dabbed across her brow where she lay. Lashes fluttering, she forced her eyes open. The cool cloth felt so good. She was hot, her skin sore and gritty. As her gaze focused, she realized belatedly that Sam was kneeling over her. And even more belatedly, Kate realized with embarrassment that she'd fainted.

"Just lie still," Sam urged quietly. He poured a little more of the precious water from his canteen into his bandanna and wiped the sides of her face. Her eyes were half-open and filled with confusion. He saw her lips twist wryly.

"I don't believe it. I fainted. I've never done that, ever...and I've been in a few tight spots before. I must be getting old...."

Her voice was wispy and weak, completely unlike her. Sam placed the bandanna across her furrowed brow and unbuttoned the two top buttons on her shirt, pulling her collar wide. He'd removed her gloves and set them nearby, propping up her feet so that the blood flowed back into her head and upper body.

"Almost getting killed brings on a lot of reactions," he grunted.

Kate's lashes dropped shut as Sam carried her out of the sun and placed her beneath the spreading arms of a mesquite tree. Languishing there, grateful for his care, Kate slowly realized that she'd told Sam she loved him. Instantly, she opened her eyes and stared up at his hard, uncompromising face.

"The horses...are they okay?"

"Fine. It's you I'm worried about."

Pushing herself up on one elbow, Kate managed a broken smile. Sam helped her sit up and she leaned her elbows over her knees, hugging her head between her legs. Color was rushing back to her face now, and Sam knew she'd be all right. He tucked the damp bandanna into her hand.

"Keep wiping your face down and cooling off."
He rose to his feet.

Kate looked up and did as she was instructed. Sam
went over to Bolt, who stood no more than six feet
away. She wanted to cry as she saw about a dozen
puncture wounds across his massive chest from his
run through the Mormon tea. Trickles of drying blood
made vertical stripes across his powerfully muscled
body. Sam spoke gently to the gelding as he slowly
ran his hand over the animal's chest in examination.
Every once in a while Sam would jerk out a thin,
needlelike spine causing Bolt to flinch.

Getting to her feet, her knees still a little weak,
Kate moved over to Cinnamon, who had sought the
shade of the mesquite tree as well.

"Let me check her over," Sam said from behind
her, his hand settling on her arm. "Sit back down,
Kate. Just rest a minute."

Ordinarily, Kate would have protested, but the sand
and the shade looked awfully inviting. "Okay…"

She watched as Sam discovered at least thirty cactus spines in Cinnamon's belly, where she'd brushed
the prickly pear in her lifesaving leap.

Sam crouched down, carefully picking the spines
out one by one. Cinnamon never moved a muscle.
"She did one hell of a job jumping that patch. I didn't
think she would make it." He glanced over at Kate.
She had gone pale again and he saw her lips compress
at his statement. "Bolt *might* have made it, but I
never thought this little bay Arabian could do it.
When I saw you make the decision, I thought you
were dead."

Kate wiped her brow with her trembling hand. She

was still amazed at her reaction to the event. But then, she reminded herself, she'd never been the target of a two-thousand-pound bull intent on killing her, either. "I didn't have a choice. Cinnamon knew that."

Sam patted the mare affectionately after he'd removed all the spines from her belly. "She saved the woman I love," he told her huskily.

Kate swallowed hard as she watched Sam approach her. Her eyes filled with tears as he knelt down on one knee and touched her cheek, cupping it and making her look directly into his eyes.

"I'm going to tell you something, Kate. And maybe it's too soon and I'm out of line, but I just damn near lost you, so I'm saying it anyway." He held her glistening blue gaze as her tears trickled downward, meeting his palm as it lay against her cheek. "I never stopped loving you either, Gal. Not *ever*." Sam bowed his head, emotions overcoming him. When he got a hold on them, he looked up again, his voice oddly husky. "You've got more courage than brains in your head, you and that little horse you ride. My God, I thought you were crazy for coming back down that slope after us."

Surprised, Kate whispered, "Sam, One Horn had you trapped! What else could I do?"

His mouth twisted into a half grin. "Stayed up on the knoll and watched, you crazy woman."

Incensed, Kate sputtered, "Like hell, Sam McGuire!"

"You came down because you love me."

She stared into his stormy gray eyes and realized how upset he was. "Yes, I did. I didn't see any other options, Sam."

"When I saw you come riding hell-bent-for-leather down that slope, sand and gravel flying, my first thought was that you were crazy, until I realized why you were really doing it." With a heavy shake of his head, Sam rasped, "Kate, you're the bravest woman I've ever known. I think you knew One Horn would go after you. Didn't you?"

She shrugged helplessly and slid her hand against his roughened one. "If he didn't, *you* were going to be killed." Her voice cracked. "I—I couldn't stand the idea of that. I just couldn't...."

Pushing aside the damp strands of hair that clung to her cheek and temple, Sam whispered unsteadily, "I know...I know...."

Sniffing, Kate said, "All I could think about, Sam, was you—what we'd had a long time ago. When you came and picked me up at the halfway house, I felt so many things. I never stopped loving you even though you married Carol. It was probably just as well Kelly broke my nose and I missed those last six weeks of school. I couldn't have stood seeing you in the halls or the cafeteria...anywhere."

Sam eased back on his heel and watched Kate fighting her tears.

"And I never got to tell you back then the *real* reason why I married her," he rasped apologetically.

"You tried and Kelly stopped you," Kate whispered, wiping her tears away with her fingers. "It was just as well, Sam. You did the right thing. It's all in the past."

"Well," he murmured, his fingers grazing the slope of her dirty cheek, "what I'm interested in is you, me and our future, Gal." He lifted his head and watched the two bulls, which had found some dried grass in the gulch and were grazing peacefully. Turning his attention back to Kate, he smiled tenderly down at her. "We got some unfinished business to attend to first before we can really sit down and talk. You up to helping me herd these two thickheaded bulls to the pastures?"

Kate put out her hand as Sam rose to his full height, drawing her up with him. Warmth flowed through her fingers and up her arm as he held her hands, momentarily erasing all her aches and pains from the fall. "You know I am," she answered. "This isn't the first time I've been thrown off a horse, Sam McGuire. It won't be the last." Kate saw a one-cornered grin tug at his wonderful mouth. A mouth she wanted to kiss endlessly until the last breath left her body.

He led her over to Cinnamon, picked up the reins and placed them across the animal's neck for her. "Climb on," he told her, and helped her mount by cupping her elbow to steady her. Kate was quickly bouncing back from the incident. He saw the light shining in her eyes and the love there—for him alone. Sam felt like he was walking on air. Nothing else really mattered, but they had to keep their heads and get ranch work done first.

Giving Bolt a well-deserved pat of thanks, he remounted his rangy gelding, pulling the brim of his hat low on his brow to protect his eyes from the blistering sun overhead. He watched Kate rebutton her shirt, tug her leather gloves back on and settle her black Stetson firmly on her head. What a brave, gutsy woman she was. With a shake of his head, Sam moved his gelding over to where she sat.

"Let's go, Gal. After we get these bulls put away, I want to go home and get these horses cared for properly."

Kate nodded. The horses were their very next priority. She leaned over and gave Cinnamon an affectionate pat on the neck. "Let's go," she whispered. The animals' wounds would be cleaned, and then the horses would be washed down with a hose and carefully examined for any other cuts or cactus spine. Finally they'd be rubbed down, given a good ration of oats and released to the corral for a well-deserved rest.

As they moved the two remaining bulls out of the gully and up the steep slope of the hill, Kate's heart flew like an eagle soaring in that dark blue sky above them. Sam loved her. He'd said the words that she'd dreamed about so many lonely nights throughout her life. Barely able to deal with her wild flood of emotions, Kate forced herself to focus on the bulls. The danger wasn't over yet. Bulls were never to be trusted. Tonight, when the last of the demanding ranch activities were finished, she would have a long, searching talk with Sam—about their future. Never had anything been more tantalizing or hopeful in Kate's life.

The lights were low at the ranch house as Sam approached. It was dark now, nearly nine p.m. Ranch chores were not only demanding, but long. With only two people to do the work of six, it was a harsh way to exist, but he really didn't mind it. Freshly showered, shaved and wearing a clean set of clothes, he climbed the wooden porch steps two at a time. Taking off his hat at the door, he knocked against the screen. Soft, low music drifted from the front room as he walked. Kate come around the corner.

He couldn't help but smile in approval. She was dressed in a soft pink cotton skirt that fell to her ankles. The short-sleeved white blouse she wore had lace around the neck and exposed the delicious curve of her neck and collarbones. Her hair was washed and hung in soft curls just above her shoulders. She was beautiful.

"You clean up pretty good," Sam said in greeting as she opened the screen door to allow him entrance. He saw a flush creep into Kate's cheeks. She smiled shyly, a smile that tore at his heart and touched his soul. Here was the Kate he'd known as a teenager, but all grown up. Her sky blue eyes danced with warmth and welcome. When she reached out and slid her fingers into his, he gave her a tender look.

"I can say the same of you, cowboy. Come on in...." Kate felt a flutter of nervousness as she led Sam into the semidarkened living room. The music soothed her, as did Sam's long, easy stride beside her. She felt his fingers flex more strongly against hers. It was a small gesture, but an important one. His dark hair gleamed from a recent shower, and Kate was surprised to see he'd shaved. Generally, by this time of night, Sam's five o'clock shadow gave him a dangerous look. He wore a clean set of Levi's and a white, short-sleeved cotton shirt. Dark hairs peeked out at his throat, emphasizing his blatant, powerful maleness. She ached to love him, ached to become one with him.

As Sam settled on the couch next to Kate, she

turned to him and tucked one leg beneath her, relaxing fully with him.

"Can I get you anything to drink?" she asked, realizing she was forgetting her manners.

Chuckling, Sam shook his head and gathered her hands into his. He liked having her leg tucked against his thigh, the pink of her cotton skirt outlining her firm, strong body beneath it. "No, Gal. Everything I've ever wanted I'm holding right now." He lost his smile and looked deeply into her eyes. Sam felt Kate's nervousness and the fine tension in her fingers. "We don't ever have much time around here," he began huskily, "and I don't want to waste it on preambles." Searching her shadowed features, he saw her lips part. Lips he wanted to capture and make his forever.

"I've got something I wanted to give to you for twenty-some years," he said, releasing her hand and digging into his jeans pocket. Producing a small, ivory-colored box, he slid it into Kate's hand. "Go ahead, Gal. Open it up."

Shocked, Kate stared down at the small cardboard box, which had yellowed from age. She stole a glance at Sam. His face was grim. She saw pain in his eyes and tension at the corners of his mouth. Stymied, she placed the box on her lap and carefully pried it open with her trembling fingers. Even in the dim light, she saw the beauty of a small, slender ring inside. Gasping, she removed the lid. There, nestled in the center of the box, was a sterling silver ring with blue turquoise set in a channel setting.

"Oh, Sam...." She touched the ring gently with her fingertips.

He turned and placed one arm on the couch behind her. "It was the wedding ring I was going to give you after we graduated, Kate. I had it made by one of our Navajo friends up on the Res. I told her I wanted a ring with no edges or anything that could catch on something. Around here, with ranch work, jewelry takes a beating." He smiled at her, at the tears glimmering in her eyes. Taking the ring out of the box, he picked up her left hand. He saw the bruises and cuts on her skin from today's near miss with death. Gently, he eased the ring on her fourth finger. It fit perfectly. That was a miracle to him, after all these years.

"I had planned to ask you to marry me the day after graduation, Gal," he told her in a low, off-key voice. "I had everything set. I had a part-time job up at the Maitland ranch waiting for me. I'd signed up to go to the university there. I'd planned on working during the day and going to school at night to earn my four-year degree. I'd talked to Steve Maitland, the owner, and he'd promised you a job if you wanted one. I'd even gone so far as to sign a lease on a little apartment up in Flagstaff. A place where we could settle in and make our first home."

"Oh, Sam...." Kate cried softly. She pressed her fingers to her mouth. Pain surged through her—the pain of a broken past. She saw him shake his head and felt him holding her hand gently with the ring around her finger. A wedding ring.

"I blew it," he rasped. "One night. One drunk. One mistake that cost me you. I know your running away wasn't the fault of my actions. But if I'd been more mature, less the egotistical football hero, I'd have waited for you and not fallen into Carol's arms because I felt sorry for myself."

Sam lifted his gaze and held Kate's. Her hand was damp and cool inside his warm, dry one. "Kate, I can't undo what happened. I was hoping when you came back that maybe, just maybe, there was a chance for us. It was a crazy wish that refused to die in me all these years. And since you came home, from time to time I thought I saw love for me in your eyes. Most of the time, I thought it was my imagination, because I wanted you so badly. But today—" he breathed raggedly "—today I knew. I knew without a doubt of your love for me. You proved it in a way that I never expected. There aren't too many women on a little bay horse that would take on a one-ton bull to save the man she loves, is there?" His mouth stretched into a tender smile.

Shaken, Kate sniffed. "I never thought of it that way, Sam. I knew you were in trouble. I couldn't stand the thought of you being killed by that bull. I had to do *something.*"

Releasing her hands, Sam cupped her face and looked deeply into her teary eyes. "And you did. That was when I knew, Gal, that you loved me beyond your own need to protect yourself. The ring is yours, Kate. It's always been yours. I want you to keep it. I know we just got back together and I know we— you—need more time." He stroked her cheek with his roughened fingertips. "That's a wedding ring, Gal. It's my pledge to you. Someday, when it's right for you, I want to marry you. I want you to share my name. To share our future—together...."

Whispering his name brokenly, Kate leaned forward, sliding her arms around his strong neck. She felt Sam's arms lock around her, and the air rushed out of her as she buried her face against his. "I love you so much I ache," she whispered unsteadily. "Love me, Sam…just hold me and love me. It's been so long…I need you so badly—so badly…."

Within moments, Kate felt herself being lifted off the couch and into Sam's arms. Contentment thrummed through her as he walked down the hall to her bedroom, to that old brass bed with the colorful quilt across it. Moonlight sifted throughout the lacy curtains at the window, a warming breeze moving the filmy material now and then. As he laid her down on the bed, his large hands bracketing her head, she looked up, up into his dark, stormy eyes filled with desire—for her.

It was so easy to lift her hands, place her fingertips across his barrel chest and open his shirt, button by button. With each of her grazing touches, she saw him wince. But it wasn't a wince of pain; it was the raw pleasure of her touch he was absorbing. The moonlight carved shadows against Sam's hard, weathered face. Her lips parted as his hand moved slowly downward to caress and cup her breast beneath the soft material of her blouse, his own touch evocative, teasing. A small moan escaped her.

His smile was very male as she helped him off with his shirt. Her fingers trembled badly on the belt buckle, so he helped her with that. Instead of shedding his jeans, he turned his attention to her as they sat on the bed next to one another. His fingers burned a path of need as he outlined her collarbone beneath the lace.

"You're a wild and beautiful mustang, Kate," he

rasped as his fingers trailed downward. "Let me taste your wildness, woman..." Then he leaned forward, capturing her parting lips. He took her hard and fast, pulling the breath from her. His callused hands caressed her breasts, and a cry of pleasure rippled through her, a cry of mounting, fiery need. He coaxed off her blouse and she saw him smile as he explored the silky quality of her white camisole. In moments he'd eased that from her, too. Her breath became ragged and her hands moved of their own accord across his massive chest. With each touch, she felt his muscles bunch and harden in response. She was barely aware of her skirt being pulled away from her ankles. His hands slid provocatively up the expanse of her thighs and she lay back, her lashes closing.

A hot weakness enveloped her as he followed the curve of her thighs. As her silky panties were eased away her skin burned with need of Sam's continued touch. She felt him shift and move, and she looked up appreciatively as he stood beside the bed and got rid of his Levi's and briefs. Her mouth went dry as she stared up at his strong male form. Sam was nothing but hard muscle shaped and formed by the unforgiving land and harsh weather. She saw many white scars over his body, reminders that ranching was tough and demanding and took more than a pound of flesh from those who rose to the challenge. As Sam eased back down beside her, she gloried in him, in his embrace.

She felt his insistent hardness pressing against her flank as he settled next to her, his arm beneath her head. Stretched out beside him, she turned toward him, a soft smile on her lips. Grazing his cheek with one hand, Kate could feel the brand-new stubble prickle her exploring fingertips. "I love you, Sam McGuire," she whispered, "with all my heart, my soul. I always did. I always will...." Then she sought and found his hot, hungry mouth, pressing herself against him. Her breasts met his chest, her hips grazed his and she felt his maleness meet the soft curve of her abdomen. Sliding her arms around his neck, she felt the ragged beat of his heart against hers, felt the iron bands of his arms encircling her, crushing her against him.

Taking, giving, his mouth slid wetly across her lips. The heat of his tongue thrust into her mouth and she moaned. Her thighs parted and she felt the delicious weight of him move on top of her. It was so right. So natural. She clung to his male mouth as she felt his hand slide beneath her hips, raising her just enough to welcome him into her awaiting depths. The ache in her lower body intensified almost to pain in those fleeting, heated seconds before she felt him move against her. Her nipples hardened against the wiriness of his chest hair. She moaned and flexed her hips upward to receive him fully. Unconditionally. No longer did she want to wait. She wanted him. All of him. Now. Forever.

The power and heat of his thrust made her arch her spine and throw back her head. Her cry shattered the silence, but it wasn't one of pain. It was one of glorious welcome. She felt the grip of his hands on her hips, guiding her, establishing the rhythm. In moments, they were melting into one another and she felt his body cover hers like a hot, hard blanket. She looked up as he framed her face with his hands, up into his stormy eyes glittering with love. She felt each thrust, moved with him, took him more deeply into her with each fluid movement. The ache turned to fire, and then to a burning longing. She saw a partial, triumphant smile tug at his mouth as the heat within her exploded violently, in a rush, like a volcano too long lain dormant.

Crying out his name, she gripped his damp, tense shoulders, her body pressing against his as the liquid heat flowed powerfully through her like lightning striking during a violent storm. Only the storm was one of raw need for Sam alone, the desire to feel his maleness mated with her femininity once again. She clung to him, gasping. He whispered her name, found her mouth and took it relentlessly as he thrust his hips more deeply, prolonging her pleasure. Moments became sparkling rainbows of color and light beneath her closed eyes as the heat peaked and then began to spread throughout her taunt, quivering form. Then she felt Sam turn rigid, a groan tearing from him, his hands capturing her face and holding her beneath him.

A few minutes later, he moved aside and then brought her up against him. They were breathing raggedly, and he could feel Kate's heart beating against his. He absorbed her soft, cool touches—on his face, shoulders and arms. How good she felt in his embrace! Opening his eyes, Sam stared into her blue ones, which danced with gold flecks of joy. He knew it had been good for her. He had made himself a promise that when it came time to love her, his needs would be secondary to hers. Kate was the one who had suffered all these years. She deserved the best from him now. No longer was he the selfish, egotis-

tical football captain. No, he was a mature man who
had made plenty of mistakes, and somehow he was
going to make up for every one. One small gift was
to make sure she enjoyed their lovemaking as much
as he did.

Lifting his hand, Sam brushed several tangled
strands of hair away from her damp, flushed cheek.
His words came out low and husky. "I love you,
Gal."

"I know that now," she whispered, touching his
cheek. Kate felt her body tingling in the aftermath
and she absorbed the pleasure of just being in Sam's
arms, pressed against his hard, muscled form.

He ran his hand lovingly down her rib cage and
across her hip. There wasn't an inch of fat anywhere
on Kate. Ranching life guaranteed that. He saw the
ring on her finger, the moonlight making the silver
glint for a moment. Catching her hand in his, he
brought it against his chest. "Just tell me that we have
a chance, Kate. I don't want you to think that I'll bed
you and that's it. Someday I want you for my wife.
When you're ready."

Closing her eyes, Kate rested her brow against his
chin.

"I never thought," she admitted hoarsely, "that
you would ever be my husband, Sam. I've dreamed
it over and over throughout the years, but I never
thought..." She lifted her head and sighed softly.
"This is all so new for me...."

"I know it is," he rasped. "Take your time, Gal.
We've got it now.... You're home. You're where you
belong. And you're with me...."

Epilogue

"Well, Jessica's got her greenhouse," Sam drawled with a smile as he placed the hammer back in his toolbox.

Kate smiled back and looked on admiringly at the small eight-by-ten-foot building of plate glass. "I think she'll love it, Sam." Much of a cowboy's work was repairing and building things around the ranch, and Sam had done a fine job making the little structure for her sister. Jessica had over fifty orchid varieties that she used in her natural essences, and was driving them down from Canada. In less than three days, her little sister would arrive at the Donovan Ranch to continue her successful business. In her spare moments, Jessica would help out with the demands of the ranch.

Sam grinned and wiped his sweaty brow with the

back of his hand as he studied the building, which stood partly beneath the shade of an old cottonwood, near the rear of the red flagstone house that Jessica would live in. Jessica had sent him dimensions, details and the money to buy the necessary items to build a house for "her girls," as she called her orchids. Pleased with his work, he glanced toward Kate, who had helped him. His body held a warm glow and his heart became suffused with love for her. She stood so proudly and tall as she surveyed their mutual handiwork. It made him feel good that she thought so highly of his skills.

The June sun had risen at five-thirty, its golden rays starting to heat up the land. There were no clouds in the flawless turquoise sky. The scorching drought would continue for another unrelenting day. They would have to wait until July, when the monsoon rains arrived, driving thunderstorms and moisture out of Mexico sweeping northward into Arizona. Hopefully, plenty of rain would fall. Worried about the slowly lowering water table, a huge lake that lay beneath the Sedona-Verde valley, Sam picked up his toolbox.

"Breakfast about ready?" he teased, placing his arm around Kate's waist. They walked slowly toward the ranch house. What they needed was enough money to hire a full-time cook and housekeeper. Both of them ended up doing housekeeping chores, but haphazardly at best. Their fourteen-hour days were wearing on them after six months without help. Jessica would be a welcome addition, but Sam knew she would have to work hard to get her company set up, fill orders from around the world for her natural essences, and pay her own bills. Still, he felt Jessica's ebullient, bubbly presence would further heal Kate of her past wounds, because she was very close to her little sister.

Automatically, Kate fell into step with Sam. He always shortened his long, rolling stride when he was walking with her. He was always sensitive to her needs, she thought as she leaned against him, resting her head briefly against his shoulder. ''We're so lucky....'' she whispered, a catch in her voice as she looked up. Drowning in his tender gaze, Kate tightened her arm around his waist.

''The luckiest,'' he agreed huskily, leaning over and pressing a quick kiss to her flushed cheek. He saw her eyes dance with joy. So much of the old Kate was unfolding daily before his eyes. Sam knew it was because their love was allowed to take root once more and thrive. This time he was older and wiser. This time he wouldn't throw away the woman he loved.

They walked around the ranch house after he put his tools away. It was still early and he could hear the lowing of the cattle, the soft snorts of the Arabians nearby. Overhead, Sam heard the shrill call of a red-tailed hawk. Looking up, he saw two of them and pointed them out to Kate.

''Husband and wife,'' he said. Red-tails mated for life and this pair nested on the black lava cliffs above the ranch house.

Kate shielded her eyes with her hand as she watched the two hawks circling lazily five hundred feet above them. ''They're catching the rising thermals.''

Sam placed his arm around her shoulder and

watched the birds gracefully flow on the unseen heat currents starting to rise from the earth as the sun grew warmer. "The Indians would say it's a good sign. They're in the East."

Kate nodded. "East is the direction of new beginnings. Creation."

"Jessica's coming," he said, grinning.

Kate nodded and relished his closeness, his protective arm around her shoulders. "Jessica is so close to Mother Earth."

"I think that of the three daughters, Jessica has your mother's close connection with the soil." He looked at Kate. "Not that you don't, but it's expressed in a different way."

She nodded. "I always used to worry about Jessica. She was so flighty and couldn't ever finish anything she started. Something would catch her eye and she'd take off in this direction or that. I often wondered what she'd grow up to be."

"She runs her own company," Sam murmured. "I'd say she's pretty steady and has a good head on her shoulders despite her wandering ways."

Laughing, Kate agreed. They walked toward the ranch house. She would make them a hefty breakfast and then they'd begin the daily chores of feeding the animals. Today the blacksmith was coming out to trim thirty of the Arabians' hooves. At six dollars apiece, the bill would run up quickly. In his spare time, Sam would do trimming, but he was spread thin as it was, with the weight of the ranch falling on his shoulders.

"Jessica's so excited about coming home," Kate said as they climbed the wooden steps to the porch.

"When she called last night, she was worried her orchid girls wouldn't make the trip. I guess they need moisture in the air and the temperature can't be too hot or too cold."

Sam opened the screen door for her. "Coming to Arizona is going to be hard on them."

"Jessica thinks she can manage it with that greenhouse we just built."

"It sounds like she's going to need a full-time helper," Sam said, taking off his hat and placing it on a wooden peg behind the door.

Kate took her own hat off and hung it beside his. Both were dusty, beat-up and desperately needing a good cleaning. Money was tight. Hats weren't high on the list of priorities.

"She said that she's going to have to hire someone to help her, and we're to try and think of someone who might fill the bill." Kate went to the kitchen. While Sam went to the fridge to get the bacon and eggs, she retrieved the cast-iron skillet from a cabinet next to the stove. Their morning routine was wonderful and she loved working closely with him. He'd shred the cheese for their omelets, cut up red and green peppers, chop up some onion and broccoli while she got the eggs ready for the skillet.

"I've got an idea," Sam exclaimed, placing the eggs and slab of bacon on the counter next to Kate. He pulled the rest of the items from the refrigerator and shut the door. Washing his hands in the sink, he said, "There's a half-Navajo, half-Anglo by the name of Dan Black who *might* be the person Jessica's looking for. He's Indian, has close ties to the land, understands and accepts like Jessica does that plants have their own spirit and energy.''

Kate nodded and broke a dozen eggs into a big blue ceramic bowl. ''Dan Black—that name is sure familiar. Where have I heard it?''

''The Black family up on the Navajo Reservation,'' Sam told her, wiping off his hands with a towel. He picked up the grater, unwrapped a block of sharp cheddar cheese and methodically began to shred it. ''His mother is a real famous Navajo rug weaver. She just received an award of recognition at the White House for her artistry. And Dan is one hell of a wrangler. We can use one. Besides, Gan needs to be gentled and trained. Right now, he's dangerous to everyone.''

She put the bacon in another skillet. ''If I remember right, they called Dan the 'stallion tamer'?''

''Yes, he's got a good reputation for taming wild mustangs, especially mean studs like Gan.''

''So what're his bad points?'' Sam was excellent at assessing people.

His mouth quirked. ''He's got a few problems.''

Kate glanced at him and poured the beaten eggs from the bowel into another skillet. ''You're hedging, Sam.''

Quickly cutting up the vegetables for their omelets, Sam said, ''He was in the Marine Corps for a long time. He went through the Gulf War, Desert Storm. They medically discharged him after that.''

''Why?''

''Mental problems.''

Kate rolled her eyes. ''Mental problems? And you

want to hire him to work with Jessica and tame Gan?''

''Now, calm down,'' Sam murmured, placing the vegetables in a bowl so that Kate could add them to the cooking eggs. ''He's not crazy, Kate. Just a little introverted and a loner since coming back, that's all.''

''That's nice to know. We have enough problems keeping this ranch afloat without hiring someone who has mental-health problems.''

''I knew Dan over at the Maitland ranch in Flagstaff. He worked as a wrangler for me before joining the Marine Corps. He was a hard worker, took orders well and took pride in his work,'' Sam said, watching her cook. Kate's black hair was brushing her shoulders now. It made a beautiful frame for her incredible sky blue eyes, which he regularly lost himself in when they made wild, unbridled love. ''I haven't seen him of late, but I did see him right after his discharge. I think he's got PTSD.''

''Post-traumatic-stress disorder?'' Kate put the lid on the omelets to let them cook for a moment and turned her attention to the pan of bubbling, fragrant bacon.

''I think Dan's problems are controllable. He was a pretty outgoing young kid at Maitland's ranch. The war changed him.''

''What war doesn't change a person?''

He nodded. ''Let me do some snooping around about Dan. Fay Seward, the saddle maker, knows the family real well. I might stop in there and have a chat with her.''

''If I had my way,'' Kate said, scooping up the finished omelets onto plates that Sam retrieved for her, "I'd hire people with Indian blood in them. They never lose their connection with Mother Earth. They have a harmony I want to reestablish here."

Sam put the plates on the table and poured coffee into some white mugs. "I don't have any," he teased.

Kate sat down and grinned. "You're Native American in your heart."

"*You* have my heart, Gal."

She loved this time of morning with Sam. They sat with their knees touching beneath the old wooden table. How many times had Kate looked at the ring she wore on her left hand? She wanted to marry Sam after all her sisters were home. Jessica would arrive in May, and Rachel would be home in late November, or early December at the latest. Already the three of them were planning for Kate's coming wedding. It wouldn't be an expensive event, but a small, quiet one. Money was hard to find, and Kate certainly wasn't going to spend it on the wedding gown she'd dreamed of so many years ago. Sam agreed to the wait in order to meet the driving demands of the ranch.

"That's got hot peppers in it," she warned watching Sam as he spread salsa over his omelet.

"Makes it good."

Grinning, Kate said, "Mexican food is the way to *your* heart, cowboy."

Chuckling, Sam dug into the omelet. "Guilty as charged. I was raised on the stuff."

Who wasn't out in Arizona? Kate smiled and absorbed the taste of the omelet.

"So," Sam murmured, "your sisters got the details of our wedding worked out yet?"

Kate grinned. "Most of them. Rachel is so glad we're waiting until she can be here as the maid of honor. I don't know who is more excited, them, you or me."

He felt a bit of heat in his cheeks. Kate's eyes danced with merriment. Stilling the fork, he caught her gaze. "I probably am."

"No, I am." Kate laughed, thrilled with the thought that by the end of the year she would be Mrs. Sam McGuire. The idea always made her feel euphoric. She saw the happiness reflected in Sam's gray eyes, too. She picked up a piece of bacon and thoughtfully chewed on it.

Sam sipped his coffee, his gaze resting tenderly on Kate. "One time after we made love, early on, you told me that you had all these dreams about a big wedding. You had the dress all picked out. You showed me that scrapbook you'd made up when we were going together in high school. You put it together, dreaming of marrying me someday. I know you and your sisters are pinching pennies and you're not going after the wedding you really wanted."

A rush of love flowed through her as she saw Sam's gray eyes grow tender. How much she loved him! Kate had always imagined what it might be like to be married to Sam, but never in her wildest dreams had she thought it would be possible—or this wonderful.

"It would cost too much to put on the wedding I'd originally planned, Sam. It's okay. Really, it is. Don't be giving me that look. I can do a lot on a shoestring, believe me."

She watched him shake his head. "No, I want to

see you have the one I saw in your scrapbook. I've been giving this a lot of thought and I think I've come up with a way to have it happen. Let's sell one of your best broodmares. She should fetch at least five thousand dollars. That should be enough for that fancy dress you showed me from your scrapbook."
He saw the tears gather in Kate's eyes. How soft and loving she'd become in the past months. The change was startling and wonderful.

Wiping her eyes with a look of embarrassment, she said, "I never thought of that angle." The fact that he wanted to give her a beautiful wedding dress instead of what she was planning on wearing—a cream-colored wool suit—made her love him even more fiercely.

"That's my job," Sam drawled, giving her a one-cornered smile meant to tell her he loved her.

Kate closed her eyes. "I've always dreamed of a beautiful white wedding dress like that...."

Sam nodded, feeling his heart expand with joy. Kate's voice reflected her sudden enthusiasm. Jessica coming home made Kate happy. She could hardly wait for her "Little Sis" to arrive. "Well, let's see what we can do then, about expanding plans for that big wedding you always dreamed of instead of the shoestring-budget one, shall we? We might be living hand-to-mouth right now, but things could change by the time your sisters get home. Besides, dreams need to be fulfilled." Especially Kate's dreams. Sam had stopped dreaming long ago and Kate had already given him back that gift. He could do no less in trying to fulfill her dreams, too.

Kate knew that with the ongoing drought, any bit

of excess money they had saved was being eaten up in feed bills to keep the cattle from starving. "Okay," she whispered. "I'd love to wear a dress like that for our wedding day." How thrilled Jessica and Rachel would be about this news! She saw the love in Sam's eyes, his thoughtfulness toward her sending a wealth of emotion through her.

Slowly rising, Sam picked up their plates, took them to the sink and rinsed them off. "Good. Then it's settled. I've already got a buyer for that one black broodmare." He silently congratulated himself for giving Kate another gift she so richly deserved. He'd taken one look at the scrapbook that she'd pulled out and shared with him many months ago, and had realized the depth of her love for him was more than he thought possible. Kate had cut out photos of the dream house she'd wanted as their home, a lace-and-pearl adorned wedding dress, the white-and-purple orchids for the bouquet she'd wanted... They'd been the dreams of a young teenage girl, dreams that he aimed to fulfill because he loved her. She was giving him a second chance. He wasn't about to ruin it this time around. Now he had the capability of helping all her dreams come to life, and that made him feel good about himself for once.

Sam captured Kate's hand as she rose from the chair. In one smooth motion, he brought her into the haven of his arms. She felt good to him as she leaned against him, her hands resting on his arms as she smiled up at him.

"Miracles," he whispered, catching her mouth and kissing it softly, "happen every day of our lives when I'm with you." Her lips were pliant and sweet beneath his. He caressed her mouth and murmured against it, "And I want to stay in your life and show them to you every single day, Kate Donovan—for the rest of our lives...."

* * * * *

Don't miss Jessica Donovan's story in
STALLION TAMER, the second book in
Lindsay McKenna's exciting miniseries,
COWBOYS OF THE SOUTHWEST, *coming*
in May 1998, only from Special Edition!

Take 4 bestselling love stories FREE

Plus get a FREE surprise gift!

BEVERLY BARTON

**Continues the
twelve-book series—
36 Hours—in April 1998
with Book Ten**

NINE MONTHS

Paige Summers couldn't have been more shocked when she learned that the man with whom she had spent one passionate, stormy night was none other than her arrogant new boss! And just because he was the father of her unborn baby didn't give him the right to claim her as his wife. Especially when he wasn't offering the one thing she wanted: his heart.

For Jared and Paige and *all* the residents of Grand Springs, Colorado, the storm-induced blackout was just the beginning of 36 Hours that changed *everything!* You won't want to miss a single book.

Available at your favorite retail outlet.

Silhouette®

Silhouette®

SPECIAL EDITION™

COMING NEXT MONTH

#1171 UNEXPECTED MOMMY—Sherryl Woods
That Special Woman!
And Baby Makes Three: The Next Generation
Single father Chance Adams was hell-bent on claiming his share of
the family ranch. Even if it meant trying to seduce his uncle's lovely
stepdaughter. But when Chance fell in love with the spirited beauty for real,
could he convince Jenny to be his wife—and his son's new mommy?

#1172 A FATHER'S VOW—Myrna Temte
Montana Mavericks: Return to Whitehorn
Traditional Native American Sam Brightwater was perfectly content
with his life. Until vivacious schoolteacher Julia Stedman stormed into
Whitehorn and wrapped herself around his hardened heart. With fatherhood
beckoning, Sam vowed to swallow his pride and fight for his woman and
child....

#1173 STALLION TAMER—Lindsay McKenna
Cowboys of the Southwest
Vulnerable Jessica Donovan sought solace on the home front, but what she
found was a soul mate in lone horse wrangler Dan Black. She identified
with the war veteran's pain, as well as with the secret yearning in his eyes.
Would the healing force of their love grant them a beautiful life together?

#1174 PRACTICALLY MARRIED—Christine Rimmer
Conveniently Yours
Rancher Zach Bravo vowed to never get burned by a woman again. But he
knew that soft-spoken single mom Tess DeMarley would be the perfect
wife. And he was positively *livid* at the notion that Tess's heart belonged to
someone else. Could he turn this practical union into a true love match?

#1175 THE PATERNITY QUESTION—Andrea Edwards
Double Wedding
Sophisticated city-dweller Neal Sheridan was elated when he secretly
swapped places with his country-based twin. Until he accidentally agreed to
father gorgeous Lisa Hughes's child! He had no intention of fulfilling that
promise, but could he really resist Lisa's baby-making seduction?

#1176 BABY IN HIS CRADLE—Diana Whitney
Stork Express
On the run from her manipulative ex, very pregnant Ellie Malone wound up
on the doorstep of Samuel Evans's mountain retreat. When the brooding
recluse delivered her baby and tenderly nursed her back to health, her heart
filled with hope. Would love bring joy and laughter back into their lives?

She's a woman without a future
because of her past.

THE
DAUGHTER

At fifteen, Maggie is convicted of her mother's
murder. Seven years later she escapes from
prison to prove her innocence.

After many years on the run, Maggie makes a
dangerous decision: to trust Sean McLeod, the cop she
has fallen in love with. She knows he can do one of two
things: he can turn her in or help her find her mother's
real killer. She feels her future is worth the risk....

JASMINE
CRESSWELL

MIRA

MJC425